IF GOD WAS A BANKER

IF GOD WAS A BANKER

Ravi Subramanian

RUPA

Published by
Rupa Publications India Pvt. Ltd 2007
7/16, Ansari Road, Daryaganj
New Delhi 110002

Sales centres:
Allahabad Bengaluru Chennai
Hyderabad Jaipur Kathmandu
Kolkata Mumbai

ISBN: 978-81-291-1147-0

Thirty-fourth impression 2020

40 39 38 37 36 35 34

The moral right of the author has been asserted.

Printed at Shree Maitrey Printech Pvt. Ltd, Noida

1
New York

It was 5.45 a.m. on a Monday morning. New York city was dark and cold. The sun was yet to leave its heavenly abode. A few cars could be heard in the distance. Early risers, who had to travel a long distance to work, were making their way to office.

Rrrrrnnng... Rrrrrnnng... Sundeep was wide awake. Yet, he could not hear the alarm bell go off. He hadn't slept the whole night. His eyes were tired but open. By this time he knew the entire topography of the Greco-Roman chandelier, which hung from the roof of his modern five-bedroom apartment in Manhattan. He himself had no idea of how long he had been staring at it... the whole night maybe! Numerous questions were flashing in his head. What would Natasha think of him? Will she accept him? What will the kids say?

'Sundeep, will you please turn it off.' It was Natasha, his wife of nineteen years. She had just woken up, her sleep disturbed by the constant ringing of the alarm. Sundeep stretched out his right hand and pressed the button on top of the alarm clock to stop the irritating buzz. Natasha went back to sleep almost instantly. She was normally the first to get up. But today was not a normal day. Sundeep hadn't slept at all.

It was not the first time that Sundeep had been awake all night. Any other day, he would be the last to leave the dance floor at any party. He would breathe life into any gathering. His admirers said that Sundeep's parties began only after midnight. But today was not 'any other' day. Today was indeed very different. There was no party tonight. Life could change dramatically for Sundeep in the next eight hours. He was a worried man.

It was only after six long hours that the Greco-Roman chandelier ceased being the centre of Sandeep's attraction. He glanced to his left and looked at Natasha. She looked like an angel in her sleep. The silky linen added a heavenly touch. Even in sleep, her lips curled up in a delicate smile. Sundeep knew that Natasha had not the slightest clue about what awaited her before she would hit bed again on Monday night.

Natasha was a bomb. Once a beauty queen, she had been attracted to the frail frame of Sundeep twenty years ago. Attracted to power, to fame, to adulation. Since then she had become quite used to it all, and probably enjoyed it too. Of late, signs of age had begun to show on her face. Her skin had started withering. Slight wrinkles could be spotted on her forehead. But, even today, only a madcap could have suggested that she was a day older than thirty.

Sandeep had not told her anything till now. But he knew that this wouldn't last. Sooner or later she would get to know. Should he tell her now and prepare her, or should he tell her after everything was over, after the verdict was out. After all, he was a very senior guy and there was just that small chance that he might get past the entire problem unscathed. But he knew it was extremely unlikely.

Staring at the chandelier all night hadn't helped him make up his mind.

He let out a deep sigh and stepped out of bed. His feet felt the exquisite texture of a Persian rug, imported from Tehran and gifted to Natasha on her thirty-fifth birthday by his NRI banking team. She was the wife of the Business Head, wasn't she?

'I will take a chance,' he muttered under his breath. His mind was made. Natasha was not to be told.

By 6.45 a.m. Sundeep had showered and got dressed in his impeccable pinstripes. He was wearing the red tie that Natasha had picked up for him from Harrods about six months ago when they had gone to London on a holiday. Their last holiday together. Sundeep was lecturing at a leadership course in London and had taken Natasha with him. That was around the time his problems had deepened. Things hadn't improved since.

He looked back over his shoulder. Natasha was still asleep. Sundeep walked up to her and kissed her on the cheek. Natasha smiled back. 'Come back soon,' she murmured, unmindful of the fact that he might be coming back for good.

'Hmm...' Sundeep turned and walked out of the room. On his way out he glanced into his children's bedroom. Alka and Ajay, six and seven years of age, were firmly tucked into their beds, fast asleep. Unlikely to be up before ten. Schools were yet to reopen after the Christmas vacations, and they were in no hurry to go back to their classrooms. 'God bless,' muttered Sundeep as he made his way down the hallway to the garage, where his prized possession—a recently acquired BMW 9S—was parked.

He would have to give it all up, unless the gods decided to side with him today. 'But why would God even think of me?'

It suddenly struck him that he was thinking of God, for the first time in, he couldn't even remember how long.

'Even God needs to be spoken to, else he'll forget that you exist,' his mom had once told him when she caught him running away from a *pooja* at a family function. How he wished he had heeded her advice.

Within fifteen minutes, Sundeep's car pulled into the basement of the sixty-two-storied building that housed the headquarters of New York International Bank (NYB), the world's fourth largest financial services conglomerate. The moment they saw his car, the guards at the gate stood up and released the lever, activating the access-controlled door for a special floor, that served as the parking lot for the Group CEO and his direct reports. A reserved parking here marked one's arrival into the Ivy League of New York International Bank.

Sundeep eased his car into the slot marked Managing Director-Retail. This slot had become his when he moved into New York twelve months ago. To manage the retail business of New York International Bank in the emerging markets, the Group CEO had handpicked him from a shortlist of fourteen candidates across the bank.

He got off his car, a beep signalling that the car had been locked. The same beep also activated a device in the parking lot, sending out a signal to his secretary on the sixty-second floor that her boss was on his way. She would get about three minutes before her boss walked into the office.

'Morning, Mr Srivastava,' said Louisa as Sundeep stepped out of the express lift and took measured steps towards his cabin. A hot cup of black coffee, without sugar, was waiting for him on his table. Natasha had insisted that he cut down on his sugar intake. He was getting old and she wanted him to control his diet for better health.

He had hardly settled into the plush leather chair when Louisa walked into his room.

'Michelle called a couple of minutes before you arrived.'

'Thanks, Louisa.'

'She has left a message for you. Mr Bridge wants to meet you in the boardroom at 9.45.'

'Hmm... thanks,' was all that Sundeep managed to say. He could feel his heart sinking. His worst nightmare was about to come true. Tedd Bridge was the Group CEO of New York International Bank. If he wanted to meet Sundeep with Michelle, it spelt disaster for him.

It was 8.30 and he still had seventy-five minutes before the scheduled meeting.

2

'Ladies and gentlemen. It gives me great pleasure to call on stage the winner of the Director's Gold Medal for the Best All-round Performance in the batch of 1986,' a beaming M.R. Rao announced over the public address system. He was the Dean at the Indian Institute of Management, Bangalore—a premier MBA college in India. The occasion was the convocation for the outgoing batch of 180 students. Ratan Tata was handing out the degrees to the dreamy-eyed students who were embarking on a long and arduous journey into the corporate world.

'Please put your hands together for Sundeep Srivastava.' The moment Rao finished saying this, the audience erupted. Sundeep was very popular among his classmates and was liked by one and all. Son of an Army Major, Sundeep was fiercely combative. He typified the aspiring middle class in the country.

The women in Sandeep's batch adored him. Without looks that would put Tom Cruise to shame, it was his aggression and intelligence that won him friends.

Sundeep walked up to the stage with a swagger like Viv Richards'. He exuded tremendous confidence while accepting the gold medal from Ratan Tata. Then, departing from laid out protocol, Ratan Tata took the microphone.

'Hey, young man. Congratulations on winning the Director's Gold Medal.'

'Thank you, sir.'

'Sundeep, I am sure you have worked hard for this medal. How do you feel?'

'Great. It's an honour. Winning this medal was very important for me.'

'Did you think for a moment what you would have done had this medal gone to someone else?'

'Pardon me sir, but that option never existed. I play to win and not only for the spirit of the game,' said Sundeep, with the attitude of a veteran.

'That's excellent, Sundeep. I like people who play to win. I am sure you will too. This attitude will take you a long way. Could you tell us what you aspire to achieve over the next ten years... in the next decade?' asked Mr Tata.

'I would like to be standing here and asking the same questions that you are.' He was getting cheeky now. Everyone in the audience was shocked. Such impudence was very unlike Sundeep.

'I am sure you will. Thank you, young man. Congratulations again.' Mr Tata, visibly embarrassed, cut short the discussion and handed the microphone back to Rao.

This was the first time the world had got a taste of the real Sundeep. The Sundeep they had not seen till now. The successful Sundeep Srivastava had marked his arrival in style.

3

In the mid-eighties banking in India was dominated by state-owned banks. These banks were slow and laid back. Customer service was not a word from their dictionary. Archaic technology, lack of customer-oriented processes, and antique products were their hallmark. Foreign banks were very small. They had very few branches and operated in a heavily regulated environment.

Banking was synonymous with pinstripes-clad corporate bankers. Retail banking hadn't made its presence felt. The small individual customer was not on anybody's mind.

These banks made so much money from large corporations that it was not worth their while to invest in building relationships and to run after small customers. No one in India even considered retail banking a viable option. That is, before New York International Bank (NYB) proved them all wrong.

World over, banking had metamorphosed. Corporate banking had lost its sheen. Large corporations had started squeezing banks on margins, and the banks had little choice but to comply with the demands of these giants, or else exit the business. There were always ten banks waiting at the doorsteps of the corporations, each willing to lend at rates lower than yours.

Every bank worth its dime in the developed world had transitioned from servicing high-end corporates to higher margin retail customers. Banks in India were slow to catch on. They were still running after the miniscule margins they were making on the large Tata and Birla companies. They couldn't see the change coming in at breakneck speed.

And that's where New York International Bank saw a golden opportunity. It decided to step in and fill the gap in the retail banking sector in this country.

The NYB local management, however, was from the old school of thought. They were all corporate bankers with no exposure outside the country. They had obvious reservations on the launch of retail banking. Convincing them was taking so long that NYB decided to hire a completely new team for this purpose.

Retail banking needed a new aggression, and a thought process different from what was found in the world of Indian corporate banking.

Aditya Rao moved from New York to India, with a mandate to launch NYB's retail banking business in India. Aditya needed energy, passion, and drive in his team, and decided to hire fresh talent from premier institutes. It was thought that anyone from outside the banking industry would come in with new ideas that could redefine banking. Along with energy and aggression, the team members had to possess high intellectual calibre. Where else would they find it, but in the top MBA institutes in the country.

In 1986, NYB decided to hire the top five students from every IIM in the country.

Sundeep, IIM-B topper, was one of those who got an offer. He did not have to think twice before accepting, despite an ordinary pay packet. Smart Sundeep could read the future.

His decision was driven by the challenge of doing something new and different. Something that hadn't been done in India before: setting up the retail bank franchise of one of the largest retail banks in the world. He was confident that, with the bank's global expertise, it won't be long before it made its presence felt in Indian retail banking. And this, he was sure, would catapult his career into the stratosphere.

So, in May 1986 Sundeep joined New York International Bank as a management trainee in the newly set up Retail Banking Unit.

4
New York

'You don't look OK, Sundeep. Are you unwell? Should I get you something?' Louisa interrupted Sundeep's thoughts.

'Sundeep, it's a call from home. Your wife. I didn't get you on your extension and walked in,' Louisa's voice was full of concern.

For a moment Sundeep was surprised. Natasha would not normally call him so early in the morning. 'Put the call through.'

'Natasha, what happened? Hope all is fine.'

'Yeah. Ajay has been insisting on going to the zoo. I am taking both the kids there. Will eat out. Was planning to watch a movie at the dome with the kids. Will only be back by six. Just wanted to check if that's fine with you. You would anyway be back only after that.'

'Of course, Nattie. It's perfectly fine. I would also have come, had it not been for...'

'Sundeep... do you remember the last time we went out. I have stopped expecting you to do these things. Be back by dinner time. See ya.' Click. Natasha hung up before Sundeep could say anything further.

5

Monday. 6 May 1986. Sundeep Srivastava walked up to the gate of the NYB office at the busy Nariman Point area in Mumbai's central business district. It was a quarter to eight in the morning, too early for an induction programme for new recruits, which was to start only at half past nine. The bank offices had not even been opened. A towering security guard, rifle in hand, refused to let him in. The guard insisted that the gates could only be opened after an authorised personnel came in. And corporate bankers were not known to be ones who came on time. They normally stumbled in well past the official bank reporting time of 9.00 a.m. Sundeep tried out his best powers of persuasion on the guard, but to no avail. So he decided to make himself comfortable on the bench just outside the building.

The bench had been put there for the guards to sit for a while when they came off their duty. No more than three people could squeeze into it.

He cursed himself for having come so early and turned towards the wooden bench. Sitting on the bench was a young man, roughly the same age as Sundeep. Wearing an oversized coat, he was deeply engrossed in reading a copy of the *Economic Times*. He had plonked himself right in the middle of the bench, leaving no space on either side for anyone to sit.

'Will you move a bit to the side and allow others also to sit.' Sundeep's tone and manner was curt and unnecessarily aggressive.

'Yes, of course,' said the person sitting on the bench, taking his eyes off the newspaper and looking up for the first time. It was only then that Sundeep noticed the file in the man's hand. It had a letter that looked quite similar to the one Sundeep had got at the time of his appointment. He quickly realised that the person sitting on the bench had also come to join NYB. He had, in fact, reached earlier than Sundeep. The *vibhuti* mark on his forehead, and his well-oiled and combed hair gave him away as someone from the south of the Deccan. 'Looks like a Tam-Brahm,' thought Sundeep. Tam-Brahm was slang for Tamilian Brahmins—upper-caste people from the South Indian state of Tamil Nadu, belonging to the Brahmin community. Tam-Brahms were known to be highly intelligent, honest, and not so aggressive.

'Sundeep. My name is Sundeep Srivastava. Am joining NYB today as a management trainee. I can see from your letter that you have also come in to join today. Have you been waiting here for too long?' Sundeep's tone had mellowed down the moment he realised that the guy on the bench was a fellow NYB employee.

'Hi. My name is Swaminathan. I am also joining NYB as an MT today,' said the man sitting on the bench. The tone was typically South Indian. Now Sundeep was sure that here was a southie.

'This is my first time in Mumbai. I do not know anyone here. I had no idea how long it would take to reach this place. So I left the hotel at 6.30 a.m. Didn't want to be late on day one.'

And they continued to chat.

'IIM Ahmedabad. Passed out this year,' said Swaminathan.

'IIM-B, same batch,' said Sundeep.

'Where are you from?'

'Delhi. And you?'

'Chennai. Have lived my life there.'

'I can see that.' Sundeep smiled.

Swaminathan didn't mind and smiled back. He was used to people commenting on his appearance when they met him for the first time.

Thus began a legendary partnership in NYB—the fast and aggressive Sundeep versus the mature and sensible Swami.

6

Swaminathan was a merit student at the Indian Institute of Management in Ahmedabad and was acknowledged as 'the brain' of the campus. Swami was also the eldest son in a family of modest means. He was barely two-years old when he lost his father. His father, a clerk in the rural development ministry, had struggled to feed a family of four with his measly salary. With no savings, the small pension was just not enough, and the retirement benefits went into paying off the mortgage on their one-bedroom house in Mylapore, a middle-income locality in Chennai.

Bringing up Swami and his sister was not easy. Their mother struggled hard to put them through school. She would cook at various Brahmin households and marriages to raise money for their education. Both the children never made her feel that what they had was not enough. Swami was an intelligent and hard working student who always topped his class. When he reached college, he was lucky to get a scholarship. That was a big relief for his mother, because her earnings were just not enough to manage the expenses for both the children.

Swami was quick to realise that his mother would not be able to manage the ever-increasing expenses, despite his scholarship. He got himself transferred to an evening college.

This gave him an opportunity to work for a few hours during the day and supplement his family income.

He started off by keeping accounts for Nalli's, a large chain of sari stores in Chennai. He would spend 9.00 a.m. to 1.00 p.m. everyday at the Chettiars' office and then would attend college from four to nine in the evening. The salary that he earned from Nalli's was just enough to ensure a normal life for the three of them.

Graduation completed, Swami was faced with a dilemma. Should he continue his studies, or should he give it all up and take up a full-time job to provide for his family. His mother made the decision easier. She insisted that he should study further. She had somehow managed for 19 years, with occasional support from Swami. She didn't want to stumble at the final milestone. She knew that another two years and Swami would make it. She had great faith in Swami's commitment and intellect, and was hopeful of him getting a scholarship.

True to her expectations, Swami got into the Indian Institute of Management, Ahmedabad, the best management institute in the country. At the end of his first term there, when the scholarship list was announced, Swami's name was right on top. He won a full waiver of his tuition fees. When he broke the news to his mother, she couldn't hold back her tears. She wept continuously that whole day; if only Swami's father were around, how he would have swelled with pride.

Like Sundeep, NYB was Swami's first job too. He had made it by the whisker. When NYB came out with the first list of five hires from IIM-A, Swami's name was not there. He was sixth in the merit list at his institute and NYB was hiring only five. However, a batch mate of his, Sandeep Runwal, who was third on the merit list, decided to join his father's booming construction business, and opted out of campus placements. This piece of good luck made a huge difference to Swami's life. Swami, who was sixth on the merit list, made it as a reserve candidate. It meant a lot to him.

Once he got out of the institute, Swami had no money. While at IIM-A, he survived on scholarship, and his family survived on the money he had saved earlier. His sister took tuitions and earned some money to supplement their mother's income. Life was not easy in those two years. But all along he knew that there was light at the end of the tunnel.

'Once I finish my MBA, you Amma, and Ambujam, my dear sister, will live a life of luxury,' he had told his mother when he joined IIM. All that was about to come true. Their lives were going to change on joining NYB.

There was a two-months gap between the time Swami finished his MBA at IIM-A and the day he was to join NYB. Swami had spent these two months doing odd jobs. He saved enough to buy himself a good set of clothes. After all, he was joining a foreign bank.

Foreign banks in those days were a designer's paradise. Pinstripe suits, jackets and exotic ties were in vogue. The dress code prescribed in the appointment letter was 'business formals.' Business formals in banking parlance meant suits or jackets. He couldn't afford one. So he borrowed a jacket from a friend who was eighty pounds heavier than him. That explained the oversized jacket that Sundeep saw Swami wearing on the day they joined NYB.

7

Sundeep and Swami got up together and walked into the bank at 8.45 a.m. This time, the guard didn't stop them.

Day one of the induction began with Aditya Rao addressing the gathering. Aditya had a reputation of being a tough boss. A banker with a reputation to protect. A person who was heavily focused on the task at hand, and for whom career was everything.

New York International Bank had hired thirty-eight new recruits from the premier MBA campuses that year. They had actually hired forty new recruits, but two of them didn't join NYB on the appointed day. All of them were ushered into a conference room that could barely accommodate twenty-five people.

'Good morning, everyone,' Aditya's voice rang in everyone's ears. 'New York International Bank welcomes you all to hell.' For a minute there was stunned silence in the classroom. As if Osama had walked into George Bush's meeting in the Oval Room at the White House. Aditya deliberately paused for a minute before he spoke his next line.

'Yes gentlemen, all of you have entered hell,' he roared. 'For the next twelve months, as we set out on a journey to launch consumer banking in this country, life will be hell for us. We are going to start a war. And in war, there is no family and there are no friends. In war, there is only the enemy and the mission. We cannot rest until we win,' he roared.

Swaminathan was sitting in the first row, listening intently. He was overawed by the tone and the energy in the message. Sundeep was his usual overconfident self, sitting the farthest from the firing line. While Aditya Rao continued elaborating his vision for the bank, Sundeep gently tapped the shoulder of the PYT (pretty young thing) sitting in a row ahead of him. She was Sundeep's batch mate from IIM, Bangalore. Kalpana was her name.

'Kalpana, I think Aditya is kidding.'

'What?'

'With you around, how can this place be hell,' Sundeep whispered in her ears.

'Very funny,' was all that Kalpana could say to this. Sundeep had always flirted with her through the two years at campus, but that was something he did with many women. She never took him seriously. But Sundeep was not the one to give up.

'Thank you, gentlemen. Together we will build the best consumer bank in this country. Congratulations on joining me here. I hope each one of you handpicked guys has a wonderful career at New York International Bank.' Aditya walked off the podium. Swaminathan, sitting in the first row, clapped till his hands got tired and he realised that he was the only one still clapping.

The session broke for tea. Tea and biscuits were being served in the lobby outside the conference room. Swaminathan was completely overawed by the occasion. Aditya Rao's words kept ringing in his mind: 'In war, there is only the enemy and the mission. We cannot rest until we win.' How true it was. Hadn't his life been a war all along? Survival was his mission, and he was close to achieving it. His hand went inside his coat pocket and out came a handkerchief, which wiped a tear that had sneaked out from the corner of his eye.

While Sundeep was having tea during the break, a khaki-clad peon came and handed him a small chit. He opened it and was taken aback. The chit read: 'SEE ME IN MY CABIN

AFTER THE PROGRAMME—ADITYA.' Sundeep didn't know what this meant for him. Was it good? Did it spell disaster? He had no clue. His heart started pounding faster. First day in office and the unit head sends out a note to meet him. He had no choice but to wait, wondering what was in store for him.

8
New York

Knock! Knock! Sundeep's journey back in time was abruptly disturbed by a knock on the cabin door.

'Hi, Michelle.'

Michelle was the Head of Human Resources at New York International Bank. She had shut down her flourishing HR consulting business to join the bank when Tedd Bridge took over as its CEO. She had a tremendous faith in his leadership and business building capabilities.

Michelle was the one who had, in fact, recommended Sundeep's name, when Chetan Bindra moved out to take over as the Global Head of Retail Banking. It was not too difficult to swing the job for Sundeep as he had successfully delivered in roles across the globe.

'How are you, Sundeep?'

'Could be much better,' said Sundeep, in a nervous tone. 'Definitely much better.'

'You should not have done it, Sundeep. Not when you are at this level. I can't protect you even if I want to.'

'I am being framed. You know that,' said Sundeep, in a voice that belied his own confidence in what he was saying. 'Everyone hates my success. Why don't you understand someone is playing me? Anyway, a lot has been said on this. What's the verdict?'

'It will have to wait, Sundeep. Tedd wants to meet you today. By the way, I came to tell you that Tedd can only make it at 3.45. The meeting at 10.30 will now be held at 3.45. Just came to check if that suits you.'

Sundeep nodded his head, as if he knew what was in store for him. Michelle left, leaving him alone in his cabin—just he and his thoughts.

'Coffee?' Louisa came in to drop some papers.

'No, Louisa. Thanks. Please hold all calls till I tell you to put them through. I am not to be disturbed for the next two hours.'

9

When day one of the training programme for new recruits entered the last session, Sundeep's heart was hammering away. Kalpana, who was still sitting in front of Sundeep, could sense that something was wrong with him. He had not tried flirting with her in the past three hours. Though she would never accept it publicly, she quite liked Sundeep's attention. She turned around and looked at him a couple of times, but Sundeep didn't respond. He was lost in his own thoughts. Thoughts of what was in store for him in Aditya's room.

The last few minutes of the day were spent in discussing logistics for the next day and the schedule for the next week. It was a month-long training programme, with a week of classroom training, and three weeks of 'on the job' training, in which the new recruits would spend time at the branches of New York International Bank and observe how work gets done. At the end of one month, they were to reassemble, assess what they have learnt, and list out their preferred areas of work. This would form the basis of their final assignments.

'That's it for the day, guys. We will meet tomorrow morning at nine, in this very room. Our party tonight will begin at 8.30 p.m. at the ballroom of the Taj Mahal Hotel. Brian Close will address you. Please be on time. Formals please. Don't forget your jackets. See ya there.' The moment the speaker closed the evening, Sundeep dashed out of the room. He was extremely nervous and didn't want to stay back and speak to anyone. He headed for the den of the don Aditya Rao.

On his way he saw a rest room and ducked into it. He washed his face and freshened up. He wanted to be sure that he was properly groomed before meeting Aditya for the first time.

For the first time in his life Sundeep was nervous before a meeting. It was the fear of the unknown. Why had Aditya called him? This question was gnawing his brain. But he knew one thing for sure: at the end of day one, if Aditya remembered anyone's name from the list of new recruits, it was his. For good or bad, he didn't know, but he had to capitalise on this.

'I am here to see Mr Rao. My name is Sundeep Srivastava.' Natasha, Aditya's secretary looked up when she heard this.

'Oh yes, Sundeep. He is expecting you. Please wait for a second while I check with him,' said Natasha. She was an attractive young woman, surely not older than twenty-one, and looked like someone straight out of college. Natasha got up from her seat and walked into Aditya's room. Sundeep couldn't help noticing how attractive she was.

Sundeep surveyed the secretary's workspace. She had a large cubicle. In other organisations, six to eight employees would be seated in the space that she occupied. There was a plush leather sofa, definitely an imported item. He tried guessing the place of origin of the sofa. UK, Germany, probably Greece! He couldn't make up his mind and eventually gave up. If the secretary had this kind of space, he could well imagine the size and furnishings of Aditya's office. Despite his nervousness, he couldn't help being distracted by these thoughts. 'One day, I will make this my own office.' He was already imagining the day when he would walk into this office and call it his own.

'Aditya will see you in five minutes. Can I get you something?' Sundeep didn't seem to notice when Natasha returned from Aditya's room. 'Oh no. Thank you. I will just wait here.'

Natasha looked at Sundeep from the corner of her eyes and was reminded of the conversation that Aditya had with her a few hours back. He had just walked back from the induction programme. 'Natasha. There is a guy in there called Sundeep. Please send a note to him and ask him to see me after the session ends for the day.' He had seemed pissed and had walked into his room in a foul mood. He had called her again within the next three minutes and crackled over the speakerphone: 'Before he comes in, can you please get me his CV from the records.'

Secretarial work was new for Natasha, but she was a fast learner. She had been in the organisation for no more than thirty days and had already become indispensable for Aditya. Knowing Aditya, she was feeling a bit sorry for Sundeep. She was beginning to like him.

10

Swaminathan was looking around for Sundeep after the day's training got over. He was looking for familiar faces in an alien crowd. Being an introvert, it was a challenge for him to go and talk to people on his own. He was standing alone in the corner of the training hall, holding the study material that they had been given. It was 6.45 p.m. and the party was at 8.30. He had nowhere to go. 'Might as well go through the study material,' he thought. He walked back into the classroom and opened the spiral bound books. They were actually not books, but collations of the various presentations that the seniors from the organisation had made to the group. He was soon completely engrossed in his reading material.

'Hi, scholar.' Swami was startled when he heard a voice from behind. He looked up through his thick glasses and found Kalpana staring down at him. 'You are Swaminathan, right? I saw your picture on the notice board for our batch.' Swami nodded his head. They hadn't spoken to each other despite being in a small group of thirty-eight people. Swami was too shy to initiate a conversation with anyone, and if it was a woman, Swami would stay a mile away. 'Kalpana,' she continued, pointing at herself. 'You have a whole life to read all this boring stuff. Let's go and get ourselves some fresh air.'

The building that housed the office of New York International Bank was on Marine Drive, overlooking the sea. The Marine Drive promenade offered a breathtaking view of the whole of south Mumbai. For years, Queen's Necklace, as Marine Drive was otherwise called, was dear to the heart of every *Mumbaikar*. Pick up any magazine on Mumbai and you would find it on the cover. The place is particularly engaging at the cusp when day bids adieu and night takes over. Hordes of people gather to see the spectacle of the lights coming on one by one in a gigantic semi-circle—the glittering pearls on the Queen's necklace of lights.

Kalpana literally dragged Swami to Marine Drive, from the confines of the training room. At IIM-A, Swami was rarely seen in the company of women. While all his classmates would actively seek out female company, Swami would be happy in the world of books, spending all his free time in the library. This single-minded dedication had partly to do with his modest means that didn't allow him to spend money on girlfriends like most of his friends. He didn't want to be embarrassed, and so stayed away.

Marine Drive was extremely windy. The waves were lashing against the rocky shore. Water was splashing all over the promenade. Kalpana and Swami were chatting and strolling on the path alongside the shore. Swami was a little worried about his borrowed jacket getting wet; he would have to wear it again tomorrow. But he was embarrassed to mention it. He quietly moved as far away from the water as he could without making it obvious to Kalpana.

Kalpana, however, saw through his effort. 'How sweet!' She was impressed by his gentle mannerisms. 'What a nice guy!' she thought.

'Swami, have you had *bhelpuri* here? There's a fundo shop on the other side. Let's go there.' She figured out a way to take Swami away from the water without embarrassing him.

'Any place where I can get some *kaapi*?' asked Swami.

'Independence Café. Let's go,' she responded spontaneously.

'How do you know this place so well, Kalpana?' asked Swami.

'I have lived half my life here, Swami. I have roamed these streets for years. I know every street, every nook and corner. Leave me in any *galli*, and I will find my way back home.'

Kalpana was born to Rajasthani parents. Her parents moved to UK when she was very young. They spent a few years there, but finding it difficult to bring up a child in alien surroundings, they moved back to India and set up shop in Mumbai in the early seventies. They opened a small electronics goods store. Their business grew rapidly, and now they had a chain of twelve stores in Mumbai alone. Planning to make their chain a nationwide success, they were also talking to a number of foreign brands for collaboration. Kalpana was their only daughter.

Independence Café was a small joint just off Marine Drive. It was frequented by college goers and had a relatively young crowd patronising it.

'I had been frequenting this place for over four years, before moving to Bangalore for my MBA,' Kalpana was telling Swami while the two of them walked in. They looked around and settled for a table in the corner, away from the door.

'I always try and get this seat if it is free. It's away from the door and there is less disturbance here.'

Swami was very happy when he saw the menu. The first item on the menu card was 'South Indian Filter Coffee.'

There were two basic things in life, which no South Indian will ever compromise on: *The Hindu* newspaper, and his morning cup of coffee. Ever since he landed in Mumbai, Swami had got neither.

A shabbily dressed waiter came to the table. 'Yes, maam.' Kalpana did the ordering. 'One cup of strong South Indian filter coffee for sir, and one watermelon juice without sugar for me.'

'Anything else, maam?'

Kalpana looked at Swami and then back at the waiter. 'No, that would be it,' she said.

Swami waited till the waiter was out of earshot. 'Why no sugar? Are you worried about your sugar levels or is it plain calorie consciousness?'

'No! No! Not at all,' laughed Kalpana. 'It is only because sugar spoils the taste of watermelon. I am not calorie conscious at all.'

'You don't need to. You look good anyway.' Swami was shocked at himself for having uttered this. Was he flirting with Kalpana? He had never done such a thing in his whole life. Clumsy though he was, Kalpana couldn't resist a smile, and Swami was embarrassed. He didn't know what to say.

Kalpana found his embarrassment quite amusing. She was beginning to like his simplicity. Swami came across as an honest, down-to-earth guy. No one makes guys like these nowadays, she thought. 'How do you like Mumbai, Swami?'

This was just the beginning of their conversation. They talked about nearly everything under the sun. The weather, their families, their aspirations, their lifestyles, and more. Completely oblivious of the passage of time, they seemed to be enjoying each other's company.

Kalpana just happened to glance at her watch and exclaimed, 'Oh my god! It's 8.30 p.m. We will have to rush immediately.' Kalpana picked up the tab on their way out. Swami couldn't have paid for the three rounds of coffee and watermelon juice.

By the time they reached the ballroom, it was 8.35 p.m. They were five minutes late. Everyone else from their group had arrived. Brian Close, the CEO of the bank in India was yet to show up. Swami looked around the room trying to find Sundeep, but there was no trace of him. Sundeep was with Aditya Rao.

11

'Aditya will see you now, Sundeep,' said Natasha. 'I will show you to his room.'

Sundeep had been waiting outside Aditya's room for quite some time now. The five minutes that Natasha had initially indicated stretched to forty-five minutes. But Sundeep just had to wait. He could not push his way through here, especially since it concerned Aditya Rao.

'Good evening, sir,' said Sundeep as he walked into Aditya's room.

'Call me Aditya. There are no sirs here.'

'Sure, Aditya.'

'Take a seat, young man.'

'Thank you.'

Aditya Rao pulled out Sundeep's CV from the folder in front of him and looked at it, feet nonchalantly placed up on the table. Sundeep was shivering in his pants. What had he done?

'Sundeep Srivastava, BE, MBA, Gold Medal at IIM-Bangalore. Topper at IIT. Good. Army major's son. Mother, a doctor. Impressive, very impressive young man. Summer training at ANZ Grindlays Bank. Quite an impressive pedigree, son.'

'Thank you, sir.'

'But what was definitely not impressive was your behaviour in the training session this morning.'

Sundeep didn't know what to say. He chose to keep quiet, lest he said something wrong. Obviously, something he had done in the morning had pissed off Aditya.

'What do you think you were doing, Sundeep? You were extremely distracted on the first day of your job. I noticed that you were also disturbing those who wanted to learn something. This is not acceptable, my friend.'

It was clear that Aditya was unhappy. But Sundeep was no idiot. He realised that this was his only chance—not only to make up for what he had done, but also to leave a lasting impression on Aditya. If he managed to pull this one through, he would always be on top of mind as far as Aditya was concerned.

Sundeep apologised for his behaviour. He realised that this was the best thing to do. 'Aditya, I was slightly excited and didn't realise what I was doing. I am sorry.' Aditya too had cooled down since morning and didn't push the case.

'Sundeep, when you join a new organisation, it is very important to understand the organisation and imbibe its culture. You should try to know your colleagues, realise their strengths and weaknesses, and focus on the task at hand. This will help you go a long way in any organisation. First impressions last long. Always remember this.'

'I will ensure that you do not have a reason to complain, sir. I will take utmost care in the future,' responded the ambitious Sundeep to his boss' sermon. Sundeep wanted to leave Aditya with a good feeling. No point getting egoistic with the boss.

Aditya had made his point and was a bit relaxed now. 'Good, did you get a chance to go through our retail launch strategy,' asked Aditya. The retail launch strategy paper was a document given to all new recruits as a part of their joining kit.

'I briefly read it in the break.'

'What do you think of it?' Aditya was testing Sundeep.

'Aditya, with due respect, I have a concern on the launch strategy outlined in that document.' Sundeep was taking a risk. He had decided to challenge Aditya on this.

Aditya looked at him disdainfully. 'Go on, you have five minutes of air time.'

'Sir, this morning, you talked about our launch plans. I remember you mention that we were planning to launch credit cards first, before we launch any other product in the retail segment. I have serious doubts about whether this would work in India. That's why I quickly went through the strategy paper during the break, to figure out the rationale. Even after reading the document, I am not convinced.'

Aditya was listening. Sundeep had his complete attention. 'Why do you think so?'

This was Sundeep's chance. He said:

'There is no doubt that we will be able to launch cards in a big way. We will get customers and will also manage to get them to use our cards. In the process, we will build a huge client base that will be the envy of every other organisation. In fact, so huge a customer base that our existing infrastructure and technology will not be able to support it. Our overburdened service delivery system will creak, and we will give away all our goodwill and market to the next player who comes in with better services and systems.

'We need to launch, in the short run, products and services that are supported by the available technology and systems. And use that to build our brand in the retail space. This will give us some time to set up the required infrastructure.

'In our country, we have seen a number of nationalised banks launching big products with half-baked processes and failing miserably. We cannot afford to do that. Sir?'

'Aditya! Not sir.'

'Sorry, Aditya. If you were to ask me, the first product I would launch in this market would be car loans. It is a product which is backed by security, and there is no large player in the market. If we do it well, it will establish us as a leading player in the market, and give us some revenues to play around with.

'Every automobile manufacturer worth his name will queue up for tie-ups with us. We will get enormous media presence. Every car ad will scream: "Auto loans from New York International Bank." We will ride their campaigns, on their expense. They will spend the money and we will book the loans. This will give us time to set up an infrastructure to sell credit cards. We will then be able to sell cards from every car dealership in the country. Just imagine the distribution capability we would have set up. Imagine a situation where we start selling cards through eight hundred car dealerships across the country. If each dealership sells a hundred cards a month, we would have sold eighty thousand cards a month, which will propel us to a different level altogether.'

All this while Aditya Rao hadn't moved. His eyes didn't leave Sundeep for a minute. Was this a rookie speaking, or was this an experienced professional? Aditya was completely floored. Aditya believed in debate. He did not propagate a dictatorial approach to business. He was willing to learn, even if it was from a rookie. However, no one had ever come up and told him that he was wrong. When Aditya had set out to build this business, his thinking was exactly the same as Sundeep's. Somewhere down the line, it got diluted and he decided to place his faith in NYB's expertise in cards in other markets. But what Sundeep was saying made eminent sense to him.

But what Sundeep did not tell him, and did not intend to, was that his last trimester project at IIM-B was on 'Emerging Retail Banking in India.' He had done an extensive study on this subject, and, hence, knew almost everything that he needed to know. Surprisingly, in his project report Sundeep had argued that the launch strategy for any retail bank in India had to be driven by its credit cards product.

Then why did he change his stance now, and say exactly the opposite to Aditya?

Well, no one knew.

The discussion between the boss and the new recruit went on and on, and neither was in a mood to stop it.

Just then the door opened and Natasha came in. 'Aditya, you are getting late for Brian's address at the Taj Mahal Hotel.'

'Oh yes. I completely forgot about it. Thanks, Natasha.'

He looked at Sundeep, then back at Natasha, and said, 'Will you please call the hotel and get a message delivered to Mr Close that I, and this young guy here, will not be attending.'

Natasha raised her eyebrows, but couldn't question her boss. 'Sure, Aditya.'

Sundeep and Aditya's discussion went on for another three hours. By the time they finished, it was well past 10.00 p.m.

'Well done, young man. I must say that your CV is not the only thing that looks impressive. You have an impressive mind too.'

On his way out, Aditya looked at Natasha. 'Natasha, if you are not doing anything tonight, why don't you take this young guy out for dinner and send me the bill. I have not only made him miss Brian Close's address, but also his dinner.' Before Natasha could respond, Aditya was out of the door, leaving Sundeep behind with her.

'You are stuck with me tonight.' Natasha just smiled at this cheeky remark from Sundeep. Wasn't she happy to be stuck with him?

'Do you normally leave this late?' Sundeep tried to start a conversation, as Natasha was shutting down her computer.

'Not everyday. But at least twice a week. Aditya normally works late and expects you to work late too. His earlier secretary,

Leena, used to work really hard. She would do everything on time, but had to leave at six everyday. She had a problem. Her daughter was in a day care, which would shut down at 6.30 p.m. I have picked up from others that she was the most efficient secretary to have ever worked in New York International Bank. Still, Aditya didn't like her. She resigned about two months ago. For Aditya, if you leave before him, you haven't worked hard enough.'

Sundeep had just learned his first lesson: Do not leave before Aditya does. If that was the culture in New York International Bank, he better follow it.

The two of them stepped out to Kala Ghoda in the Fort area of Mumbai for a quick bite. They had an uneventful and quick dinner. Both were tired at the end of a long day.

Natasha quite enjoyed Sundeep's company. Sundeep, on the other hand, kept comparing her with Kalpana. Natasha would run Kalpana close on almost every aspect, but Sundeep was biased in favour of Kalpana.

By the time they finished their dinner, Sundeep had gathered that Natasha was single and did not have a boyfriend. He could also make out that Natasha kinda liked him. He invited her to dinner on Saturday evening, which Natasha promised to consider. She couldn't have said yes at the first instance, and Sundeep knew that.

12

Most of the foreign banks in those days had expat CEOs. NYB was no exception. Expat CEOs in the Indian financial services market had a typical problem. They failed to see the Indian market as something different from the developed world they came from. It beat them why a customer in Delhi could not access his account from Mumbai. Technology drove banks in the developed world; in India everything was pretty much manual. It was difficult for them to understand why it was impolite to push an Indian customer to an ATM for withdrawing cash, when in the US, not to have ATMs was simply inefficient service delivery. They couldn't grasp why, in a country with over a billion people, it was difficult to find thirty smart, educated persons.

They also got into another usual MNC rut. Converted into dollars, the money an organisation would make in India after tremendous struggle would hardly stack up. India would contribute only a miniscule proportion to an MNC's global profits and hence would be way down in the pecking order. This would hurt the expat's self-esteem and they would want to go back to their home country.

Things have changed a lot since then, but when Swami and Sundeep joined New York International Bank, things were still pretty much gloomy. The hierarchies in every multinational was reminiscent of the days of the Raj; the *brown* Indians would never get the top post. A foreigner needn't be a top performer to become a CEO in India. An average performer willing to go to India stood a good chance to get the job. India was perceived to be a difficult and hostile country to work in. Punishment posting, it was called. Expats sent to India also got a hardship allowance for having agreed to work here.

Brian Close too was one such banker. He had joined NYB over three decades ago, as a teller—the ones who count cash behind the counter whenever you walk into a bank—and was close to retirement. India was his last assignment and he was due to retire in nine months.

Brian Close's speech was nothing great. He was one of those expat CEOs who begin to think of themselves as rock stars the moment they get the microphone, and think that the Indian employees are suckers who would gleefully lap up any Hindi word thrown at them in an anglicised accent.

'Naaamaastey Iiindiaaaaa,' shrieked Brian Close. He expected the new recruits to jump in ecstasy at his Hindi. That didn't happen. Still he went on for over forty-five minutes, without conviction. When he stepped off the podium, there was a thunderous applause. One thing was not clear though: Did the new recruits applaud him for a fabulous speech, or were they simply relieved that the torture had ended! Brian thought it was the former, while the look on the faces of Swami and Kalpana made one believe that it was definitely the latter.

Kalpana was glued to Swami for almost the entire evening. She had begun to admire him. Swami was a humble human being, with a deep intellect and a clear thought process. When Brian came and met them after the address, Kalpana was impressed by the way in which Swami spoke with him—crisp, concise, clear, and, most important, honest. She couldn't help comparing him with the aggressive, arrogant, and brash Sundeep. Swami clearly stood out.

On her way home, Kalpana couldn't stop thinking about Swami and Sundeep. Natasha too was lost in thoughts, but she had only Sundeep on her mind.

13

On day two of the induction, both Sundeep and Swami came on time—not like the first day when they both were two hours ahead of schedule.

'Didn't see you at Brian's party last night. What happened?' asked Swami, the moment he saw Sundeep. The latter was not listening. His eyes were focused on the door. Kalpana had just walked in. She was looking stunning in a violet sari. Her free flowing hair added to her girlish charms, leaving Sundeep speechless for a minute. 'Sundeep!' Swami called out again. But Sundeep was already heading towards the door.

'What a bomb!' murmured Sundeep when Kalpana passed him. She heard him but decided to ignore it. She went straight to the vacant seat next to Swami.

Sundeep realised that Swami was asking him something and turned towards him. 'Oh yes, Swami. How was the dinner last night?'

'Sundeep, I was asking you why you didn't come for the dinner.' This time Sundeep heard him. 'Oh, Aditya had called me.'

'Why?' Swami was worried that Sundeep had screwed up something.

'He wanted to talk about the retail launch strategy.' Sundeep was showing off. 'He wanted to know our views.'

'Hope you told him that the launch strategy was flawed and it should not be a credit cards led strategy. Did you tell him about our lunch time conversation yesterday that the launch paper is not a well thought through document, rather a hastily made one that will not cut ice in the market.'

'I didn't get a chance,' lied Sundeep. He hadn't taken his eyes off Kalpana. 'She is looking terrific,' he murmured.

'Yes, she is.' When Sundeep heard Swami say this, he realised that his murmur was a bit too loud.

Sundeep did not tell Swami anything about his discussion with Aditya. Everything he had told Aditya the previous evening were actually ripped from his lunch time conversation with Swami. Sundeep had chosen not to mention Swami and had passed off everything as his own thoughts. He had no qualms about seizing the opportunity to impress Aditya.

Swami would never get to know of the discussion Aditya had with Sundeep. Round one had gone to Sundeep, without Swami even realising it.

14

Aditya was late for office on Tuesday. He had reached home quite late, well past midnight, after his crazy discussion with Sundeep. 'The guy has balls,' thought Rao on his way home. He could not help being impressed by the young talent he had unearthed.

He stayed awake for a long time, thinking about Sundeep's point of view. There was significant merit in what he said. For long, Aditya's office had resembled the sets of *Yes Minister*, the popular British soap. But finally someone from outside had come in like a whiff of fresh air. He will go a long way, thought Aditya, as his eyes closed involuntarily.

It was 4.00 a.m. when he slept. As a consequence, he overslept and was late to work. Normally, Aditya would leave early in order to beat the heavy morning traffic. Today, however, he was late and had to contend with twenty-five extra minutes of driving through the maddening Mumbai traffic.

When he reached office, there were three messages from Brian Close waiting for him. 'What's it about?' he asked Natasha when she gave him the messages.

'Don't know. I asked him, but he wouldn't tell. He seemed quite easy and had even dropped in once to see you. He requested that you call him once you get in. Didn't seem to be anything urgent.'

'Thanks. How was dinner, sweetheart?' He was surely teasing her.

'Was very good. In fact, Sundeep couldn't stop singing ballads about your conversation with him last night.'

'Good. An intelligent young man he is. A bit arrogant though.'

'Can you please line up dinner for him with me on Saturday? At my place.' Natasha couldn't hide her disappointment. She was looking forward to dinner with Sundeep on Saturday, but now her boss had usurped him. She didn't say anything. Her look said it all.

'Well, if I have upset any plans that you might have already made, may I invite you to join us too.' Aditya was too perceptive.

'Also check with Brian, if he is free. I will drop in and say hello.' Aditya walked into his room while Natasha dialled Brian's extension.

'Mr Brian on his way to see you.' Natasha breezed into Aditya's room and announced. The very next moment, Brain walked in.

'Aditya, I must tell you this. At the dinner last night, I met these two young recruits—Swaaamee and Kaalpaanaa. Very bright guys. I had an interesting conversation with them. While I was speaking with them, they mentioned that we should not launch credit cards without building a service infrastructure. Instead we should launch other quick revenue generating products. Quite interesting that they should mention car loans. They were emphatic that we should stay away from credit cards till we have strengthened our branch infrastructure and service delivery channels. I found that discussion quite intriguing.

Couldn't wait to mention it to you. It is worth your while to have a chat with those blokes. Not sure, but something tells me that we might have missed a trick or two.'

Aditya couldn't hide his surprise. 'Brian, it is quite a coincidence that you should mention it now. Around the same time yesterday, I had a chat with a guy called Sundeep and he had a similar view. So taken in was I by this discussion, that I couldn't cut it short and attend your address. But yes, I will speak to these guys as well.' He then buzzed Natasha to join them.

'Natasha, will you please ask Swami and Kalpana also to join Sundeep for the Saturday night dinner with me.' Natasha nodded.

15

Aditya's home was a 20th floor penthouse apartment in a posh sea facing apartment complex on Carter road in Bandra. Huge by any standards, it covered 4,500 square feet. The sprawling living room alone could play host to over a hundred people. It had three seating bays, with carpets imported from Afghanistan providing comfort for the feet. Antique furniture brought in from the villages of Tanjore gave it a rich feel. Many visitors to his house often wondered how Aditya stayed here all alone.

Aditya had separated from his wife Mandira after twelve years of marriage. Not many people in New York International Bank knew about his wife or had met her. The separation, which happened over two years ago, when both of them were in the US, was bitter and financially draining. Despite that, Aditya had enough to last him a lifetime. The talk was that after he joined New York International Bank, Aditya had little or no time for his family, and slowly both of them started drifting away. The fact that they had no children didn't quite help either.

He had a cook who stayed with him. He had taken good care of him for over a decade now.

Kalpana was the first to arrive, followed by Sundeep and Natasha. Natasha had picked up Sundeep on her way. Swami was the last to arrive. Unfamiliar with Mumbai, it had taken him some time to locate the building.

Aditya was a great host. Natasha helped him and played the role of a good hostess to the core. This was the first time that any new recruits had been invited to Aditya's house for dinner within a week of their coming on board. Something had to be different with these guys.

'Where's your drink, Sundeep?' Natasha asked. 'I will just get up and fix myself one,' he said. Sundeep didn't need any invitation for booze.

She turned to Swami, 'Where's yours?'

'I do not drink. I will have a Thumbs Up.' Those were the days when Coke and Pepsi had not re-entered India. Thumbs Up and Campa Cola dominated the soft drink scene.

Everyone looked at Swami as if he was from a different planet. He was embarrassed. 'I have never felt like drinking,' he said.

Aditya sensed his discomfort and quickly changed the topic. 'So Swami, your parents are in Chennai?'

'My mother, sir. Dad passed away when I was two. He died of cancer.'

'I am so sorry, Swami,' said Aditya. 'Your mother must be extremely proud of all that you have achieved in a short while. I would like to meet that lady one day.'

'Thank you, sir,' said Swami. He couldn't take all the adulation. All this embarrassed him.

Meanwhile, Sundeep was ogling at Kalpana. She was wearing a red top with a plunging backline over a pair of Levi's. Sundeep couldn't take his eyes off her. She looked stunning. Ever since Kalpana had started spending time with Swami, she had been ignoring him. Sundeep was getting a bit worked up on that. Whole of this week, he had been trying to ask her out for dinner and she had been constantly putting it off.

Natasha was constantly observing Sundeep. In a world of middle-aged pot bellied bankers, Sundeep was one young dude she was looking forward to. She had spent hours getting ready, trying out numerous outfits before she settled on one, and Sundeep was not even looking at her. She was looking forward to this night, but it seemed to belong to Kalpana. She had offered to pick up Sundeep, despite the fact that the place where Sundeep stayed was out of the way for her. Sundeep was very quiet all along the route. He could sense the widening chasm in his relationship with Kalpana. Natasha tried to cheer him up. She flirted with him, but the normal Sundeep was missing.

'You seem to be lost somewhere,' said Aditya. 'Is everything fine?' He was looking at Sundeep. Natasha was not the only one who had noticed.

Once he had everyone's attention, Aditya started talking about the plans for New York International Bank. 'Brian and I had separate conversations with you on the launch of our bank's retail business. All of you had some interesting thoughts. The purpose of tonight's meeting is to brainstorm and lay out the broad priorities for the launch. Global HQ wants us to be self-funding in three years time. That is, we will have to generate the required investments from our profits in three years time. Natasha will take notes.' The preamble was set. This was followed by a long and arduous discussion. It was good that none of them had to go back to their families as they kept no track of time. Sundeep, Swami and Kalpana battled it out with Aditya on the product sequencing of the launch.

All three were very passionate about what they felt. Aditya was playing a smart game. He contested even those points of view that were not divergent from his. He played the devil's advocate. He questioned every simple logic. He made sure that they thought through every option and every consequence of their actions. It was five in the morning when they called it quits.

Sundeep was completely drunk. The adrenalin rush of the discussion had kept him going. The moment it was time to pack up, he couldn't take it any more and collapsed.

Aditya called for his cook, 'Ramu Kaka, please take him to the guest room and leave him there. He can find his way back to the hotel tomorrow.'

'It's OK, Aditya. I will drop him at his hotel,' said Natasha. Aditya just smiled and nodded.

Ramu Kaka helped Sundeep get into Natasha's car. Natasha then drove towards Sundeep's hotel.

Swami and Kalpana left together. Both were sober.

16

Kalpana and Swami decided to take a walk on the beach. The mild chill in the winds, the lonely stretch of the early morning beach, a few joggers strolling around, and the mild roar of the waves dying on the beach made it a very romantic setting. They found a clean stretch and settled down.

A young boy with a kettle in hand came running to serve some tea. Swami looked at Kalpana and she nodded. A couple of rupees exchanged hands, and Swami and Kalpana got two *kullars* (clay cups) of steaming hot tea.

'Have you always been so shy?' asked Kalpana.

'I don't know,' said Swami. 'But why?'

'Did you ever have a girlfriend?'

'Never,' said Swami, his eyes riveted on the sand.

'Why?'

'Never found one. And I don't have the personality that women look for these days.'

'Rubbish. Don't lie.'

'Well, Kalpana, I couldn't afford one. Taking care of my family and meeting my basic expenses never left me with any money to spend on girlfriends. So I stayed away from them. Women don't like paupers for boyfriends, do they?'

'This woman does not mind a pauper for a boyfriend,' Kalpana said. Swami, for the first time, moved his eyes from the sand and looked up. Kalpana was smiling.

He did not know what to say. The visit to the café last week was the first time in his life that he had gone out with a woman, and here she was already proposing to him. He was too stunned to react. This had never happened to him. His eyes went back to survey the sand.

'Swami, ever since meeting you, the one thing I have admired about you is your humility. Anyone else with even half your intelligence would be screaming from the rooftops, stinking of arrogance. But you are different, Swami, and that's the reason why I like you. If there is anyone I have met so far, with whom I feel like spending the rest of my life with, it's you.'

Swami looked back at her, at a loss for words.

'You need not give me an answer right away. You can think it through. We can remain good friends till then. We will remain great pals even if your answer is a no.'

Swami was listening. He was confused. All this was a bit filmy for him. He did not know what to say. He had a mother and a sister to provide for. His sister had to be married off. True, he too had started liking Kalpana, and looked forward to spending time with her. But this was too fast for him.

The fact that Kalpana was a Rajasthani and from a very well off family was not making matters any easier for him. What will his mom say? She had lived her life for him. It was payback time. How could he be so selfish now?

Swami knew that Kalpana was the kind of girl he would like to take home to his mother. But she was a Rajasthani. His mother was a conservative South Indian. What would she think of him?

He did not want to say no. His heart wanted to say yes. Yet he couldn't. Kalpana understood the turmoil going on within his mind. She put her arms around him and held him tightly. 'Come, let's go. My heart is lighter, now that I have told you what I wanted to. I will not bring it up again till you want to. I will wait for your decision.'

They got up and walked silently next to each other. They would have hardly walked two hundred metres, when Kalpana felt something moving next to her hand. She was startled and looked to her left. A smile came to her lips. It was Swami. He was clumsily trying to hold her hand. When he finally managed to, he looked up and smiled at her. They walked back hand in hand. Swami had made his decision.

17

Natasha parked the car in the porch of the hotel where Sundeep was staying. The doorman helped her carry Sundeep to the room. Both of them carefully put Sundeep on the bed. Sundeep had passed out and had no clue what was happening. Natasha gave the doorman a twenty-rupee note before he left, closing the door behind him. Natasha looked at her watch. It was 5.30 a.m. She didn't feel like leaving, as she didn't want to leave Sundeep in this state. Had she fallen for him? Of course, she had!

She plonked herself on the sofa in the room and switched on the TV. She surfed all the channels and settled on an old Hindi classic that was running on one of the hotel channels. The next thing she knew was someone shaking her, asking her to get up. She had fallen asleep while watching the movie. Sundeep had gotten up and was surprised to see her sleeping on his sofa.

'What are you doing here? I was waiting there for you all night,' said Sundeep pointing at his bed.

'Very funny, Mr Srivastava! The least you can do is thank me. You were drunk and out of your senses when I brought you here,' said Natasha. She was not upset with Sundeep for his comment. Sundeep smiled. 'Thank you, sweetheart,' he said and kissed Natasha on her left cheek.

It was Sunday morning. There was no pressure to go to work and hence both of them were very relaxed. Natasha taunted him about how he landed in bed last night.

'What about Kalpana?' asked Sundeep.

'Swami went to drop her home.'

Sundeep's face shrunk. He was not too happy about the budding relationship between Swami and Kalpana.

'Any plans for breakfast?' Natasha's question brought Sundeep back to reality.

18

Aditya was in office very early on Monday morning. He was thinking about his discussion with Sundeep and Swami on Saturday. Retail banking was new in India. Experienced talent was in short supply. He had tried to go out and hire from competing banks. He had been unsuccessful. No bank had enough people who knew how to run a retail bank. He had the option of getting in expats from US to help set up the business. But that was an option he didn't want to consider, as it would render the project a non-starter. The expats would apply an American solution to an Indian problem. He knew that this would only lead to more heartburn, frustration, and complete failure of the project.

And here were two young men with the energy, the will, and the commitment to drive this new initiative for New York International Bank. While they had thirty-six other colleagues who had joined with them, these two guys were different. Their intellect was far superior, and their understanding of business complexities supreme. These were people who could earn the respect of their colleagues in no time.

Yet, they were untested. Should he take a punt on these two guys? Would it work, or would it bomb? He couldn't make up his mind. The organisation had approved a plan to launch credit cards in the first quarter of 1987. These two prodigies were recommending that they launch retail loans before anything else, and, heart of hearts, he agreed with them. Why not challenge them with the loans business while someone else goes about launching credit cards. It would at best prepone the launch of retail banking in India. They could, irrespective of what Swami and Sundeep did, go ahead with the cards launch in March 1987 as planned. He required an organisation buy in for this. Brian had to be on his side.

'Natasha, get me Brian on the line,' Aditya's voice crackled over the speakerphone.

Natasha called back within thirty seconds: 'Brian on the line, sir.'

Aditya spoke to Brian at length about his plan. The conversation went on for over thirty minutes. Brian's room was on a floor above Aditya's. 'Aditya, why don't you come up. Let's talk this through and close it,' Brian said.

'In a minute, Brian.'

Aditya disconnected the phone and ran. He did not want this break to disrupt his thought process. When he stepped into Brian's room, he was panting.

'Relax Aditya, relax,' this statement from Brian irritated him, but he didn't say a word. After all, Brian was his boss.

The discussion was extremely animated and lasted another forty-five minutes. 'Thank you, Brian. I will ensure that I am on top of this. It seems to be the right thing to do. I will also ensure that there are no surprises in this before your successor is in place. I have lots at stake,' said Aditya as he stepped out of Brian's room.

19

Sundeep and Swami were in their second week of training. Mr Sawant, the training head of the bank, was taking a session on 'career progression.'

'Excuse me, Mr Sawant,' Natasha knocked on the door of the training room.

Sawant excused himself and came out of the room. 'Aditya wants to meet Sundeep and Swaminathan, ASAP,' said Natasha. ASAP meant As Soon As Possible, and Mr Sawant, an old hand, did not require anybody to tell him that when Aditya said ASAP, he meant NOW.

When Sundeep and Swami walked out of the training hall, both thought: 'Now what?' Natasha had disappeared and hence they couldn't even ask anything. They were nervous. 'I haven't done anything wrong today. Hope it is not about my passing out on Saturday night,' said Sundeep.

'If I understand Aditya correctly, he wouldn't have pulled us out of a training programme for that. And why me? If he wanted to speak to you about Saturday night, he should have called you and not both of us.' Swami had a point. But that couldn't satisfy Sundeep. He was tense again. He was beginning to wonder why he was getting tense every time Aditya called.

'Come in, boys,' said Aditya as soon as he heard the knock on the door. 'Natasha, can you please organise some coffee and join us. This is going to take some time. And before you come in, please get Kalpana also to join in.'

Swami and Sundeep gave each other blank looks. They were wondering what the hell was going on. Natasha came in. The coffee came in another six minutes, around the same time that Kalpana joined them. All this while, Aditya was doing his mail and hadn't spoken a word. This was adding to the suspense.

'OK guys,' said Aditya, getting up and moving away from his IBM notebook. 'I have something interesting to talk about, and if you guys are ready, we can start.' Everyone in the room looked at each other, then at Aditya, and nodded in unison. No one spoke.

'I had a chat with Brian. I mentioned our discussion on Saturday night. He has agreed to a change in the launch plans,' he announced. 'We will no longer launch credit cards in this market. We will first launch our loans business and then decide what we want to do next.' 'Fabulous,' everyone said at almost the same time. This was turning out to be their first strategic victory ever. Everyone's face lit up.

'I have agreed with Brian that we will launch car loans, cash loans, and, as Swami mentioned, we will get into the mass market with motorcycle loans and employee loans for corporates.' Then Aditya paused.

The statement was a very simple one, but its meaning was profound. Here was an organisation, which was willing to value a new thought process, new ideas, new principles, and a new approach, even if they came from someone who had no exposure to this business.

'That's not all,' continued Aditya. 'There will be a team of five working on this project, and all five are in this room. This will be the core retail banking team for our bank.' Sundeep jumped out of his chair. 'Eureka! If there is anything better than sex on the beach, this is it.' Pin drop silence followed. Sundeep suddenly realised the inappropriateness of his statement and quietly sat down.

Aditya burst out laughing. Everyone else followed suit. This was the most thrilling day in the life of each one of them. To be part of a launch team for one of the largest banks in the world, and that too within two weeks of joining. They couldn't have asked for anything better.

'Swami,' Aditya continued, 'You and Kalpana will work on launching loans for two-wheelers, both scooters and motorcycles, and personal loans for corporate employees, and Sundeep, you will work on the launch of car loans.' Aditya's voice was music to everyone's ears.

Aditya went on to explain: 'We have a ninety-day deadline for the launch of these two products. In the next three months we have to get these products up and running. We are in May right now. I have committed to Brian Close that we will launch these by the end of August. We will have till the year-end to make these into successful revenue generators for the bank. Come January, we are committed to launch credit cards in this country. This is a commitment made at the board level, and we cannot go back on it. If we do not make your products a success by January, we will have to shift our focus to credit cards.'

The others in the room could not believe their ears. April got over twenty days back, so Aditya couldn't be playing an April fool prank on them. Swami was almost in tears. Natasha began to wonder what her role was, when Aditya continued: 'Since we have a lots to do and we do not have time on our hands, Natasha will be an assistant for the entire group. She will cease to be my secretary from this very instant and will move to a project role for the next three months.'

'Will we begin work on this post our training?' Kalpana asked him.

'Are you kidding? If you guys needed training, you wouldn't be here. All of you are off training from this very instant. If we harness any dreams of launching these products in the next ninety days, we cannot afford to waste a single moment from now on. I have spoken to Sawant and he has agreed to release the three of you right now,' said Aditya.

'Get cracking, guys. We will meet everyday in the evening to take stock. We cannot afford to fail. I have stuck my neck out and believe me when I say this—I do not like my neck tickled.'

20
New York

'Are you fine, Sundeep? Shall I get you something for lunch?' Louisa was getting a bit concerned since Sundeep had been behaving quite weirdly since morning. 'It's an hour past noon and you haven't had anything. Natasha called about an hour back. She wanted to know if you have eaten something, since you left quite early and didn't have breakfast at home.'

'I am fine, Louisa. I will have my regular veg sandwich, without any butter. And brown bread, please.' That was Sundeep's regular lunch, ever since he had landed in New York.

His health had been a bit erratic of late. Fluctuating sugar and cholesterol levels, sedentary lifestyles, and thirty cigarettes a day didn't look like a healthy package.

Natasha ensured that he took care of his health. She also insisted on regular medical check-ups. Sundeep was smart. He would start controlling his dietary habits a week before his regular check-ups. This would ensure decent medical reports and keep Natasha happy.

When Louisa interrupted him, he was thinking about his initiation into the world of corporate success. His first champagne toast had come within two weeks of his reporting for his first job. He was wondering how could he make that count?

21

Kalpana, Swami, and Sundeep slogged their butts off. Aditya was constantly on their backs, driving them crazy. But they did not mind it. They were here to learn the trade and this was an opportunity even a mad man wouldn't give them.

Sundeep, who had to launch car loans, visited every single car dealer in town. He also started making rounds of car manufacturers for exclusive financing tie-ups.

For the car manufacturers, all this was new. No bank had ever approached them, leave alone pamper them. Sundeep was able to wrangle out special customer-friendly schemes for financing new cars. The manufacturers were quick to jump on to the bandwagon as they saw great value in some financier coming along to push car sales in order to pump his loan numbers. Sundeep convinced the manufacturers that they would be able to double their sales if the easy financing options which NYB was willing to offer was bundled with the car sales.

Swami and Kalpana on the other hand started visiting large corporates and public sector units for cash loans to their employees. Who wouldn't want a loan? Those were the days when banks were deposit gatherers and lending was only done to large corporates. So when the young guns of NYB went around with their loan schemes, people queued up to hear them. Only politicians and film stars were supposed to elicit such an overwhelming response. In one unit in the Kolar Gold Fields near Bangalore, there was a virtual stampede to avail NYB loans. At the end of every day, Swami and Kalpana would wonder why anyone hadn't done this earlier in this country.

The two businesses were a hit from the very start.

There, however, was one casualty. Sundeep could see that Kalpana was losing interest in him. She was no longer responding to his advances. She would spend all her time with Swami. 'They are working on the same project,' thought Sundeep and consoled himself.

In the first week of August, Aditya was called to New York. He left on a Thursday. 'Today's evening meeting has been called off, since Aditya is off to New York. He asked me to call all of you and pass on the message,' said Natasha over the phone. This was a god sent message for Sundeep.

'Have you told Kalpana?' asked Sundeep.

'You are the first one I called, heartless.'

'OK. Don't bother calling her. I will call her and inform her. I will pass on the message to Swami too.'

'Thanks. Call me if you need anything.'

Sundeep kept the phone down and called Kalpana's extension. 'Hey, glad I caught ya. Today's meeting is off.'

'Oh. Because Aditya is away in NY,' Kalpana said. 'I was hoping that we guys would meet up and talk without Aditya.'

'If you got nothing to do tonight, how does dinner sound?' Sundeep was hoping Kalpana would say yes. 'It's been a long time since we did this.'

'Dinner with you! Never,' said Kalpana.

'What the fuck is your problem?' retorted a furious Sundeep.

'Just kidding ya! I have already committed for dinner with someone else. Sorry, sweetheart. If you have time, let's pick up a quick coffee right now.'

Sundeep was quite put off, even though he realised Kalpana said that in jest.

'I am a bit caught up now. Need to go. Talk to you later.' He said and hung up.

Later he realised that he was guilty of not spending time with Kalpana. He promised himself that he will find time to ensure Kalpana gets back to him.

Natasha had just come up to Sundeep to hand over a few documents, which Aditya had given her. She had overheard Sundeep's side of the conversation with Kalpana. She could make out that Sundeep was not happy with the outcome. She was feeling bad for him and decided to step in. She invited him for dinner. 'It's been a while, Sundeep. How about tonight? I am free.' Sundeep, was quite pissed with Kalpana, and, on rebound, decided to go out with Natasha.

Natasha knew that she was not Sandeep's first choice, but she didn't mind. All through dinner, she kept wondering why Sundeep liked Kalpana so much. There were moments when she felt like expressing her feelings to Sundeep, but the fear of rejection stopped her. She preferred to wait and watch.

After returning from New York, Aditya announced at the Monday evening meeting: 'New York is extremely happy with our progress. We have managed to create a stir in the group's management. They are all waiting for the initial results. You guys are going to become stars. We cannot fail.'

After this initial euphoria, it was back to business. 'Can I now get some updates from you guys,' demanded Aditya.

'We are meeting Brij Mohan Munjal day after tomorrow. Will you be able to come with us, Aditya?' said Swami.

Brij Mohan Munjal was the Chairman of Hero Honda Motors Ltd., the largest manufacturers of motorcycles in the world. Getting a chance to meet him was a special opportunity, not to be missed at any cost. If they wanted a deal, they had to get it now. There would be no second chance.

'No, Swami. I won't be able to come with you. Why don't you go with Kalpana?'

'In case Aditya is unable to come with you, would you want me to come with you, Swami? I have worked with car manufacturers in financing tie-ups.' Sundeep was not really offering help; he wanted to somehow stop Kalpana from going alone with Swami. He had noticed her interest in Swami, but had ignored it, assuming that their closeness was purely professional.

'I think we should let the two of them go,' Aditya quickly interjected. 'You already have your plate full with car loan deals, Sundeep.'

Sundeep didn't like the thought of Swami and Kalpana being away together for three days, but he could do nothing now.

After the meeting, while they were leaving Aditya's room, Sundeep walked up to Kalpana, held her by the elbow, and said, 'When you are back, we need to sit and chat.'

'What's the matter, Sundeep? Anything I need to know?'

'I would rather talk to you when you have some time for me.'

Kalpana was a bit taken aback by Sundeep's abrupt manner. She and Sundeep went back a long way.

'Sundeep, you appear to be quite stressed out. Come, let's get ourselves a cup of coffee. The coffee at India Coffee House is good. Swami and I have been there a few times.'

The mention of Swami irritated Sundeep a bit, but he did not let it show. The India Coffee House was in Nariman Point, two blocks away from their office. On their way out, they met Natasha in the lift lobby.

'Hey guys, headed home?'

'No, we are just going to get ourselves some coffee,' said Sundeep.

'Would you guys mind if I join in?' Natasha blurted out. 'I have a splitting headache and a cup of coffee will do me good.' But later she saw their grim faces and realised that it was a mistake.

'Of course not.' Kalpana was forced to lie, as she couldn't afford to be rude to the boss's secretary. Sullen faced Sundeep headed with the two beauties to the India Coffee House. Sundeep was thoroughly pissed. He went out to buy a packet of cigarettes, while the other two stayed inside sipping their coffee. The next fifteen minutes were spent in silence, occasionally disturbed by two lines of pleasantries followed by monosyllabic answers.

Sundeep finally gave up and said that he had to go. He left in a huff. Kalpana was concerned. What did Sundeep want to talk to her about? Why was he so stressed out? She wanted to call him back and drive him to his hotel, but before she could do that, he was gone.

Sundeep spent the next three days on a bed of thorns. He was not at ease with himself. He had to talk to Kalpana. Was it too late? Would she be interested in him? He tried calling her once or twice in her room at the Delhi hotel, but couldn't speak to her, since she was never in her room. Once he even called well past midnight, but to no avail. Kalpana wasn't in her room. 'What the fuck is going on? Is the bitch sleeping around?' he wondered. 'With Swami?' He felt disgusted. 'Na. She wouldn't even look at the South Indian uncle. He is not her type.'

Despite the self-assurance, he picked up the phone to call the hotel.

'Good morning. The Imperial Hotel, Delhi. May I help you?' the telephone operator came on line.

'Can you put me through to room number twelve forty-eight, Mr Swaminathan.'

'Who should I say is calling?'

Sundeep thought for a moment and banged the phone down. He couldn't bring himself to call up Swami's room, to check on Kalpana. What if she was indeed in his room?

Something was not right, but he didn't know what. He couldn't even ask anyone.

22

Swami and Kalpana's trip to Delhi was a great success. Hero Honda agreed to an exclusive two-year, all-India arrangement for the financing of Hero Honda two-wheelers with New York International Bank. This was fabulous. Hero Honda sold over two hundred thousand two-wheelers every month, and this deal gave NYB access to the entire Hero Honda customer base. This was a deal any bank would kill and die for.

There was more good news for NYB. Sundeep had managed a tie-up with Maruti Suzuki for car financing. To say that Aditya was thrilled would be an understatement. His hand-picked team had given him two of the best possible deals. What more could he ask for?

They decided to celebrate, just the five of them. The celebration was planned for Saturday at Aditya's penthouse.

On Friday, the day before the scheduled bash, Sundeep got a call from Swami about thirty minutes before the daily evening debrief.

'Aditya asked me to call off the meeting. He has something else that has come up.'

At around 7.30 p.m., Sundeep went up to Aditya's room to have a word with him. His room was closed and there was someone in his room. He looked at Natasha, eyebrows raised.

'The two have been inside for the last two hours.' Natasha had understood his unsaid query.

'Which two?' Sundeep was beginning to get curious.

'Aditya and Kalpana.'

'What? Why? What happened? Where is Swami?' Sundeep inundated Natasha with a barrage of questions.

'He was here about thirty minutes back. Just left.'

There was a blank look on Sundeep's face. Natasha hurriedly clarified: 'Swami. He was here. Aditya had called him in.'

'Anything serious?' Sundeep's eyebrows fell and wrinkles appeared on his forehead.

'Yes. Apparently Kalpana wants to quit.'

'For god's sake, Natasha. Get serious,' Sundeep was losing control. The last thing he wanted now was someone playing games with him.

'I am not kidding. Swami told me so.' It didn't take Sundeep too long to realise that she was not kidding. He could sense something was wrong. He felt helpless, and he didn't like it when he was not on top of things.

'Swami had to make a few calls, so he has gone back to his desk. Said he might be leaving for his hotel soon.' Natasha explained.

Sundeep had no clue what was going on. He started prancing up and down the lounge waiting for these guys to come out.

'Do you want me to get Swami on the line?' Natasha could see his anxiety and wanted to help. She pressed the speakerphone button and started dialling without waiting for Sundeep's answer.

'Hi, you have reached the voice-mail of Swami...' Swami's voice-mail came on after six rings. Swami had left and there was no way to contact him. He would be on his way to the hotel, and at this hour it would be a good fifty minutes before he reached. There were no mobile phones in those days.

Sundeep was very fidgety and nervous. He kept pacing up and down the lobby outside Aditya's room, like an anxious father-to-be outside the delivery room. Why did Kalpana want to quit? Was Aditya not happy with her? What about Swami? Did things go wrong professionally between the two of them? 'I am sure this fucking Swami would have tormented her and pushed her to the limit, because of which she now wants to quit.' Numerous possibilities flashed through his mind. Poor thing, she would be in tears. He just wanted to rush into the room and take charge of the situation.

At that very moment, the door to Aditya's room opened and he peeped out.

'Natasha, coffee,' demanded Aditya and then looked at Sundeep. Kalpana was sitting with her back to the door and hence Sundeep couldn't exactly tell what was going on. Was she crying?

'Hey, Sundeep. What are you doing here? Come on in.'

'Things don't look so bad. Else Aditya won't be smiling. Everything looks fine,' Sundeep heaved a sigh of relief as he walked into the room.

'Natasha, coffee for my friend too.' Aditya was addicted to coffee. His mind wouldn't work without a coffee every half an hour.

As he strode past Kalpana to occupy the sofa on the other side, he saw that she was smiling. A big grin on her face told Sundeep that everything was indeed fine. 'What's going on? What's the fuss about?' he wondered.

'Young man, this lady here wants to quit, and I don't know how to stop her,' these words from Aditya reinforced what Natasha had told him. 'Maybe you can try?' he added.

'But why? What's wrong with you, Kalpana? We have just about started getting somewhere in this business and you want to quit. You cannot just walk out on us like this.' Sundeep was extremely anxious. He couldn't hide his desperation. Or was it frustration?

'This has been going on for some time. I have been mulling over it and talking to Aditya and Swami for over a fortnight now.'

'Swami again!' wondered Sundeep.

'It has now reached a head and we have to take a decision one way or the other,' Aditya was quick to inform him and looked at Kalpana and smiled at her. Kalpana grinned back.

This was irritating Sundeep no end. Everyone but him seemed to know what was going on. Were they serious, or were they playing him on? 'Kalpana, enough of fun. It's close to eight in the evening. Can we get serious?' He was not amused one bit.

'I am getting married, Sundeep.' This blew the wind out of Sundeep's lungs. Sundeep felt like he was at the epicentre of a nuclear blast. He was now sure that they were having fun at his expense.

'Kalpana, for god's sake, get serious. If you guys wanna have fun, I am not interested. I'm leaving. See you tomorrow.'

'I am not joking, Sundeep. I am getting married. In forty-five days time.'

'And who is the lucky guy?' Natasha asked as she walked into the room with some coffee. One glare from Sundeep told her that he did not find it funny. Sundeep turned towards

Aditya with a questioning look, hoping that he would respond.

'Don't look at me. Ask her who the guy is. I will not spoil her surprise.'

Sundeep looked at Kalpana. 'Out with it.'

Sundeep was waiting with bated breath for hearing the name. But he went momentarily deaf. He could see the movement of her lips and knew that some words were being formed, but he couldn't grasp them. Maybe he didn't want to hear the name.

'Swami!' shrieked Natasha. 'You are getting married to Swami. Wow!' Natasha's excited yell brought Sundeep back to ground zero. He blacked out for a moment, lost his balance and stumbled backwards. The sofa stopped him from falling flat on the floor. He was quick to regain his composure and looked at Kalpana. 'Kalpana, you never cease to surprise me. That's great news. WOW! How did this happen?'

Kalpana smiled. 'It just happened, Sundeep.' She was grinning from ear to ear. She didn't realise the pain in Sundeep's heart, and couldn't see through the lie in his words. Natasha did. Boy, wasn't she pleased that Kalpana was getting married to Swami. Yes, Swami was a good guy, a guy you would like to take home to mom, but that was not why Natasha was thrilled. Kalpana was out of reckoning now for Sundeep. At least now she had a chance. She moderated her ecstasy in the fear that Sundeep may not like it.

After that, Sundeep was lost in his own thoughts. Why did this have to happen to him? And why Swami? He did not have looks, charisma, aggression. Nothing at all. How did Kalpana fall for a Tam-Brahm? And where did he falter? He was utterly disappointed.

Natasha felt sorry for him, but at the same time she was glad that now she would have Sundeep all for herself.

When Kalpana and Swami decided to get married, Swami's conservative mother was surprisingly happy. She did not have any issues with a Rajasthani daughter-in-law. Kalpana's parents, however, were initially against this marriage. Swami was not from the same economic background that they came from. However, once they met Swami, they too fell in line. In him they saw someone who would be honest and dedicated to his family, and, most importantly, someone who would keep their daughter happy.

Kalpana was very clear that she would not work in the same organisation as her husband. She also wanted time to adjust with this change in her life before she caught on with her career. Despite Swami's advising her against it, she decided to take the next couple of years off, to focus on her married life. She was the one who took the call and Swami respected her decision. Aditya, of course, tried to talk her out of it, but when she didn't budge, he let her go.

Meanwhile, Swami returned to Aditya's room. He had, in fact, just stepped out to meet somebody, while Natasha thought that he had gone back to his hotel.

Inside Aditya's room was a private cabinet. Inside the cabinet was a well stocked bar. Aditya would throw it open on special occasions. Today was one such day, as he was extremely happy for Kalpana and Swami. Aditya took out a bottle of Don Perignon. He had bought it on his way back from New York. 'Special moments call for special champagnes,' he said as he uncorked the champagne.

Sundeep was quite distressed at this sudden turn of events. He couldn't even show his displeasure. 'Who am I to approve or disapprove of her decision?' he thought and picked up his first glass of champagne.

Before Natasha, who was next, could pick up her glass, Sundeep had gulped down his first one. As he reached for the next one, Natasha knew that this was going to be a difficult night for him.

After downing another glass, Sundeep held Swami by his elbow and said, 'Well done, my pal. This is the biggest deal you have struck ever since you joined New York International Bank. Cheers to the two of you.' He gulped another glass. Natasha nudged him, trying to stop him from picking up one more. Sundeep didn't bother and helped himself to another drink. Swami knew that Sundeep had a soft corner for Kalpana; so he did not respond to his taunt. He liked Sundeep and respected his intelligence. He thought of him as a good friend.

23

By the time Swami and Kalpana left, it was well past ten. Aditya too left after instructing Natasha not to let Sundeep drink too much. But Sundeep was already sloshed and on the brink of passing out.

Natasha got up and went towards Sundeep. The moment she held him, trying to help him stand up, he pulled her down. 'Now listen to me,' he screamed at the top of his voice. 'What is wrong with me?'

'Nothing, Sundeep. You are absolutely fine.'

'Then why did that bitch do this to me? Why? Tell me why?' He was screaming at the top of his voice, shivering in anger. He had controlled himself in the presence of Aditya and Kalpana. The moment they had left, the bubble burst.

'Women. All you women are like this. Bitches. Never to be trusted!'

'You never bothered to tell her about your feelings for her, Sundeep. How can you expect her to reciprocate?' Why was Natasha even trying to reason with a drunk Sundeep?

'Shut up, you bitch. You don't even know her. She is a fucking whore. She flirted with me for two years and now she wants to hump that son of a bitch. How could she? How could she? I know. You are also like her. All of you are the same. Fucking whores.'

Natasha was getting irritated by his language, but she was also feeling sorry for him. Sundeep was in a pitiful state. She hugged him tightly.

'All of you are the same. You will also leave me. I know. I just know it.' Sundeep was wailing like a child who had lost his favourite toy.

She hugged him even tighter, trying to console him. 'Do not worry, Sundeep. I will take care of you. I will always stand by you. I will never let you feel her absence in your life. I love you, Sundeep. I love you.' She wanted to make him feel good.

For a minute there was silence. Sundeep's wailing stopped. He didn't know how to react. He didn't look at her. He was scared. Kalpana spurning him for Swami had offended his male ego. He had never faced failure in his life, but the first big desire in his personal life had just ended in a catastrophe. He wanted to prove to Kalpana that he could live without her. Natasha provided this perfect opportunity for him. All these thoughts zoomed through his mind in an instant. What a creep he was!

He turned his face upwards and looked into Natasha's eyes. All this while, his face was snug against her breasts. Her eyes couldn't hide the fact that she was madly in love with him and wanted him desperately.

Her face was right above his, their lips separated only by a few inches. Sundeep took the initiative. Natasha closed her eyes in anticipation. Sundeep kissed her on her lips. Natasha hugged him even more tightly, but didn't open her eyes. Sundeep didn't stop. He was a devil. He had been spurned and had found a girlfriend almost on the rebound and he was going to make the most of it. Sundeep's roving hands were all over Natasha. One hand started to unbutton her blouse while the other raced up her velvet thighs.

When his hand reached the heaven between her legs, she suddenly opened her eyes and stood up. 'No, Sundeep. Not here.'

'Why? There's no one in office.' Sundeep knew that the chances of anyone being in office at 11.00 p.m. was remote.

'No, Sundeep. Not here. It's not right,' she said and ran straight to the rest room.

'Come back. I said come back.' Sundeep ran after her.

She stood in front of the rest room mirror, staring at herself and her clothes, which were in disarray.

'What am I doing? I have waited for this for three months, and now when it's going to happen, why am I scared of it?'

Sundeep was inside in less than three seconds. He hugged her from behind, and kissed her on the back of her neck. Involuntarily her eyes closed. She wasn't able to resist anymore. Sundeep moved in for the kill. His hands moved to fondle her breasts. Natasha couldn't control herself and neither could Sundeep. 'Make love to me,' Natasha demanded as they got down to the floor.

Suddenly the door opened and Aditya walked in. 'What's going on?' he thundered as he walked into the loo. The moment he saw them on the floor, he quickly covered his eyes.

'Oh my God! Looks like I walked in at the wrong time. Keep at it! Just watch out for the security cameras.' And he walked out with a chuckle.

Aditya had gone down to the parking lot and then realised that he had forgotten his car keys in his office. On his way out after collecting the keys from his desk, he had heard some strange noises from the ladies toilet. Thinking that someone was in distress, he had just looked in to see if everything was fine. He was in for a shock when he peeped inside. But he had pulled himself up quickly and had left the room, trying not to embarrass the two lovers.

But Natasha was extremely embarrassed. 'Tomorrow the whole office would know about it. Well, maybe not. After all, Aditya is a gentleman. He will not make life uncomfortable for me.'

The passion suddenly evaporated. The mood was gone. Both of them got up, wore their clothes, and stepped out of the women's rest room. They walked down to the parking. No one spoke. Sundeep knew that this was not his day. He had lost out twice. With Natasha, he knew, he would get many opportunities. Kalpana was gone for good.

24
New York

'Why did things have to reach this stage?' thought Sundeep as Louisa brought in his sandwich. She had also got him a cup of black coffee. She knew that he would ask for it.

He had a great career. Both he and Swami had a fabulous run at New York International Bank. They had been recognised for the success of the India retail business. Huge bonuses and stock options had come their way.

Both of them had big, well-paying jobs. Both of them had good, happy families. Then why did this happen?

He had himself to blame for this. Everything he could aspire for was within his reach: money, power, fame, career... Everything was going fine until Suneel Dutt arrived on the scene.

25

The next twelve months were very hectic. NYB's aggressive foray into retail business was spearheaded successfully by Swami and Sundeep. International recognition came their way. With Aditya, both of them won global accolades for having built their success story on limited resources.

Swami and Kalpana got married in a small ceremony in Woodlands hotel in Chennai. Kalpana's parents wanted an extravagant wedding, but Swami insisted that it had to be a simple affair. He was worried that the extravagance might put off his middle class relatives. Kalpana's parents were happy to oblige. Aditya attended the wedding along with Sundeep and Natasha. Even Ramu Kaka had accompanied them. Swami was his favourite.

Swami and Kalpana had chosen Kodaikanal, a small pristine hill station in the hills south of Chennai, for their honeymoon. Swami couldn't afford anything more extravagant and Kalpana was quite happy to go to Kodai.

But, on their second night together, Swami was being apologetic about being unable to take Kalpana to an exotic foreign locale. 'How does it matter? I would be disappointed if you had any sightseeing plans on our honeymoon?' Kalpana was trying to be at her seductive best and smiled at Swami as she switched off the lights.

26

Swami and Sundeep become hot commodities in the global community of NYB. Aditya had ensured that they get the required recognition and visibility internationally. They kept getting invites for various seminars and conferences across the globe. 'Retail Financing in Emerging Markets.' Swami could now deliver a lecture on this topic even in his sleep.

At the Annual Retail Banking Conference, a conference for the Country CEOs, Swami and Sundeep were special invitees. The global chairman of NYB presented both of them with a *Rising Star* award. They had finally arrived.

Barring the Sundeep-Kalpana hiccup, life had been very kind to all of them.

Sundeep and Natasha got engaged and married after six months. Probably the guilt of getting caught in the loo pushed them into marriage so soon.

The initial success in the automobile loans business gave NYB confidence in its ability to deliver in retail business. Credit cards was next in line. Aditya had set a precedent with the businesses that he had begun. The group started expecting such high results from India in almost all the businesses. Aditya had become a rock star head of business.

One day, Sundeep got a call from Aditya. 'What are you doing, my friend?' Sundeep knew that Aditya spoke like this only if something was troubling him. 'Nothing, Aditya. Just closing things for the day. Lots of pending work.'

'Why don't we go for a drink on the way out? Just you, me and Swami.'

'Sure, Aditya. Anything you want us to come prepared with?' Sundeep wanted to be sure.

'No, Sundeep. We haven't gone out in a while. That's all. Will you be able to make it?'

'Sure, Aditya.'

'Will you inform Swami? He is not at his desk right now.' Then he hung up.

The three of them left office at 7.45 p.m. and headed to the *Rain Tree* bar at the Taj, next to their office building. They were the only ones in the bar. It was too early and a weekday too. Aditya ordered a screwdriver for himself, whisky with soda for Sundeep, and a Thumbs Up for Swami.

'Why has he asked us out?' Both were wondering at the same time.

'Guys, both of you have been very close to me. I look upon you not as employees of NYB, but as my own younger brothers. You have in a short while become a part of my world. I didn't want you to hear this from someone else. That's why I have called you here.'

Both Swami and Sundeep were fearing the worst. Was Aditya being called back to New York?

'I am quitting NYB,' Aditya dropped his bombshell.

'What?' the two of them exclaimed in unison. 'You can't be serious,' Swami went on. 'Is something wrong, Aditya?'

'No.'

'Then why, Aditya? Where is the need? Everything is going on so well.'

In private, Aditya had harnessed a dream for over a decade. A dream of running his own company and turning it into a successful venture. He didn't want to continue working for someone else for long. He had always wanted to be his own boss. Aditya took pains to explain to them his dream, his aspiration, and his desire to create something from a scratch.

But the two of them were in no mood to relent. They would have nothing of it.

Both Swami and Sundeep felt they would be orphaned by his exit. Aditya had protected them all along and they could focus on the task given to them. But now, with Aditya going, they were also wondering what would happen to them.

By the time they left the bar, Aditya was literally in tears. He had no answers to Swami's and Sundeep's questions. The fact was that he wanted to quit and start a new business when his confidence and market reputation were on a high. And given his recent achievements at NYB, this was the best possible time for him to quit.

Two weeks passed. No one spoke about the discussion at the *Rain Tree*. They were hoping that if they ignored it, it would go away. That was not to be. When two uneventful weeks went by, Swami was sure that Aditya had canned the idea of leaving them.

On an afternoon like any other, Swami had come down to see Natasha after lunch, and they stepped out into the compound for a stroll. Suddenly they saw Aditya's Mercedes pull up into the driveway. Aditya got down from the left. Swami was surprised to see a tall gentleman step out from the right. He had never seen him earlier and was wondering who he was. Aditya and the new guy walked straight into the building and disappeared into the lift.

'Swami, did you see the guy with Aditya? Do you know who he is?'

'No. What about him?' Swami asked.

'I saw him for the first time this morning when he walked into Aditya's office. They have been closeted since. They stepped out for lunch a while ago. They are probably returning from there now.'

'Is there anything I must know?'

'I don't know, but Aditya has been asking for all your files and is showing it to him.' Though it was not right on Natasha's part to discuss this with Swami, but she felt obliged to do so. 'I thought you might know him. Don't know why, this time, Aditya didn't even introduce me to him.'

'Come, let's go. Let's try to find out,' said Swami and started walking briskly towards Aditya's room.

As he entered the floor, Aditya saw him and shouted, 'Hey, Swami! Come on in.' As Swami walked into his room, the other man there looked up and shook his hand.

'Hello, Swami. Good to see you. Have heard a lot about you from Aditya.' Swami looked perplexed because he didn't know who that guy was.

'Suneel, Swami will be one of your key guys going forward.' Swami frowned at Aditya's stress on 'your' and started wondering what was going on.

'Swami,' continued Aditya, 'Suneel is our new Country Head for Retail Banking. He is going to take over from me.'

'Oh! Good afternoon, sir. Glad to meet you. And now if you would excuse me, I gotta run.' Swami was curt and abrupt. It was clear that he didn't really like Suneel replacing Aditya.

When Swami left in haste, Suneel was visibly pissed. 'This bloke didn't seem too thrilled to meet me. That's kinda strange. Does he have a history here?' He wanted to know if Swami was a problem creator. Even before it began, the relationship had strained.

Aditya smiled and let it pass, because he understood Swami more than anyone else.

Back home, late in the evening. Swami confided in Kalpana and told her about his first meeting with Suneel Dutt, his future boss. Kalpana knew that Swami's reaction was not because of his dislike for Suneel, but his extreme devotion towards Aditya. Aditya was the one who gave him his career. Aditya was the one who gave him his stock options worth millions. He owed a lot to Aditya.

She tried to reason with him. 'Look, it's quite possible that Suneel is not such a bad guy. One does not choose one's boss.'

This reasoning didn't impress Swami, but he said nothing.

Sundeep's introduction to Suneel was quite different. The slick Sundeep managed his first meeting brilliantly, impressing Suneel and oozing positive energy. When he left, Suneel couldn't help wonder: 'What a guy!'

As far as first impressions were concerned, Sundeep had won, Swami had lost out. But with Suneel, Swami didn't want to win. No logical reason, but Swami simply didn't want to win. He just didn't want to be a 'Suneel guy.'

That evening Swami and Sundeep went out for a drink. Sundeep for his screwdriver and Swami for his Thumbs Up. Despite all the complications in their lives, they remained friends. More so because their families, that is, Kalpana and Natasha, got along really well and their relationship continued even after Kalpana had quit and Natasha got married.

'The guy is a creep,' began Swami. 'I can't stand him. He suffocates me.'

'He is still your boss, my friend, and when it comes to bosses, we seldom have a choice. When I had met Aditya for the first time, I had thought the same about him as well.' This was the same logic that Kalpana had thrown at him.

'I do not want to work with Suneel. After having worked with Aditya, I just can't.'

'We are at a stage where we cannot make these choices.'

'Why can't we join Aditya in his new venture?' the loyalist in Swami spoke.

'Because he is too small right now and cannot afford you guys.' They looked at each other, because neither had spoken. The answer irritated both of them.

'Who the fuck asked you!' they shouted and turned around. Aditya was standing there.

'Natasha said I could find you guys here, so I came down.'

'Grow up guys. I am flattered by your attachment to me, but remember, you can't always tag your careers to mine. Yes, I gave you guys the opportunity, and you guys grabbed it. I gave it to you also because I needed you at that time. I needed your fire to take us to our goal. But you guys have to break free now. I am starting my software and processing business. It's a fledgling business and needs time to grow. Till it grows big, I will not be able to afford you.'

Neither Sundeep nor Swami said a thing.

'Guys remember, I have made my money. I have saved enough to be comfortable all my life, even if this venture of mine fails. If you guys join me, you will have to forego your stock options in NYB. Are you willing to do that? Come on, guys. Stop kidding yourselves. I have done what I wanted to in a large corporate. Remember Swami, if you join me and I fail, you will have to start all over again in your career. God forbid, if you have to do that, I cannot live with that guilt.'

No response still.

'And now folks, will you guys keep staring at me or will you order my whisky.'

They kept drinking till two in the morning, and by the time the bar took the last order, both Sundeep and Aditya were dead drunk. Swami dropped them home in his new Maruti 800.

Next morning, as Aditya was clearing his mailbox, a new mail popped up on the screen, titled 'URGENT AND PERSONAL.' It was from Swaminathan.

Dear Aditya,

The two years of working with you were full of learning and fun. You trusted us with large deliverables and we came good on each one of them. For us, your decision of leaving and starting your own company came as a big shock. We have now reconciled to your leaving us and going away.

However, I have a small request to make. With you not being around, I will not be able to work in the same role. The credit for my success in this position largely goes to you. I do not see how I could possibly continue delivering in this role, once you have gone. I would like to request you to move me out of retail into some other unit, before you leave this organisation.

I leave it to you to decide what is good for me. However, if it is not possible, I will not raise it till your last day at New York International Bank. However, the day after that, I will put in my papers and chart a fresh course for myself. I really do not see myself here without you.

Regards,
Swami

'What an emotional fool!' Aditya knew that Swami was a guy who was seldom wrong and so it was next to impossible to make him change his view on anything.

Aditya didn't have an option. There were another fifteen days before Suneel moved in to take complete charge. Before he came in and took over from him, Aditya moved Swami to a plum role in Treasury. Sundeep took charge of Swami's portfolio.

27

Suneel Dutt was not new to India. He had worked in India in the late seventies and early eighties, before going to New York on a foreign assignment. He was said to be very close to Joseph Fernandes, who was the senior most Indian, and a very influential one, in the higher echelons of power at New York International Bank. When Aditya made his intentions on quitting known, Joseph had personally seen to it that Suneel got the top job in India.

Suneel had a gorgeous Norwegian wife and two lovely young daughters Karen and Celina, aged eight and five respectively. Suneel's wife had refused point blank to come with him to India. After a lot of deliberation, they came to an arrangement that Suneel would go to India for two years and would go alone.

Sunil was not a clean guy and his reputation preceded him. Bit of a wheeler-dealer, he would do anything to get his work done. For him, self was above everything. He was the kind of guy who would sell his wife to get a deal through. More akin to Sundeep than to Swami, he had the reputation of a Casanova.

The Insomnia pub in the Taj Mahal hotel was host to the impressive welcome party for Suneel Dutt, which Aditya had organised. The top team of NYB was present in full strength. The key employees were invited, along with their spouses.

Kalpana and Natasha were meeting after a long time. Both looked ravishing. Kalpana had put on a little weight, but it was fine. Any more of it and she would look fat. Today she was looking gorgeous.

After all the welcome speeches and the goody-goody noises, the party was thrown open. Booze was on tap. The latest Bollywood numbers were rocking the floor. Zeenat Aman was the MC for the night. Suneel Dutt had marked his presence on this event too. He did everything in style. His parties were the talk of the town for a long time. When it came to parties, it was said, Suneel wouldn't compromise.

Sundeep and Natasha set the dance floor on fire. Swami and Kalpana were standing by the side, Kalpana sipping her wine and Swami Thumbs Up as usual. Kalpana wanted to dance, but since Swami didn't really enjoy dancing, she went ahead and joined the crowd.

Suneel walked up to Swami. 'So young man, will you ignite the fire in the treasury department as well.'

'I will try my best.'

'On a prom night, Swami, people who do their best always whine. The winner takes the prom queen home,' said Suneel at his arrogant best. The dialogue was a straight lift from a Hollywood flick.

'Kalpana was a prom queen, Suneel,' retorted Swami. Thanks to Kalpana, he had seen the same Hollywood flick starring Nicholas Cage. He honestly didn't care too much because Suneel was not his boss anymore.

Suneel was pissed, but couldn't do much about it. 'I'll finish you,' he muttered under his breath as Swami walked away.

The dance floor was jam packed, like a peak hour Mumbai local, when Suneel pushed his way through. He found Sundeep and Natasha grooving and joined them.

'Suneel, where's your drink?' asked Sundeep.

'I'll get one when I am off the floor.'

'What do you want, I will get it for you,' said Sundeep. 'The regular whisky and soda?' Suneel nodded as Sundeep dashed off the dance floor, leaving Natasha with Suneel.

'Dance with me?' asked Suneel. Natasha didn't quite mind, as she was anyway grooving away furiously. Suneel matched her step for step. With every move of his, Suneel started moving closer to her. Natasha was a pro at handling advances. She was quick to notice and took preventive action. She was hoping that Sundeep would come back with the drink soon, but he was taking too long. Her eyes scanned the crowd to look for him, but she couldn't find him. Suneel realised that her attention was diverted, and, in one move, his hand went behind her waist and drew her to him and then released her almost immediately. This was just a sampling move. He was only testing the waters. Natasha was taken aback for a moment, but when Suneel released her, she relaxed a bit.

When Suneel saw that Natasha didn't react, he started getting bolder. He moved in for the kill. He was so close to her now that Natasha could feel his breath. Suneel was a professional wooer. He was making it seem like a dance step, but it was not. No one around could realise what he was up to. Only Natasha knew. His hand was all over her back. When he pulled her close to him one more time, Natasha could make out that he was aroused. 'Where the fuck is Sundeep?' she thought in desperation.

Kalpana was dancing next to Natasha and could make out from her expression that all was not hunky dory. She stopped dancing and went up to Natasha. She clutched her hand, looked at Suneel, and said, 'Suneel, will you please excuse us?

I need to talk to her for a minute.' Suneel couldn't refuse. She dragged her away from the floor, just as Sundeep returned with the drink. 'Anything wrong?' he asked Suneel.

'Well, no. Nothing. Just as the mood was building up, your wife went away with some lady. Maybe she thought I'm a lousy dancer,' he said. The sarcasm in his voice was evident. Suneel didn't like to be turned down.

Later that night, Sundeep and Natasha had a huge showdown. Sundeep was upset that Natasha had walked away from Suneel on the dance floor. Natasha kept explaining what Suneel did, but Sundeep did not listen. He felt she was overreacting.

For the first time in eighteen months, Natasha felt that Sundeep was not the kind of guy she thought he was. 'Did he marry me because he really loves me, or was it something else?' Natasha wondered as she hit the bed that night.

28

Life in office became tough for Natasha. She was finding it difficult to cope with Suneel. This man was known to be a vindictive guy. He had not forgotten the dance floor snub and would make snide remarks at Natasha once in a while. Natasha decided to bide her time. Sometimes, when it became unbearable, she would call Swami or Kalpana and cry her heart out. She didn't say anything to Sundeep. She knew he wouldn't empathise with her. He was out to build a relationship with Suneel and was blind to everything that would make it difficult.

In the next few years, many other banks also got into the loans business. But given their long history as deposit gatherers, with limited exposure to lending, they were extremely conservative in their lending policies. It was a horror for customers to avail of loans. To get a cheque in hand one had to survive a tortuous process from the time of application for a loan. Reams of documents would be collected from the applicant for a loan worth a few lakhs of rupees. A customer would end up making five to six trips to the bank, sometimes even more, for just one loan. If they managed to get a housing loan approved in a month, it meant the bank manager had decided to do them a favour. Normally, banks took their own sweet time. Those days banks would sell loans directly to customers, without any intermediaries.

In this scenario, NYB made a breakthrough by pioneering a concept called DSAs: Direct Selling Agents. Suneel introduced DSAs for NYB's personal loans and home loans business in the four big metros in India. The DSAs worked for a fee as intermediaries between the customer and the bank. They helped the customer complete the documentation required by the bank and ensured that the loan application was made in a form acceptable to the bank. They also did the running around on behalf of the customers. It was a win-win situation for both the bank and the customer.

Suneel liked to keep his hand on the pulse of the marketplace and hence reviewed his businesses with the heads once in a month. During one such review with Sundeep, Suneel steered the discussion towards DSAs. 'Sundeep, there is an acquaintance of mine, Ram Naresh. He is a chartered accountant in Kolkata, and is very well networked there. He wants to become a home loans DSA for us. Why don't you meet him and see what you can do with him?'

29

This was how Sundeep first met Ram Naresh, a typical *gujju bhai* who was a third generation Calcuttan. It didn't take long for Sundeep to figure out that Ram Naresh was more than an acquaintance for Suneel Dutt. Ram Naresh knew a number of people within the NYB circuit. And he had no qualms about using these contacts for his benefit. He was a more than useful guy. Definitely more useful that he had imagined.

Drooling over chicks and constantly talking about them was this *gujju bhai's* trademark. He would drop names at every opportunity—names that meant something to Sundeep. 'How do you think Suneel went to the US? Didn't he tell you?'

Seeing a blank look on Sundeep's face, he added, 'Didn't he tell you that I had spoken to Joseph to get him the job in the US, when he was struggling here in India.'

'Joseph?'

'Joseph Fernandes, your vice chairman.'

'Oh, you did that? It was very kind of you to have helped him.'

'Don't worry, Sundeep. We will do something for you too.'

Sundeep hit it off with Ram Naresh in a big way. They had found some common links in the army. And that was not all. They also realised that some of Sundeep's family friends had studied with Ram Naresh at Lovedale in Ooty. Moreover, Naresh's father was a teacher there and had also taught Sundeep, who was alumnus of the same school.

Naresh wanted NYB to cover the cost of setting up his DSA. Naresh spent a lot of time explaining how the financials would work. Sundeep was getting more and more interested. By lunchtime Sundeep had lapped up the idea.

This discussion had taken place in the bank's conference room. Naresh invited Sundeep to come in and see his office. They stepped out for lunch and then drove to Naresh's office.

Naresh's office was in a small dingy lane. The lane led to the back entry of a ten-story building called Everest Towers. He led him up to the second floor and into his gaudily decorated office. In the corner was a cricket bat autographed by all the members of the Indian team that had won the 1983 World Cup. Occupying the pride of place on one of the walls was a stick-on board that had pictures of every one of Sundeep's seniors at New York International Bank who were now in senior positions overseas. The pictures were taken at various times on their visits to Naresh's office. The seat of honour went to a picture of Joseph Fernandes hugging Ram Naresh. They went and sat down on Naresh's nicely laid out table.

'You haven't met my secretary, right,' said Naresh, as if the secretary was a piece of art.

'No. Not yet,' said Sundeep, and added, 'Do you mind if I smoke here?'

'Please go ahead. Here you can do anything you want. Absolutely anything.' And almost as an afterthought, he said, 'Wait, we will get her to light it for you.'

'Monica.'

'Oh, that's the secy's name,' thought Sundeep.

A cute, twenty-something girl walked into Naresh's office. She was wearing a figure-hugging, red coloured t-shirt with a miniskirt that ended a foot above her knee. Her outfit left little to Sundeep's imagination. A brief sentence of introduction later, Naresh asked her to get a lighter for Sundeep.

The moment she turned, he looked at Sundeep and licked his lips with his tongue. '*Degi kya*? You think she will give me?' he asked Sundeep.

'Of course,' said Sundeep, 'you just have to ask.'

'I am very old, *yaar*. These youngsters don't want to have fun with me,' Naresh said slyly.

Monica returned within a minute with a cigarette lighter. When she came close to Sundeep to light his cigarette, the smell of her perfume filled Sundeep's nostrils. As she bent down to light his cigarette, the neckline of her t-shirt dropped a bit, exposing what they were desperately trying to hide. Sundeep could not take his eyes off her. 'My god, is she hot!' he thought as the flame hit his cigarette.

The moment the cigarette was lit, the lighter dropped from her hand and fell on Sundeep's lap. 'Oh, I am so sorry,' she said as she slowly picked up the lighter, lightly brushing her hand against his swollen crotch. 'Will that be fine, sir?' she said, bordering on an innuendo.

The moment she left the room, Naresh looked at him. 'Which cigarette were you getting her to light?' And both of them began to laugh.

'Isn't she hot?' asked Naresh.

'Wow. Eminently humpable.'

The conversation eventually turned to the financials of the DSA proposal. Sundeep agreed to a deal heavily tilted in favour of Naresh. Well, after Monica's performance, it couldn't be otherwise.

They shook hands and parted ways. 'Sundeep, it was great meeting you. My driver will drop you at your hotel.'

'Thanks, Ram.'

The moment Sundeep had left, Naresh called out for Monica.

Sundeep reached his hotel quite late. He had a shower and changed into casual clothes. The clock on the wall told him that it was 9 p.m. He had just picked up the phone to call

Natasha when the doorbell rang. He was in for a surprise when he opened the door.

'Hey, Monica. What a surprise? What brings you here?'

'Naresh sir asked me to see you. He said there was some work to finish,' she said seductively.

Sundeep didn't understand. 'I think there has been some miscommunication. We had completed everything before I left his office. I am so sorry you had to come all the way.' She smelled good. He had liked the smell back at Naresh's office too.

Monica had already made her way into the room and was standing at the edge of his bed. 'No sir, he asked me to finish the work I had left incomplete in the afternoon.'

Sundeep was clueless. What was she talking about?

'Sir, when I dropped the lighter on you this afternoon, I figured out that you were on fire down there, despite the lighter being off. I thought maybe I could help you put out that fire,' she said and took off her sandals.

Sundeep was getting turned on.

'When I was leaving the room, the two of you were admiring my ass, why not feel them now!' She unzipped her skirt and it fell on the carpet.

The thought of Natasha back in Mumbai flashed through Sundeep's mind. But just for a moment. 'She won't get to know about this,' he told himself. Then Monica started unbuckling Sundeep's belt and he completely lost it. He quickly got rid of his clothes and ripped off her t-shirt. Soon they were on the bed, hungrily devouring each other. Monica gave Sundeep one of the best fucks of his life.

When Sundeep woke up the next day, Monica had already left. On the bed was a small note. 'Hope you had a good time. I loved it. Anytime for you, sir.'

It slowly dawned on Sundeep that it meant, anytime for Naresh sir. By sending Monica to him, Naresh had bought him for life. He had got a good deal from New York International Bank. And now he had ensured that the deal was his forever. The phone rang. Sundeep picked it up.

'*Kee haal hai*? How are you, young man? *Kudi ne ratti sohn ditta ki nahi*? Did Monica let you sleep last night?' It was Naresh on the line. Sundeep saw through the set-up. He wanted to curse Naresh. But the fact was that he had himself to blame for all this.

Naresh had his contacts in the bank, right up to Joseph Fernandes. No point screwing around with him. He could finish his career at NYB. When everyone in the bank played ball, why should he be any different.

'Yes, Ram. She was fabulous.' He was in it now. And once you are sucked in, there is no getting out. Sundeep did not realise the dangerous game he had got into. His long friendship with Naresh had begun.

30

In Mumbai the previous evening, Suneel Dutt asked Natasha to stay back late. He gave her a few dictations; a few mails to respond to; a few presentation slides to update; and a few calls to put through. Natasha did everything diligently, but when she found out that the calls were actually made to friends in New York, she started getting worried. Was Suneel planning something sinister? All the work that he gave her could have waited till the next day. But he was the boss and she couldn't have questioned him.

After finishing work at around eleven at night, he asked her out for a drink. Natasha refused. She said that she had to get back home.

'Oh, come on. I know Sundeep has gone to Calcutta. There's no one at home. What will you do there? In any case, tomorrow is a Saturday. Let's go out, have some fun, and I'll drop you back. Or if you want to come back home with me, I am game.'

'What the fuck,' she thought. Suneel was directly asking her to sleep with him. 'How dare he?' She felt outraged. She wanted to give him one tight slap, but held herself back. 'Let Sundeep come back. I will ensure you are history,' she told herself. But deep inside she knew what Sundeep's reaction would be. He would again say she overreacted.

When there was no reaction from Natasha for a while, Suneel looked at her and said, 'My bed is better than the loo. I can promise you that,' he said with an emphasis on the word *loo*. When Natasha still didn't react, he picked up his bag and left.

Natasha was shattered when he said this. She was extremely upset and shivered with fury. She collapsed on the sofa next to her workstation and tears rolled down her cheeks.

Natasha didn't know what to do. She first thought about calling Sundeep, but decided against it. Had she tried to, she wouldn't have got through. Sundeep had activated the *Do not disturb* sign on his telephone, before jumping into bed with Monica. All calls to his room would be held back.

Natasha didn't move for the next five minutes. She didn't know whom to call. Who to talk to. Finally she got up, picked up a phone, and dialled a number.

'Hello.' It was Kalpana at the other end. Natasha couldn't say a word. She started sobbing.

'Hello. Who is it? Hello... Hello... Natasha, is that you?' Kalpana was beginning to panic.

'Yes... it's me,' and the sobbing intensified.

'Oh dear. What's wrong? Where are you?'

'I am in office.'

'What are you doing there so late, Natasha?' asked Kalpana. Swami was next to Kalpana, hearing her side of the conversation.

'If she is still in office, I think I know what the problem is. Ask her to wait there. I will be there in twenty minutes,' said Swami.

'Natasha, stay there, we're coming to get you,' said Kalpana and hung up. Swami was already up and changing into his trousers.

Natasha kept the phone down, and once again contemplated calling Sundeep. She brushed away the idea.

The feeling of getting violated by Suneel Dutt's proposition was not the only thing that hurt her. She had dealt with lecherous people in the past. What grieved her even more was what Suneel said: 'My bed is better than the loo.' Suneel knew all about her romp with Sundeep in the loo. How the hell did he know that?

Besides the two of them, Aditya was the only one who knew. Even Swami and Kalpana didn't know about it. Had Aditya told Suneel about it? She had thought of Aditya as God, as family, friend and guide. And he had made a mockery of her devotion. She was pissed with him. Suneel made her angry, but it was Aditya who made her cry.

Swami and Kalpana parked the car on the street and ran into the building. '*Suneel saab kidhar hain?*' Swami asked the guard about Suneel Dutt's whereabouts.

'*Abhi bees minute hua nikalke.*' Suneel had left twenty minutes ago, around the same time that Natasha called them. The guard's answer confirmed Swami's fear. 'Bastard,' thought Swami as both of them ran up the stairs to the second floor office.

Natasha saw them and burst into tears once again. Kalpana hugged her and patted her on the back. 'Don't say anything, sweetheart. Let's get out of here.' She turned towards Swami, 'Look at her, she is shivering. Let's take her to a doctor.'

No one spoke in the car. Natasha didn't want to visit the doc, so the plan was dropped. By the time they got home, she was feeling better. Kalpana brewed her a cup of coffee, which made her feel even better. She cleared up the guest room and tucked Natasha into a warm bed. They switched off the light and came out. Both of them were feeling miserable about it.

All this while, the one who should actually be feeling the most miserable about the whole episode was enjoying his romp in bed with Monica in faraway Kolkata.

Swami was a little shaken by the way Natasha was being treated. Is this becoming a culture in the bank? Are women meant to be walked over? Is this the way all foreign banks worked? The bank may be foreign, he thought, but the people working here are all Indian. Why should a few slime balls like Suneel be allowed to bring disrepute to a bank? He didn't have the answers. Swami tossed and turned in bed that whole night, and was up the next morning before both Kalpana and Natasha. He desperately wanted to do something about Suneel's behaviour, but felt extremely helpless. He wanted to call Sundeep, but knowing his reaction to the dance floor incident, he decided against it.

Kalpana and Swami were having coffee when Natasha came out of the room. Her eyes were red and swollen. She hadn't slept well. Swami thrust a cup of coffee into her hand and said, 'Don't worry, Natasha, it will all be fine.'

No one spoke about the previous night. Natasha had lunch with both of them before they dropped her home. Since it was a Saturday, they didn't have to go to work.

Natasha found it difficult, actually impossible, to believe that Aditya had told Suneel about the most personal and embarrassing event in her life. She couldn't resist calling Aditya. She dialled his number. When Aditya picked up the phone, she hung up. What would she ask him? How embarrassing would it be to discuss this with Aditya! She finally decided not to ask him.

Sundeep got back on Sunday. Actually he was supposed to come back on Saturday night. Just as he was packing up to leave for the airport, Monica had arrived, this time in tight jeans and a tank top. Sundeep had immediately stopped packing his bag and started unpacking her. How could he have left? He called Natasha and told her, 'Not coming back tonight. Review with the sales team didn't get over.' He had then hurriedly disconnected the call, because Monica had already reached for his zippers. He did not want to give up even a minute of this heaven.

31

Swami called up Aditya on Sunday. 'You must not lose heart, Swami. One person does not make a bank. Our bank is not Suneel Dutt. It is a nice place to work.' Aditya tried to convince him. 'Sundeep and Natasha should take a strong stand on this and take it up with someone senior in the organisation. People of low integrity are definitely not good for any bank.'

'Sundeep does not know this. And Natasha doesn't want to tell him,' said Swami. He then told him about what happened at Aditya's farewell party, which was also Suneel's welcome bash.

'She doesn't want to go back to work.'

Aditya was silent for a while. 'OK. I will then try and speak to Shelly Andrade. I know her very well.'

Shelly was a senior manager in NYB's Asia-Pacific Human Resources team and was based in Singapore. She was also the Head of the Diversity Committee for the bank in the Asia-Pacific region.

The diversity committee had been formed to ensure that the bank acted as an equal opportunity employer for people from all genders, caste and ethnic backgrounds. Most of their time and energy was taken up by their effort to make the work environment more conducive for women. They took up a number of issues on behalf of women employees. Aditya had this in mind when he decided to speak to Shelly. He called her the same night.

'Hi Aditya. Good to hear from you after a long time. I was planning to call you up myself.'

'That's nice. What can I do for you?'

'I am looking for a job. Was wondering if there is a good role in your new organisation.'

'Stop kidding, Shelly.' Aditya thought she was joking.

'I'm serious pal. I put in my papers last Monday and the bank relieved me the same evening. I do not have a job now.'

'What are you saying, Shelly? After twenty years...'

'It doesn't make a fucking difference, Aditya. I have given this bank twenty years of my life. All that counts for nothing.' She seemed very upset.

'But what happened, Shelly?'

'I don't know what the bank is coming to. A few days back, I had a run in with Patrick.' Aditya knew Patrick. Patrick was the Head of Human Resources for the Asia-Pacific region and was Shelly's boss. 'He made a pass at me and when I spurned him, he called me a milch cow,' continued Shelly.

'You should have lodged a complaint,' Aditya thundered.

'Of course, I did. You wouldn't believe what happened next. Instead of acting on my complaint and taking action against Patrick, the organisation decided to ask me to go. I was given a separation package and asked to leave. I made a lot of noise about it. Finally they told me to either take the package and leave, or run the risk of getting terminated on grounds of poor performance and lose out on all benefits. I opted for the former.'

This was so depressing. What could Aditya do? He had already left the organisation. Where was corporate life heading? Aditya then decided to stay away from the politics and sleaze of the corporate world and focus on his own business. It would be better if Natasha and Sundeep handle these issues themselves, rather than expecting him to play God.

32

Monday mornings at NYB were set aside for operational review meetings. All the Business Heads of NYB met with Suneel for a review of the previous week and to give him an update of the state of their businesses. This meeting was very important for Suneel to keep his fingers on the pulse of the business. Normally this meeting would begin an hour earlier than the regular working hours of the bank. Suneel didn't want this to eat into everybody's regular working hours.

On Monday Sundeep was hurriedly getting dressed to leave for office. He noticed that Natasha was not even making an attempt to get ready for work.

'Natasha, I have the weekly Monday morning meeting today. Got to leave early. Are you planning to go late?'

'I am not going today.'

'Why? Are you fine?'

'No, Sundeep. I'm just feeling a bit under the weather. Planning on taking an off today.'

'What happened? Should we go to the doctor? Let me call and tell Suneel that I will be late.'

'No, it's okay, Sundeep. Just feeling a bit tired. I'll come if I feel better. You carry on.'

Sundeep hesitated, but eventually said, 'Okay. Take care. Call me if you need anything.' He closed the door and stepped towards his car.

Sundeep walked into the meeting five minutes before the scheduled start. Suneel was already there. He assumed that Natasha would have come with Sundeep.

'Has Natasha come in? I need some papers.'

'No, Suneel. She is not feeling well. She said that she would call you.'

'Good,' thought Suneel. He was happy that Sundeep hadn't reacted violently. This meant that he had no clue what happened on Friday. Natasha hadn't told him. But why? Why would she not tell him? While he was relieved that Sundeep hadn't been told, he was also a touch nervous. He just couldn't figure this out. Sundeep, of course, was extremely nice and cordial to Suneel.

Swami hoped that Aditya would do something to ensure that guys like Suneel do not go scot-free. When Aditya didn't call him back, he called him up on Monday evening.

'Aditya, this Suneel thing has been on my mind for the last three days. We need to do something soon.'

'I agree.'

'Aditya, you said you would speak to someone in Singapore and take this up.'

What could Aditya say? He narrated the entire incident to Swami. 'I am helpless Swami. I tried my best.'

'I don't know, Aditya. If you do not do anything, I will have to do something. I will go to the press with this story, Aditya.' He was extremely frustrated and his middle class morality did not permit him to take this lying down.

Aditya was worried now. Swami was his guy. If Swami did something stupid, he would screw up his own career, and he did not want that to happen. He did not want Swami to take it upon himself. He had to buy time till the entire issue settled down. He asked Swami for six months. 'I have moved out of the bank, Swami. To reactivate my network and move something in this bank would take six months.'

Natasha took the week off, before returning to work. 'Behave normally with everyone, including Suneel,' Swami had insisted. 'I will surely do something to address your concerns.'

It was traumatic to be back at work. Suneel ignored her and so did she. Suneel hired another secretary to do his work. He would not give any work to Natasha. He cold-shouldered her. Natasha would go to office, keep sitting, not do anything the entire day, and then come back home. This was upsetting her no end. She was close to becoming a nervous wreck. She didn't tell Sundeep anything, as he wouldn't understand. He didn't know the context.

In the next one month, an audit was to hit the Human Resources department of NYB. Audit was a very serious issue at NYB and poor audit results could badly impact career prospects.

All units that were to be audited would work day in and day out for a week prior to audit, to get their paper work, records, and trails in order.

Abhinav Mookherjee, Head of HR at NYB, was reviewing the audit preparation. He pulled out the last audit report. This audit had been done three years back. This was normally the best way to prepare for an audit—identify mistakes of the past and ensure that they are not repeated.

He went through it point by point. HR was better prepared now than they were the last time. When he reached the second last point on the audit report, he raised an eyebrow. That comment by the audit team read, 'No two people from the same family can work in the same unit and report to the same supervisor.' The auditors had then identified three such couples. In one case, the wife was reporting to the husband. These were obvious issues that had to be fixed.

'Get me a list of all employees whose spouse, sibling or child work with us. I also need the names of their supervisors,' he asked his secretary.

Within fifteen minutes, Mookherjee had a list of twelve employees whose spouse, sibling or child worked in the bank. In all but one case they were in different units and hence there was no issue. All except one.

Sundeep and Natasha worked for the same supervisor Suneel. He called Natasha. Abhinav knew that Sundeep was critical for Suneel's team and therefore Natasha had to move. He spoke to Natasha for over twenty minutes and explained his predicament. 'Which unit would you want to move to. Just checking on your preferences so that I can keep them at the back of my mind before I speak to Suneel about it.' Abhinav knew that Sundeep was close to Suneel and so he thought Suneel was very nice to her. More than what one would normally be with a secretary.

'Can we talk about this tomorrow morning. If that's fine with you. I would like to consult a few other people as well.'

'I am travelling for the next one week, so let's talk next week. I will call you once I am back.'

'Sure, Abhinav.'

When Abhinav called her ten days later, she had her answer ready. 'I would be fine moving to Treasury. The secretary's position there is vacant.'

'Let me see what I can do.'

Over the next couple of days, Abhinav spoke to Suneel and also to Sundeep. Suneel was more than happy to relieve her and let her move to another unit. Within a week, Natasha became a part of Swami's team. Swami had managed to pull Natasha out of hell. What Natasha did not know was that it was a behind-the-scene manoeuvre by Aditya.

Aditya had created a vacancy for Natasha in Swami's team. He had hired the current incumbent in his new company at double the salary and had insisted that she join within one week. Swami released her almost immediately. Once the vacancy was created, they shoved it right under HR's nose asking for the job to be given to Natasha. HR was more than happy to oblige as they were only four days from audit. All this while, Sundeep, as usual, was oblivious of everything.

33

Sundeep's trips to Calcutta became a lot more frequent. He rarely missed a visit to Naresh's office. Once he was sitting in

Naresh's room, while the latter was showing off the mini golf strip that he had laid out on his floor.

'Reshma,' Naresh shouted out for someone. Sundeep raised his eyebrow. He had only heard Naresh call out for Monica.

A young girl walked in, barely nineteen years old. '*Ji, Naresh sir.*'

'Have you met Mr Srivastava? He heads loans with New York International Bank. *Wahan pe* Assistant Vice President *hain. Jao inke liye ek cup shakkar wali special chai bolna.*'

Sundeep couldn't take his eyes off her. She had a body to kill for. When she turned, Sundeep's eyes lit up. She had the best bums he had ever seen. Naresh again smacked his lips and said, '*Yeh degi.*' Sundeep smiled. He was already thinking about his evening.

Naresh had already set up a large team for selling home loans for NYB. '*Yaar Srivastava, chaar mahine ho gaye. Kuch aur karte hain. Aisa kuch karte hain ki mazaa aa jaave.*' Naresh was bored and was looking for something more exciting. '*Mera ek call centre khulva de.*' Naresh wanted to set up a call centre for New York International Bank and explained the entire deal to Sundeep.

'Look Sundeep, I will invest in this call centre. You give me the business. I will manage the complete customer service for New York International Bank in India.' At that time there was no concept of phone banking in India. Even the now-thriving BPO industry had not reared its head. Naresh was smart. He knew how to get his work done. He knew that Sundeep could swing the deal for him.

When Sundeep started thinking, Reshma came back with the tea. Sundeep's thinking went for a toss. Then Naresh threw in the sweetener. 'I will run the call centre on paper, but we will actually own it.' Sundeep looked at him questioningly.

'Yes,' continued Naresh, 'it will be a sixty-forty partnership between us. Sixty mine and forty yours.' After a pause he said, 'Think how many Reshmas we can hire in the call centre. Everyday, someone new to fuck.'

Sundeep didn't react. Naresh knew he had won.

Naresh dropped Sundeep off at the hotel after dinner. Sundeep went up to his room and had a quick shower. He was sipping his whisky when the doorbell rang. He jumped to open the door. He was pleasantly surprised. At the door were Reshma and Monica. One look at them, and Sundeep was immediately aroused.

'Sir, I came to give a handover to Reshma,' said Monica, as she ran her fingers teasingly over Sundeep's dick. The door banged shut and the *Do Not Disturb* sign came up. Reshma was even better than Monica, and, for the first time in his life, Sundeep fucked two women in a single night.

Naresh had got his call centre and Sundeep his double fuck.

34
New York

Louisa was back in Sundeep's room. 'Mr Srivastava, your wife on the line. Should I tell her that you will call her back?'

'I will take it,' said Sundeep.

He had been thinking of his life ever since he became a banker. Even though the incidents were more than a decade old, they came back in front of his eyes, as if they had taken place only yesterday.

'Hi Natasha. How was the zoo, sweetheart?' asked Sundeep.

'The kids loved it. Though I was a little bored,' she said. 'Now they want to go to the dome for a movie. Just got a couple of minutes. Thought I would call you. Louisa told me that you were not feeling too well.'

'No, I'm fine. Just feeling a bit tired. That's all,' he lied.

'Why don't you come home early? We will ditch the movie,' said Natasha. 'I must tell you, your secy is taking good care of you, eh.'

'No sweetheart. You know...' Natasha quickly interrupted him, 'No honey, I was just kidding. You are the most caring husband anyone can ever get. I have no complaints. Even if Louisa is up to something, I am sure, I can trust you.' Natasha's words pierced Sundeep's heart.

'Wait till she gets to know everything,' something inside spoke to him.

'I will see you in the evening, babe.' He blew a kiss over the phone and disconnected.

How could he possibly tell her what he had already done with his career?

35

Sundeep was just leaving for a review when the phone rang. '*Kya kar raha hai, yaar*. You haven't come to Calcutta for over two weeks now. My secretary keeps asking me about you? Here, talk to her.' Naresh gave Reshma the phone.

'Sir, what happened? Monica told me that you came to Calcutta every week to see her. You do not like me?' Reshma asked him in her trademark seductive tone.

'I will be there this week,' said Sundeep.

He kept his promise. Naresh's limousine picked him up from the airport and took him straight to his den. Naresh came down from his office to meet him. Then they went to Naresh's house for lunch.

The lecherous Naresh kept talking about his secretaries and the fun he had with them.

'Sundeep, please change your hiring policy. The way your team hires is painful,' said Naresh.

'Why, what happened now?' asked Sundeep. 'Did any of my sales guys managing your teams screw up.'

'No, *yaar*. Your problem is that you only look at motivating your sales guys. What about my motivation? Shouldn't you be looking at that too? I must also feel happy to meet your sales managers. Today none of your managers fits the T & A criteria.'

'T & A criteria?' Sundeep didn't understand what he meant.

'Don't know T & A criteria, tits and ass, my friend. Basics in life. If they don't meet that criteria, then you should not hire them, irrespective of how good they are.'

Sundeep burst out laughing.

All this was supposedly in jest. However, Sundeep's hiring criteria did change after this. T & A criteria was informally applied to every candidate he met.

Interactions with Naresh had started shaping his behaviour. Slowly but surely Naresh was becoming an integral part of Sundeep's bank. He had grown so big that seventy percent of the business in eastern India for New York International Bank was originated by Naresh's team.

The Naresh factor had begun to impact Sundeep's personal life. He was spending less time with Natasha. He had started neglecting her. Natasha found emotional support in Swami and Kalpana.

Naresh also had a great relationship with Suneel. With secretaries like Monica, relationships were not difficult to build. Sundeep used Naresh smartly for insights into Suneel. Naresh fed him all the relevant information. If Suneel said anything good about Sundeep, he would get to know. If Suneel had a negative view on anything, Sundeep would know. This helped him to quickly fix any perception issues with his boss. Riding on Naresh, Sundeep's equation with Suneel was on a high.

It suited Naresh too. Sundeep was constantly reminded of the fact that Naresh knew his boss better than he did. If he didn't take care of Naresh, his career with NYB had no chance of taking off. Obviously, Suneel had Naresh's ear more than Sundeep had.

Business was growing. Perceptions were great. Career was galloping. Things were going fine. Till one day...

On that day Sundeep had come to Calcutta on one of his many Naresh trips. After a hectic day at work, Naresh dropped him to his hotel. Back in his room, he showered and as usual waited for Naresh's secy. This time it was Linda, a hot babe in her early twenties. Reshma too was with her, supposedly to give a 'handover' to Linda.

The next six hours were full of moaning and groaning. Sundeep spent the whole night in bed with the two women, having the time of his life.

It was five in the morning when Sundeep opened his eyes. Linda and Reshma had just got up and were wearing their clothes. He looked at Linda, stretched out his hand and pulled her down on the bed. After twenty more minutes of ecstasy, Linda wore her clothes again and prepared to leave.

Sundeep followed them to the door to see them off. It was only half past five and since he was not going to step out of the room, he didn't feel it necessary to wear anything.

'See you soon, sir. You were great,' said Linda and walked out into the corridor with Reshma. Sundeep's ego swelled and he blew them a kiss. They turned and blew a kiss back at him.

As the two women were leaving, someone walked past Sundeep's room. While they were giggling and blowing kisses at Sundeep, who was standing nude at the door, this individual looked back in exasperation. He saw the two giggly women and beyond them, a naked Sundeep peeping out from behind the door. His heart sank. A few wrinkles of concern appeared on his forehead for an instant. He just turned and walked away without saying anything.

Sundeep saw him and froze. He couldn't move. It was as if he was paralysed. Standing there in the corridor beyond the two raunch queens was someone whom Sundeep in his wildest of dreams wouldn't have imagined to be there. The door hardly did anything to conceal Sundeep's nudity. He stood there completely exposed. As he shut the door, he could see that he was shivering. The AC in the room showed twenty-four degrees.

Sundeep was booked on the 1.00 p.m. Jet Airways flight from Calcutta to Mumbai. He was initially scheduled to go back the previous night, but when Naresh told him about Linda, he had decided to stay back.

When he stepped into the flight, there was only one other passenger in Business Class. Being an afternoon flight, it was fairly light. When the captain announced for the doors to be armed for takeoff, there were still only two passengers. Sundeep was a worried man. He kept looking nervously at the other passenger from the corner of his eyes. But that guy was only interested in the scenery outside.

Sundeep waited for a few minutes after take off, but couldn't bear it any longer. He unbuckled his seat belt and walked up to the other passenger, who had his eyes trained on a fixed spot on the window. He stood there for a moment, but the other guy didn't even look at him. Sundeep placed his hand on the other man's shoulder.

'How long has this being going on?' asked Swami without even bothering to look at Sundeep.

'Three months.'

There was a prolonged silence at Swami's end.

'What are you going to do now?' asked a worried Sundeep. There was not a trace of guilt on his face. He just didn't want to be exposed, that's all.

'The easiest thing for me to do is to tell Natasha. But I won't. Not because you are my friend and I want to protect you, but because Kalpana and I adore her. She will be shattered if we tell her about this, particularly after what she has gone through.' Sundeep didn't understand the last bit. Swami was referring to the problems Natasha had had with Suneel Dutt. Sundeep just nodded.

'I will not tell Natasha anything. Relax, Sundeep. But I need to know the complete story.' Swami wanted to get to the bottom of this.

Swami could never have imagined this side of Sundeep's character. That morning Swami had set out for an early morning walk, when he became an inadvertent witness to Sundeep's escapades. How he wished that he hadn't seen that. But can you rewind your life? He thought about Natasha. What did she do to deserve this? She was such a sweetheart. She had already gone through so much trauma and, on top of that, if she got to know of this, she would surely be shattered. He will not tell Natasha anything about what he saw. Not even to Kalpana, he promised himself.

'I want the complete story, Sundeep. No short cuts.'

Sundeep told him the story, from the time Suneel asked him to meet Naresh, to his escapades with his secretaries, and the call centre deal. Swami was appalled. How could someone like Sundeep fall a prey to all this?

Sundeep hadn't told him about the financial benefits accruing to him. Swami didn't need to know.

'Sundeep, I will not tell Natasha, but under one condition.'

Sundeep nodded. Anything was acceptable to him to prevent his exposure.

'All this has to stop from this very instant. If I get to hear anything like this again, I will leave no stone unturned to get you completely exposed, despite you being my friend.'

'Trust me, Swami,' said Sundeep, trying to suppress his glee. He had succeeded in managing Swami. Not for a second was Sundeep ashamed of what he had done.

'And you will be loyal to Natasha throughout your life.'

'Hmm.' Sundeep nodded his acceptance.

'This congestion at the Mumbai airport in mid-afternoon is utter madness. I will have to tolerate Swami's sermon for at least another fifteen minutes,' thought Sundeep after the pilot announced that they were twelfth in the landing sequence.

Finally, when they landed and came out of the airport, Swami warned Sundeep for one last time and walked out to a waiting car. Back at home, Kalpana wondered what had gone wrong. Why did Swami come back so soon? This was not normal.

'Swami. What happened?' she asked him the moment she saw him at the door.

'Nothing. I was just feeling a bit unwell.' The moment Swami said this, Kalpana knew that he was lying. She did not push him because she trusted him and knew that he would not hide anything important from her.

That morning a desperate Sundeep had tried to call Naresh from his hotel room. Naresh was not at home. He had, in fact, not returned the previous night. In those days, there were no mobile phones and so Sundeep had no means of getting in touch with him.

Naresh called back in the evening, after over a dozen calls from Sundeep.

'What happened,' asked Naresh, 'you don't sound too good.' He knew, from the number of messages he had got, that something was not right.

When Sundeep told him about the incident, Naresh laughed it away. 'Is that all? You should have sounded off Reshma. She would have managed Swami on the spot. You are selfish, Sundeep. If I was you, I would have sent either Linda or Reshma to him. *Mil baant ke khaana chahiye.*' Naresh was telling him that he should have sent one of the sirens to Swami to buy his silence.

'No Ram. You don't know Swami. *Gandhi ka chela hai.* If there was a competition for the guy who is closest to Mahatma Gandhi, Swami will beat the Mahatma himself hands down.'

'There's not a guy in this bank who I can't manage,' boasted Naresh. 'Linda and Reshma are wonderful my friend.'

'You haven't dealt with Swami yet.'

'Are you worried?'

'I am not worried about today. I have somehow managed it. The concern is that he will be a constant nuisance from now on. He will always be on my trail. He and his wife are both very close to Natasha.'

'*Toh uska koi jugad kar dete hai. Tu shanti rakh.*' Naresh promised to find a way to deal with Swami.

'Don't harm him. Just get him out of our way,' said Sundeep and hung up.

Naresh didn't like bankers that didn't toe his line. This was not the first time. He had dealt successfully with a lot of bankers like Swami in the past. Just as he had made people's careers at New York International Bank, he had also screwed up careers of those who didn't fall in line.

Swami was about to witness the power of Naresh.

36

A couple of weeks later Swami and Kalpana went off for their annual vacation. A long awaited vacation for both of them. Kalpana had invited Sundeep and Natasha to join them, but Sundeep declined, stating some pressing work issues and reviews with Suneel. Swami suspected that Naresh was behind this, but didn't say a word.

Swami and Kalpana took a KLM flight via Amsterdam to reach Barcelona. They went on a weeklong cruise from Barcelona. The cruise took them deep into the Mediterranean. They visited the islands of Palma de Majorca, and Corsica. Corsica was the island where Napoleon de Bonaparte was born.

This was their first vacation after their honeymoon in Kodai. Kalpana had pestered Swami till he gave her the dates and the budget for the vacation. She had organised it entirely on her own.

Swami had taken an overseas vacation for the first time and was very excited about it. By the time the cruise docked back in Barcelona after a week, it had transported the couple into a very different world that they didn't want to come back from.

When the flight from Amsterdam landed in Mumbai at 2.00 a.m., they didn't feel like getting off the aircraft. The moment they set their foot back on Mumbai soil, it would signal the end of their vacation. Kalpana knew that the next vacation would have to wait for at least another eighteen months. They dragged themselves out of the aircraft and came back home, collecting their luggage on the way out.

The next morning Kalpana called Natasha to tell her all about the trip.

'I wish I had gone with you folks. Anyway, Sundeep was in Calcutta all the while,' said Natasha. Then she asked for Swami.

'Swami, Roger was trying to get in touch with you. I told him that you were holidaying in Europe. He has asked you to call him the moment you get back.' Roger, an expat, was Swami's immediate supervisor.

'Anything urgent?' asked Swami.

'Nothing that I am aware of. I asked the others in your team and they too didn't know. But no less than four times last week has Roger asked me to remind you,' said Natasha.

'Should I call him today?' It was a Sunday.

'I think it can wait till tomorrow morning. Just be prepared then. My intention was not to make you nervous. I just wanted to let you know.'

'Thanks Natasha. How is Sundeep?'

'He is still sleeping like a log.'

'OK. I will let him be. Let's chat tomorrow morning in office,' said Swami and hung up. He was wondering what the issue could be?

37

Monday morning, Swami was in office very early. His first day at work after three weeks. More than four hundred unread mails had piled up in his mailbox.

He was wondering why Roger so desperately wanted to meet him. By the time everyone got into office, he had read each and every mail, but except for a mail from Rogers asking him to come and see him whenever he returns from vacation, there was nothing in the mails to suggest any cause for concern.

Rogers normally came in at around ten. Natasha told Swami at around eleven that Roger wanted to see him. Swami accompanied her back to Roger's cabin.

The meeting with Roger lasted over an hour and half. Natasha could see the proceedings from her workstation, through the glass partition that separated her from Roger's room. However, she couldn't hear anything as Roger's cabin was sound-proof and the door was shut. But she could see that Roger did most of the talking. Swami was mostly sitting quiet, rarely opening his mouth. 'What's going on?' she wondered.

Two rounds of coffee were sent in. After the first two calls that she transferred to Roger, she was asked to put all calls on hold. There was no doubt now that the discussion going on inside was extremely serious. 'Has Swami screwed up something very badly? Is he going to lose his job?' Natasha began worrying for swami.

After about ninety minutes, a beaming Swami emerged from Roger's room.

'What happened?' Natasha whispered. She did not want Roger to think that she was indulging in gossip with his direct reports.

'Later.' Swami kept up the suspense.

'Should I walk up with you to your desk?'

'No. No. Later, Natasha. Actually, what are you and Sundeep doing this evening? Why don't you guys have dinner at home with us? We will talk about it at home,' said Swami, and without waiting for a response, walked away.

Natasha did not get a chance to speak with Swami the whole day.

The doorbell at Kalpana's home rang at 8.40 p.m. She opened the door to find Natasha and Sundeep. 'What a surprise?' she said, and made way for them to come in.

Natasha and Sundeep looked at each other. 'Hasn't Swami told you? He was the one who called us home for dinner.' An embarrassed Kalpana looked at them blankly. She was, however, glad that they had come. She led them to the living room and made them comfortable.

'How was the cruise, madam?' asked Sundeep. 'Will we at least get to see some photographs?'

Kalpana smiled and pulled out the photographs, which had just come in from the studio. She was showing it to them when Swami walked in.

'Look who's here!' said Natasha. She was the first to spot Swami walking in.

He handed over a large packet to Kalpana. He had picked up some food from a Chinese restaurant. He knew that both Kalpana and Natasha liked Chinese food.

'Sorry folks, I just picked up some food on the way and that delayed me. Else I would have been here before you .'

'You should at least have told me that Natasha is coming over for dinner,' Kalpana complained.

'Will you now tell us what you have called us here for?' Sundeep was extremely curious. He hadn't spoken much to Swami after they met on that Calcutta to Mumbai flight. Despite the strain in the relationship, they had to put up a pretence for their wives.

'Wait, Sundeep. Let me first settle down,' said Swami, as he excused himself to freshen up and change. He came back in five minutes and sat down on a sofa next to where Sundeep was sitting. Everyone was looking at Swami, hoping he would say something. Swami was very amused. 'What?' he asked, looking at everyone.

Natasha looked at Sundeep. 'Come, let's go home.' She got up, pretending to be annoyed. Sundeep pulled her down.

'Ever heard of ITDP?' asked Swami, looking at all three of them, one by one.

'No?' the two women said in unison. Their eyes were focused on Swami.

'No?' asked Swami, pretending to be surprised.

'What the hell, No!' said Sundeep and the other two women nodded.

'International Talent Discovery Programme, idiots.'

'What about it?' asked Natasha. Kalpana couldn't figure out what was going on.

'Wait a minute,' said Sundeep. 'You called us here to tell us that you have been nominated for the International Talent Discovery Programme, haven't you?'

Swami just smiled. Kalpana was thrilled. When she heard this, she was walking in with water for everyone and the tray nearly fell out of her hand. Sundeep's heart skipped a beat. He hadn't forgotten the past. How much he hated Swami for having married Kalpana. It was too late anyway.

The International Talent Discovery Programme needed no introduction to these guys. When Swami initially told them the acronym, the others didn't get the context and so didn't connect. Else who in New York International Bank didn't know about ITDP?

The International Talent Discovery Programme, or ITDP, as it was normally called, was one of the most sought after training programmes in New York International Bank. The bank sold ITDP as the ultimate in career enhancement at campus placement camps. It was designed to develop future leaders. Young talent from across the globe would be nominated for this programme and would undergo a rigorous one-year residential training in New York, which would prepare them for larger leadership roles in the future. After successful completion of this programme, one would become a global resource, who was deemed fit to be placed in any country across the world.

The nominations for this programme would come in from the top. Only people in country manager roles and above could nominate people for this programme. Anyone who was serious about pursuing a career at NYB would give his right arm for a nomination.

'But this year's course starts in six weeks. Have you been nominated for the one beginning next year?' asked Sundeep.

'No, we will have to be in New York in time for this year's course,' said Swami, much to Sundeep's surprise. Natasha squealed in excitement, while Sundeep felt the pangs of jealousy.

'Congratulations. This is bloody good,' he finally said.

'Does that mean both of you will go away to the US?' asked Natasha, the excitement dying a bit. Kalpana was the only friend she had in town. Swami nodded.

He had come a long way. From his modest beginnings to the ITDP at New York International Bank was a great achievement. One could have forgiven him for momentarily swelling with pride.

Swami's move to New York was the topic of discussion at the dinner table. Natasha was giving shopping tips to Kalpana.

She had been to the US years back, but on the table, she was the expert as none of the others had ever been there for more than three days.

Sundeep was extremely quiet. He had again lost out to Swami. First it was Kalpana. He had lost her to Swami. And now the ITDP nomination. Swami had got the nomination ahead of him. Why did it always have to be Swami? This was too frustrating.

Natasha turned towards Swami and asked him, 'If this was the issue, why were you having a long and serious discussion with Roger this afternoon?' That was a point everyone had nearly missed.

'Oh yes. Roger is not happy with my nomination.'

'And why the hell would he not be?' Sundeep snapped back, irritated that he might have to listen to another boring, self-effacing story.

'Because he didn't nominate me. I am going on the ITDP, not as a nomination from Treasury, but from Retail Banking.' It was getting murkier. Sundeep was in Retail Banking and Swami was in Treasury. How did he manage to get nominated on the Retail Banking quota? He was even more miserable now. If at all there was a Retail Bank nomination, it should have been his. Swami's nomination was not acceptable to him at all.

'And that's why he was quite pissed and wanted to know how I swung this deal without telling him about it. I kept reiterating that I had no clue, but he would have none of it.' Swami explained.

'But how did you manage to swing the nomination? At least tell us, we can use that strategy next year, Swami.' Sundeep was at his sarcastic best.

'I have no clue. Roger told me that Joseph Fernandes had nominated me from the CEO's quota. The Group CEO can nominate three persons of his choice. Joseph Fernandes put my name on that list.'

'And why would Joseph do that for you?'

'Suneel had spoken to Joseph personally and requested that I be nominated on this programme,' Swami defended himself. 'And that's the most surprising part. Why did Suneel do this? We don't get along gloriously. I am not sure if I will be able to figure this out.'

Sundeep heard every word with full attention. 'Why did Suneel do this?' he wondered. The smile slowly came back on his lips. He hugged Swami and said, 'Well done, friend. You have done us proud.' Then he excused himself and walked towards the washroom. His smile had turned into a wicked grin that he didn't want anybody to notice.

'What a scheming bastard!' he thought. 'How did he manage to do it so well!' He was not referring to Swami. He now knew how Swami got that nomination to ITDP. It was his dear old fixer friend Ram Naresh.

Sundeep now knew that Naresh was a very important man in his scheme of things. To protect Sundeep, and to get Swami out of the way, Naresh had spoken to Joseph Fernandes, who in turn had spoken to Suneel Dutt, and asked him to nominate Swami. And Suneel, despite his public dislike of Swami, had nominated him for the most prestigious programme in New York International Bank. 'Bastard of the highest order! Hats off to Naresh.'

This held one more meaning for Sundeep. If Naresh could do wonders for Swami's career to get him out of the way, he could definitely take Sundeep's career sky high, provided he managed Naresh well. He decided to take even more care of Naresh from that very instant.

38

When the CEO himself nominates you, others often have no choice. In the next four weeks, Swami was relieved from his job at Treasury. And the week after that, Swami and Kalpana were on a flight to New York. A new chapter in their life had begun.

Suneel hadn't spoken to Swami ever since the nomination got confirmed. Swami was completely in the dark about the behind-the-scene manoeuvre—how Naresh had packed him off because Sundeep found him to be a stumbling block to their alliance.

While he was glad that he had got nominated to the ITDP, he knew for sure that he would not be returning to India soon. ITDP participants were usually made to serve in a few other markets, before they got a posting back in their home country. The intent was to give them significant global exposure in the organisation's effort to make them future leaders. He had not mentioned this to his mother and had forbidden Kalpana from doing so.

Kalpana too had her share of insecurities. She was leaving her home country for an alien land. They didn't know many people there. While they would make enough money to make their future secure, money was not everything. She would miss her family, miss Mumbai, miss India. Swami shared her thoughts too.

There was one silver lining though. Both Swami and Kalpana wanted to start a family. They had been married for over three years. This one year away from home, with nothing much to do, provided her with the perfect opportunity to start a family.

Once Swami left, Sundeep's conscience keeper was gone. Sundeep's liaison with Naresh was on the upswing. There was no one to question him. Before he left, Swami had advised Sundeep to stay away from Naresh and not screw around in his personal life. 'It will come back to haunt you,' Swami had warned. 'You must protect your integrity.'

Sundeep did not heed Swami's advice and was on his own trip. Nothing mattered to him, except Naresh, money and women, not necessarily in that order.

39

Swami moved into a tiny service apartment in the heart of New York, just two blocks away from the training centre of New York International Bank. In all, fifty-two NYB bankers from all over the globe had come to New York for the ITDP. Swami was one of the six who had been nominated from Retail Banking. Swami had been nominated to the core talent pool of the bank.

Both Swami and Kalpana were excited by New York. The training was slow off the blocks. It would get over by 5.30 p.m. every day and Swami would be back home by six, despite walking the entire distance. Swami and Kalpana observed that people in that country valued their time. Weekends were off. Unlike India where everyone would slog their butts off even on weekends, in America, weekends were for the family. Americans respected their weekends and no one worked on a Saturday or a Sunday.

Kalpana spent the first two weeks sightseeing. She went on a day trip to the Statue of Liberty, the World Trade Centre and the Rockfeller Foundation. She walked round Times Square, and saw every other place worth seeing. She visited all the museums in town. Kalpana had brought fifteen rolls of photo film. She exhausted all of them within the first month. The first thirty days in New York reminded her of their honeymoon.

However, it was not long before she started feeling the pinch. The training was beginning to get intense. It didn't take Swami much time to create an impression. Indians generally are a high intelligence breed. Swami would rank among the top five percentile as far as the Indian population was concerned. Within a short while he was identified as an A-grade resource by the management team conducting the training. Once he was a marked man, Swami had the additional responsibility of delivering every time. He started working very hard. He would leave early in the morning and come back late at night. To lead discussions the next day, he had to prepare well. Back home, he would immerse himself in reams of paper.

Kalpana started getting extremely bored, sitting at home all day. The apartment was claustrophobic, much smaller than their apartment in Mumbai. She was beginning to feel lonely too.

She would wait eagerly for her weekly calls to Natasha. In those days international calls were very expensive. Daily calls were out of the question. Swami, like a typical Tamil Brahmin with a lower middle class upbringing, was very conscious about keeping expenses under control. 'Even if we can afford it, we should not spend more than what is required,' he would say. His days of poverty were partly responsible for this.

'Amma, I don't like it here. I am very lonely. Why don't you and Ambujam come here for a few days,' she told Swami's mom on the phone.

'Why *beta*, is Swami not taking care of you?'

'He is very busy these days. He leaves early in the morning and comes back late at night. I am on my own all day.'

'Why don't you also take up some job, *beta*,' she suggested.

'Why not?' thought Kalpana. She mentioned it to Swami when he got back from work. Swami was extremely supportive. He had always stood for Kalpana's financial independence. Her decision to quit NYB was entirely her own. In fact, Swami had even then tried to get her to change her mind.

Swami felt that the best option for her now would be to find out if an option existed with New York International Bank itself. He decided to check it out the next day.

Kalpana soon landed a job as a research assistant in the emerging markets wing of the bank. This wing was a part of the Retail Bank unit. Her earlier experience with the launch of retail banking in India helped her get this role. 'I am going back to work,' she told Natasha, who couldn't miss the excitement in her voice. The five-hour-a-day job was long enough to keep her busy, but also left her with enough time to explore America and find time for her interests.

Time just flew for both of them. Weekends were travel time. They would explore every nook and corner of New York and all other neighbouring cities along the eastern coast of America. It was a second honeymoon for them.

They had just one worry. Kalpana hadn't conceived after three years of marriage. These days couples prefer to wait much longer before having their first child, but this was different.

Swami wanted a child and they had been planning for a family ever since they landed in New York. It was over three months now, and there was no progress on that front. Kalpana started getting concerned. Was something wrong with either of them? Was it the stress at work? Was it that they were too tired by the time they got back home? She had read somewhere that excessive stress leads to a lower probability of conceiving. She started taking stress-relieving classes every day. But this didn't help. Her anxiety was adding to the stress. She was getting really paranoid about this.

40

The phone in their apartment rang one Sunday morning. They could make it out from the ring tone that it was an international call. Kalpana ran and picked it up. It had to be either Natasha or Swami's mom.

'Hello.'

'Hi Kalpana.' It was Natasha shrieking at the other end.

'Natasha, you sound so great.'

'I am pregnant, Kalpana. I am pregnant.' Natasha was almost screaming hysterically into the phone.

Kalpana burst out in tears of joy. 'I am so happy, Natasha.' Natasha was like a sister to her. She was happy for her. She was glad that at least Natasha didn't have to go through the same stress that she was going through.

'I got the report last night. I was waiting to call you.'

They talked for over an hour. Swami had to get up and make his morning coffee himself. For Kalpana, Natasha was more important than Swami, and if it was a pregnant Natasha, Swami stood no chance.

When Natasha told Sundeep about her pregnancy, he was obviously happy. It was, however, for a reason that Natasha couldn't imagine in her wildest dreams.

'Sundeep, it is not good for you and your wife to work together in the same organisation,' Naresh had once told him. 'She will get to know a lot about you through the grapevine. It will impact your life. It will be good if she quits and takes up another job.'

This was a god sent opportunity for Sundeep to get Natasha to quit her job. But he didn't mention this to her. He wanted Natasha to herself recommend this option. He was waiting for that opportune moment.

He went along with her on her next visit to the gynaecologist. He had told Suneel that he would be late. The gynae did a thorough check-up and told Natasha that she needed to put on some weight. She was slightly underweight for a four-month pregnant woman. The only way she could put on weight was by taking adequate rest. She recommended that Natasha either take leave or quit her job.

Sundeep dropped Natasha home and went to work. He had insisted that Natasha take an off that day. Once he reached his office, he picked up the phone and dialled a number.

'Dr Mehra's clinic,' said the voice at the other end.

'Can I speak to Dr Shalinee Mehra?' Sundeep asked for the same gynae that they had met in the morning.

'Dr Mehra, Sundeep here. Thank you for the help this morning. I really appreciate it.' Sundeep had no morals, no values. If he could do this to his wife, he could do this to anyone else. He had set up the gynae to recommend that Natasha quit her job and sit at home.

After a fair bit of discussion, Natasha decided to put in her papers. Kalpana had tried to convince her against it, but in front of a scheming Sundeep, Kalpana's efforts didn't make a difference. 'You know how important both you and our child are for me. I will not be able to excuse myself if something happens to you.' Sundeep pitched it at an emotional high with Natasha.

'*Bahut achcha kiya*. Well done,' was Naresh's response, when Sundeep told him about Natasha quitting her job.

Sundeep's friendship with Naresh was growing by the day. The partners in crime were flying high. Sundeep always ensured that his misdeeds didn't come out in the open. His misdeeds were restricted to those front-ended by Naresh. On the work front, Sundeep was very highly regarded and brought in an unprecedented level of energy to New York International Bank. He was the star of Suneel Dutt's team. Everyone in the bank carried the impression that it was only a matter of time before Sundeep achieved big things in life.

Both Sundeep and Swami were high on intellect. But Sundeep was a leader of men, who would inspire people to do tasks, whereas Swami was a doer. Sundeep was a transactor, while Swami was a strategist.

The two heroes of New York International Bank were charting their own course in their own ways across the continents. One was busy creating a name for himself in ITDP and the other was imprinting his name in the annals of retail banking in this country.

41

Over the next decade, NYB became one of the largest foreign banks in India. The retail business that Aditya, Swami and Sundeep had set up was among the best and the most organised in this country. They established a footprint in all businesses that one could imagine a bank to be in. Among foreign banks on Indian soil, they had one of the largest branch networks. It soon became the most profitable foreign bank in the country as well. Their cards business had taken off to a roaring start, and they had a flourishing loans business. Car loans, home loans, personal loans—name it, and they had a loan for it.

The common joke in those days was that NYB was responsible for the traffic jams in Indian metros. NYB gave every Tom, Dick and Harry a loan to buy a car, and all of a sudden the number of new cars that flooded the streets grew manifold, leading to traffic jams, and nobody had built the roads to accommodate them.

Worldwide, New York International Bank had moved up one notch and was now the third largest bank in the world. It had got there by acquiring one of the top ten banks in the US. Ahead of it were Citibank and Bank of America, the two largest banks in the world.

After a very successful stint in the assets business, Sundeep moved on as the Head of Branch Banking. He managed the largest branch distribution of any foreign bank in India for over eighteen months.

NYB in India was a mean and hungry bank. They wanted to grow quickly and had identified *Mergers and Acquisition* as the means. Sundeep led the team that acquired the South India Urban Commercial Bank (SIUCB) that had a network of twenty-one branches. In those days, the laws for acquisition of banks in India were unclear. Sundeep fought through the loopholes in the law and managed the acquisition, adding those twenty-one branches to New York International Bank's network in one go. This was another feather in Sundeep's cap. That Naresh had a large role to play in this goes without saying. Naresh had made millions of dollars in the deal.

Sundeep was considered the king of banking. He brought out innovative lending products, which were almost always, but very cunningly, bank-friendly and customer-unfriendly.

With the acquisition of SIUCB and the rapid expansion in the branch network came in a new set of challenges. Providing quality service to the ever-expanding base of customers was proving to be tough. In those days, the customers were attuned to walking into the branch of a bank for getting any service. With customer acquisition numbers going through the roof, the branches started getting crowded. The only way to service these customers was to move them to alternative channels for service delivery. Sundeep decided to set up a full-scale in-house phone-banking unit.

A phone-banking unit in those days was heavily capital intensive. Sundeep knew very well that Suneel would turn down the request for such an investment because he was on his way out after two years in India. And once Suneel turned it down, he couldn't have set it up till such time that the new head Kailash Advani came in. Kailash was a career NYB'ite and was slated to move in from America where he had been instrumental in the consolidation of the South American operations of the bank.

He decided to wait till Suneel moved out to become the CEO of NYB in Poland. Sundeep had to work in his role for a period of six months before Kailash Advani could join in. Within six weeks of Suneel's leaving, Sundeep had put in place a new phone banking set-up.

Sundeep bought out the call centre that he had jointly set up with Naresh and expanded it to meet his projected capacities. The price he paid to Naresh for buying off his unit was astronomical. Of course, part of it was to come back to him. And there was no one to question him. No one would suspect Sundeep of misappropriation. What made matters easy for him was that no one at the head office knew the revenue–expenditure dynamics in India. It was an easy battle for Sundeep to win.

But one thing was for sure—whatever Sundeep touched, turned into gold. He won the Asia-Pacific Best Retail Banker Award for New York International Bank, four times in the six years that he was in the region. NYB swept all the awards in the financial services industry in India, in the businesses headed by him. Sundeep was recognised far and wide as a star.

After spending six years in various roles, Sundeep was finally made Deputy Head of Retail Banking in India—deputy to Kailash Advani. It was a role with large strategic impact, but little direct business responsibility. It was a big day for Sundeep. The newspapers had his photos splashed on the front pages. Business magazines hailed him as the next big thing in the Indian banking industry.

Sundeep Srivastava had finally arrived. Or so everyone thought until...

42

One day Sundeep came back home very late from work. Natasha was waiting for him to have dinner. Sundeep didn't utter a word and walked straight into his bedroom. Natasha was wondering what went wrong at work. Within the next five minutes Sundeep was back and joined her at the dinner table.

'How would you like it if we were to go to London.'

'Last Tuesday you cancelled our vacation to Maldives. You said that some idiot was coming from overseas, and now you are talking about London.'

'Not for a holiday, silly.'

'Then what?'

'Kailash asked me today if I would like to head the NRI business based in London,' said Sundeep.

It was not a vacation. Sundeep was talking about leaving India for good and going to London. 'I was under the impression that you did not want to work overseas.' Sundeep had always given Natasha the impression that India was where the action is and so it would be stupid to move out, especially at a time when the country was going through an explosive growth phase.

'Yes, Nattie. But it will be worthwhile staying in India only if Kailash moves out and I get his job. But that's not going to happen soon. He has been sitting on that chair for the last four years and will be there for another four.'

Natasha was aware that Kailash was a very senior banker, a lifer at NYB, who had come back to India, to look after his aged and ailing mother in Mumbai. He was 51 years old, four years from retirement. There was only a slim chance of his moving out of India to an overseas assignment at this fag end of his career.

The next level job for Sundeep was definitely blocked for the next four years. He would constantly be the prince in waiting, a role that didn't appeal to him. An assignment in London could give him the required exposure to position him for larger roles globally. Natasha didn't argue with the logic thrown at her.

Honestly, she was indifferent. She didn't get to see much of Sundeep here and she wouldn't get to see much of him there as well. Her life revolved around Alka and Ajay, her two children. Sundeep had become a visitor in their lives.

They moved to London, where they stayed for four years.

43

Natasha enjoyed London thoroughly. The kids loved it. Sundeep travelled all over the globe. He kept his friendship with Naresh intact, even though the deals died out. There was no business now where he could cut a deal with Naresh without raising eyebrows. Both Naresh and Sundeep were too clever to do anything visibly egregious. They were not in it for short-term gains.

The NRI business flourished under Sundeep. It turned into a goldmine. Once Sundeep took over the reins, it became the most profitable business for the Indian arm of New York International Bank, and remained that way four years in a row.

But success had already made Sundeep an animal. He had lost respect for people. He had become a maniac, a successful maniac. When a man tastes continued success, he cannot take failure. This was becoming Sundeep's biggest shortcoming. The same Sundeep, whose team in the erstwhile days consisted of performers, was now constantly surrounded by sycophants. And when the flattery came from the fairer sex, Sundeep was particularly gullible.

When still in London, Sundeep and Natasha completed thirteen years of their married life. Sundeep was a doting father. Alka was his pet. Natasha was as attractive as she used to be when Sundeep first met her. The birth of two kids hadn't done anything to her almost perfect figure.

44

Swami topped the ITDP course. This brought him instant fame and recognition within the group. He got noticed and recognised by the core retail bank committee of the bank and even the Group CEO. His success never went to his head, as he had come up the hard way in life.

NYB was growing rapidly in Asia and was constantly on the prowl for acquisitions. A cards business in Korea came up for grabs. Fresh out of the ITDP, Swami was deputed by Global HQ to close the deal.

Swami and Kalpana packed their bags and moved to Korea for a short-term assignment. Kalpana was given a leave of absence by the HR head. Swami's reputation as a top-notch professional had a lot to do with it.

Swami worked hard at closing the deal with the local NYB branch in Korea. He clinched the deal in a last minute manoeuvre, even though the competition was from large, established players in the market. He then led a team of people who worked on the effective integration of the two organisations. He focused his efforts on the people aspect. He knew that acquisitions often go wrong because the acquiring bank often ill treats the employees of the acquired organisation and fails to win their trust. This acquisition was a feather in Swami's cap. Everything went as per schedule. No surprises.

On successful completion of this acquisition, Swami was sent to help turn around the branch network in South Africa. Swami had a unique, solution-oriented way of approaching problems. The South African franchise was on the roll and making money in less than a year.

Swami then got back in Chicago and was assigned to Kailash Advani's team. This team was working on the consolidation of the bank's various businesses in South America. The South American business of NYB was highly fragmented. There was no common thread. None of their various businesses across the continent was of a significant scale. Kailash and Swami worked on the entire retail strategy for South America along with a team of retail bankers. They cut down the number of products from 189 to twenty-three and realigned the employees to these businesses. They shut down a few businesses. Some tough HR decisions were taken. People with low commitment were asked to leave. In the end, the entire business got a makeover and things started looking positive. The business now had an identity.

Swami worked with Kailash for about a year and half, and most of Kailash's success there could be attributed to Swami. No wonder, when Kailash moved to India as Head of Retail Banking, he asked Swami to join him. He knew that in the Indian market a person like Swami would be of great value.

Swami had politely turned him down at that time. He was very clear that he would not be linked to personalities. He would not want to be known as Kailash's man. While it helped in the short run, he thought that in the long run there were more negatives than positives. Kailash didn't push him.

Swami's career was on the upswing. The next five years were glorious years in his career. He and Kalpana had a wonderful life. He moved across various states of USA, setting up new businesses and fixing issues in existing ones. He was the key fixer for Chetan Bindra, another Indian who was at that time the Head of Retail for the whole of America.

The only thing he and Kalpana could have complained about was their still not having a baby. Sometimes Swami's eyes would grow moist at the thought. They did all they could—went through stress-busting classes, got themselves medically examined—but nothing worked. They reconciled themselves to the fact that god does not give everyone everything in life.

45

Life often does weird things that leave one with little or no choice. One night Swami was driving back from work and got a call on his mobile. It was an international call. The caller ID on his phone didn't recognise the number, and so the number didn't come up on the screen.

Given the stickler for discipline that he was, he did not take calls from anyone while driving and so ignored the call. Within moments of the call having self-disconnected, his mobile started ringing again. This time again it was an international call. Again he didn't pick it up. The caller didn't call back.

He was listening to South Indian Carnatic music on his car stereo, when his mobile rang again. This time it was Kalpana. He intuitively realised that something was wrong. He pulled his car to a side and answered the phone.

'Swami, where are you?'

'I am on my way back. I will be home in five minutes. Why? What happened?'

'No, it's OK. Just wanted to check if I should lay out the table for dinner.' But she couldn't hide the shiver in her voice. Swami was beginning to get nervous.

'Kalpana,' he asked firmly, 'What is it?'

'Nothing, Swami. Come back quickly.' That's all she said and hung up.

Swami rushed home and found Kalpana waiting at the door for him. The moment she saw him, she hugged him and started weeping. 'What happened Kalpana? Tell me?' Swami was really worried now.

'Amma called. She was trying to reach you.'

'So it was her. The number didn't flash on the mobile screen and I was driving. I didn't pick it up. What happened? For god's sake, tell me quickly, Kalpana.'

'Ambujam's bus met with an accident on Old Mahabalipuram road. She is in the ICU at Apollo Hospital. Amma told me that her ribs have cracked and punctured her lungs. She is under observation for the next forty-eight hours. Doctors say that she is not out of danger yet. And...'

'And what Kalpana?'

'She has a skull fracture and is in coma.'

This made Swami very nervous.

'Amma is worried. She doesn't know what to do. She is all alone there.'

'Oh my God! What do we do now?' Swami was extremely upset that despite having everything in life he was not with his mother when she needed him most. Success is meaningless if you can't take care of your near and dear ones. And poor Ambu, the frail sister of Swami. How could she take all this? Poor thing couldn't even stand the prick of an injection.

He called his mother and spoke to her for over thirty minutes. Since his mother was in the hospital, he also got to speak to the doctor. The doctor was hopeful of Ambujam coming out of coma, but the conversation was not entirely reassuring.

He kept the phone down and looked at Kalpana. 'Let's pack our bags and leave. We'll take the first flight out to Chennai.'

He picked up the phone again and dialled a number. 'Hello.'

'Aditya, this is Swami.' When Swami kept the phone down fifteen minutes later, he had made all arrangements for someone to reach his mother to provide moral support till he landed back in India.

Forty-eight hours later Swami and Kalpana landed at the Kamraj International Airport in Chennai and headed straight to the Apollo hospital. Swami's mother hugged Kalpana and started weeping like a child. Kalpana consoled her, but she kept crying till the tears dried out.

Ambu was shifted out of the ICU into a private ward and after three weeks she was back at home. Though her movements were severely restricted, she was lucky to be alive. Doctors had said that it would be a good six months before she became completely normal.

46

This episode had come as a wake up call for Swami. On their first night back in India, Kalpana and Swami had talked till the wee hours of the morning. Weird that the discussion should last six hours when they shared the same point of view. They had firmly made up their mind by the time they finally went to sleep.

Swami waited for two-and-a-half weeks after they had landed in Chennai for his mother and Ambu to settle down back at home. Once that objective was achieved, it was time to act on what he had decided with Kalpana.

Swami took an early morning flight to Mumbai. Within the next couple of hours, he was standing outside Kailash's office.

'Oh, what a surprise! Swami, it's great to see you in India.' Swami's sombre smile told him that all was not well.

'Come on in. How come you are in Mumbai? Are you on a holiday?'

'I need to move back to India.' This statement from Swami made Kailash sit up and take notice.

'Swami, I was under the impression that you did not want to come back.'

Swami narrated the entire story to Kailash, including the six-hour discussion between him and Kalpana on their first night back in India. He told him firmly but politely that if NYB was not able to accommodate him in India, he would be happy to quit and find another job here.

He repeated all this over the phone to his boss in New York. Kailash asked Swami to come back and see him the next day.

Swami stayed over with Aditya for the night. Both of them were meeting after a long time and had lots to catch up on. They had been in constant touch over the phone but hadn't seen each other in a while.

The next morning, Swami was ushered into Kailash's cabin. Kailash was waiting for him. He signalled to Swami and pointed to the sofa in one corner. 'Hold all calls,' he told his secretary as he joined Swami on the sofa.

'Swami, I spoke with Tony Lewis in New York this morning and I have his concurrence to offer you the position of Head Distribution for NYB in India. This job is at a Senior Vice President level. While I do not have the exact salary details, I can assure you that you will get a good package.'

Swami knew what it meant. He had worked long enough in NYB to know what Head Distribution meant.

'Thank you, Kailash. You have no idea how much this means to me. I don't even want to talk to you on salary and other details.'

'I have not finished yet.'

Swami didn't understand.

'I have also been authorised to tell you that Global HR has requested for Kalpana to be accommodated in the HR unit in India. They made this request when Tony and I got on to a conference with HR to clinch your request. I am happy to give her the task of setting up and running the Global Compliance Hotline in India.'

Swami thanked Kailash profusely. For the first time he realised how much a positive reputation helps in an organisation. He had now come full circle. He went overseas for a global career, did very well, made his money, and now he was back to where his roots were.

All this while Sundeep was in London, firmly in saddle as head of the NRI business. For the first time in ten years, Swami and Sundeep were back reporting to the same boss. In direct professional conflict with each other. The last time round, Aditya was their boss. Now it was Kailash.

47

Two weeks later, Swami joined the Indian operations of NYB as the new Distribution Head. Swami's unit in the US was very supportive of his move and didn't even insist that he come back to New York to give a handover to his replacement. Kalpana too joined on the same day. She had decided to first complete her joining formalities and later take a month off to head to the US for winding down her house there and moving their personal effects back to India.

Swami was happy to be back in the country. Kailash had met him in the same room that Aditya used when he was Head of Retail Banking. The look hadn't changed much. The painting on the wall was in the same position, the table was where it used to be ten years ago. The only change was the absence of Aditya and Natasha.

Swami and Sundeep had occasionally kept in touch through Natasha and Kalpana who were still very good friends. They spoke to each other almost every week.

Kailash introduced Swami to his team of Business Managers: Akshay Bhalla for home loans, Vivek J for personal loans, and Anindyo Roy for auto loans. All the three had worked with Sundeep. They had heard about Swami, but had never worked with him.

The same night, Kailash organised a dinner at his house that was attended by Swami, Kalpana, Swami's direct reports, and a few other seniors from the bank. Kailash had mentioned a time of 8.00 p.m. in the invite.

Swami reached on time with Kalpana and was surprised to find that they were the only ones to have arrived.

'*Saab upar hain. Abhi bulati hoon,*' said the maid who opened the door, and went upstairs to call Kailash and his wife.

Swami and Kalpana made themselves comfortable in the living room. The maid came back with two glasses of water. 'Saab is getting ready, he will be down in ten minutes,' she said and disappeared.

The doorbell rang again. The maid reappeared and walked towards the door to open it.

The door opened and a short, slim, long-haired guy walked in with a cigarette in his hand. He looked at Swami and Kalpana and stopped in his tracks. A smile lit up Kalpana's face. Swami stood up from his chair, a smile on his lips.

'Sundeep, what a surprise!' exclaimed Kalpana and gave him a hug.

'Long time. Good to see you. Where is Natasha?' asked Swami.

'Hey folks. How come you are here? I was not expecting to see you guys here.' Sundeep was also pleased to see Kalpana, but couldn't have said the same thing about Swami. Still he went and hugged him.

'How are you, Swami?' Sundeep asked. 'I believe you moved back to India. I have been wanting to call you ever since Natasha told me that Ambujam has met with an accident.'

Swami told him the entire story about his move back to India.

'What is Kalpana going to do?' asked Sundeep, trying to start a conversation with her.

'I will be joining the HR team as compliance officer,' she said. 'Where's Natasha? She never told me that she was coming to India.'

'No. She is in London.'

Kalpana felt a touché unhappy. She was really hoping that Natasha would be there. She hadn't met her in four years now.

'Hey guys. Is this some sort of reunion happening here?' It was Kailash coming down the stairs. 'Sundeep, when did you come from London?'

'Kailash! How are you? I was in town and thought I would run around and give you a quick look in, before leaving back for London. Didn't know that you had something planned at home. I can come back tomorrow.'

'No! No! No! Don't worry. It is great to have you here. In fact, your old team is also coming in and those guys will be happy to meet you.'

Sundeep stayed back.

Swami was not a party animal and was a wee bit uncomfortable in such gatherings. Teetotaller that he was, fruit juices were his only salvation in such parties. Aerated drinks were also not his forte. He was hitting an age where they were beginning to make him uncomfortable.

Akshay came in with his wife at half past eight, followed by Anindyo Roy. Vivek had to drop his family to the airport and hence came in well past nine. Amit Suri, the Head of Cards, and Rajendran, the Head of Credit, also joined in.

Sundeep had worked with all of them. He was the centre of attraction as most of them were meeting him after a long time. Swami was feeling a bit lost.

Akshay, Vivek, Amit and Anindyo crowded around Sundeep. They were all trying to be nice and chat up to him. Gossip from overseas was indeed very interesting. Who is doing what? Who is going where? Who is joining and who is quitting? Who is sleeping with whom?

The fun of gossip apart, the other motivating factor was that Sundeep, given his contacts in London, could possibly help them land plum jobs overseas. It was important to keep him happy. Swami could wait. He had just returned—not of much value in the short run. Sundeep was getting a kick out of this. For the first time in his life, he had usurped something from Swami. The attention that would have been showered on Swami that evening was all his.

Sundeep was looking at Kailash from the corner of his eye. He had come here with an agenda, but hadn't got an opportunity to bring it up.

Rajendran, the Head of Credit, had come alone and was gulping peg after peg of whisky. Swami had hit if off very well with him when they had met in office earlier that week. It probably had something to do with their being South Indians. Swami had a weakness for South Indians. It was said that whenever Swami hired people, if everything else was equal, he would hire a South Indian. Even in the US he had managed to keep it this way.

Kailash's house was a class apart. Maqbool Fida Hussain's paintings graced his walls. He had two sections in his living room. While contemporary designer furniture adorned one section, the other had antique furniture from the villages close to Tanjore. He had carted all his furniture, specifically the antiques from Tamil Nadu, all over the globe. NYB had paid for it whenever Kailash moved homes. A picture of Kailash and his wife in their Alibaug farmhouse adorned the large wall to the right of a passage which led to the bedrooms. Kailash was one of the highest paid executives in the country at that time, and it showed. The Advanis didn't have any children.

Sundeep was in his usual high spirits. He was back with his old team, who were keeping him humoured.

'Sundeep, it's no fun without you around. *Mazaa nahin aa raha hai. Koi team spirit hi nahin hai.* Why don't you come back?' Akshay was desperately trying to suck up to him.

'*Yeh Parsi yahaan se jaayega toh kuch sochen,*' said Sundeep, hinting that with Kailash deciding to hang on, there was little hope of his coming back.

'Then why don't you get us a job there? We'll all come.' Anindyo was one who never missed an opportunity.

At that very instant, Sundeep saw Kailash heading back to his room. He quickly excused himself. '*Ek minute*, Anindyo. I will just be back.'

A deep sigh. 'He's slipped off again.' Anindyo was looking at Akshay this time.

'This is his fucking problem. He never gives a commitment. Slippery as a fish. One day he will pay for all this.' Akshay was bitching behind Sundeep's back.

'Looks like, we will have to deal with this Madrasi only,' said Akshay, referring to Swami as the man from Madras.

Even though Swami was talking to Rajendran, his eyes were on this team, which was to work with him. He was not getting a good feeling. His team was too close to Sundeep. Sundeep would always be aware of the goings-on in his domain. No one had come to him and said anything more than a cursory hello. This thought was very disconcerting. He had to deal with it. 'They are probably a little shy, that's all.' He dismissed the thought that they were ignoring him.

He saw Sundeep follow Kailash into the room and walked up to his new team. All of them had a forced smile on their faces. Swami realised that he was unwelcome in their conversation.

Amit Suri walked up to them. He was more balanced. 'So Swami, how does it feel to be back in India,' began Suri. Swami immediately felt at ease.

Sundeep had followed Kailash into his room. 'Kailash,' called out Sundeep, when they were out of earshot of the rest. 'There is something I want to talk to you about. If you have some time now, we can talk, else I will be back tomorrow.'

'What's it about, Sundeep?'

'Kailash, I was speaking to Mark Sheen in London last night. And he asked me something that got me curious,' said Sundeep, building up the suspense. Mark was the Global Retail Bank Head for New York International Bank, and was based in New York. He was in London on a business visit.

'What about?'

'He was asking me about Rakesh Makkar.'

'That's normal. Why should that raise an eyebrow?'

'No Kailash. It is not who he was asking me about that set me thinking. It was what he was asking me about him,' started Sundeep.

'What was the reason for Mark's interest in Rakesh?' Kailash was becoming more inquisitive now. Sundeep wanted that to happen. He now had his ears.

The room where Kailash and Sundeep were having this conversation was separated from the hall partly by a glass wall. Through that, Swami could make out that Kailash and Sundeep were in an animated conversation, though he couldn't hear them.

Rajendran went up to Swami. 'What's happening? Is there a problem? What is Kailash doing inside for so long?' Swami had no idea. He just shrugged his shoulders.

'Something is cooking,' said Rajendran and smiled.

Akshay, Anindyo and Atul were standing in a corner when Vivek joined them. '*Kuch gadbad lagti hai. Sundeep ki shakl bata rahi hai.*' They could make out from Sundeep's looks that some serious discussion was on. They had worked with Sundeep long enough to realise that.

Kailash's conversation with Sundeep lasted more than half an hour. Then they both emerged from the room with a smile on their faces. Almost immediately, Swami's team deserted him and crowded around Sundeep, much to Swami's irritation. Kalpana could feel Swami getting pissed, but couldn't do anything about it. Sundeep was far more flamboyant than Swami. When Sundeep excused himself and announced that he was leaving, she was very relieved. The spotlight was back on Swami.

From the moment Sundeep left, Kailash seemed quite lost. Something was obviously going on at the back of his mind. He was itching for the party to get over.

Dinner was served at 10.30 p.m. The food was mainly South Indian. Nobody liked it except Swami and Rajendran.

'*Abse to har party mein yehi khana padega.* Remember the food we used to get at Sundeep's parties. And now, this stupid curd rice.' Akshay was quite annoyed.

'Can you believe it, we are having dinner at ten-thirty. With Sundeep around, parties would begin at eleven.' Anindyo seemed to agree with Akshay.

Looked like, they were not even willing to give Swami a chance. Had Swami lost the battle even before he had started fighting? Swami seemed to have lost the battle on issues not related to banking competence.

The party folded at 11.00 p.m., almost immediately after the dinner. Swami was the first to leave. Eleven at night was well past his bedtime. When Swami went up to Kailash for the customary 'Thank you for the nice evening' stuff, Kailash didn't even make an attempt to hold him back. He wanted the party to be over soon.

48

The moment all the guests had left, Kailash picked up his mobile and dialled the third number from his fast dial list.

'The number you are dialling cannot be reached, please...'

Click! Kailash disconnected the line. 'What the fuck is he doing at this time of the night?'

He began pacing up and down the alley. He stepped out into his garden. He was fortunate to have a garden in his house in a city like Mumbai. After all, he was the highest paid executive. It was 11.30 at night. The sky was cloudy, and it was warm and humid. Anybody would sweat in this weather. Kailash's anxiety made him sweat even more.

He picked up the phone and dialled the number once more. Same response. 'Bastard,' he muttered. 'This guy is never available when you want him.' After trying a couple of times, he finally sent him a message.

He kept pacing the lawns for the next fifteen minutes when he finally decided to go in. He kept his phone firmly by his side, to ensure that he picked it up, just in case this person decided to call him back. Sundeep had told him something that was very critical. He had to act in the next twenty-four hours. There was no time.

Twenty minutes after midnight, the phone rang. Kailash picked it up after just one ring.

'How are you, my friend?' It was such a relief to have heard that voice in the middle of the night. It was Naresh on the other side of the line.

'Where were you? What the fuck were you up to at this hour?'

'Yaar, Monica had sent across a new secretary. *Usika test le raha tha!*' Naresh replied in jest.

'Ram, you need to check something out for me right now,' Kailash said.

'You seem very stressed out. What is the problem? Get a massage done. My secretary can fly down in case you want her to. You will be fine,' Naresh said with his usual wit and flamboyance.

'Sundeep came to see me today. Mark Sheen had called him yesterday about Rakesh Makkar. It seems they want to move Rakesh to New York to support the global management team in emerging markets. If that happens, Rakesh's current post becomes vacant. Only you can get it for me.' Kailash was asking Naresh to swing it for him.

'Understood. The grapevine is that Chetan Bindra is coming back as CEO for the group in India. They are meeting today to close out the moves.' Naresh knew everything. How did he manage his network?

'That's what Sundeep told me. Is there any way you can get me this job?'

'What's in it for me?' Naresh was never known to be discreet.

'How does half-a-million dollars sound? Will route it to you over the next six months.' Kailash was too keen on striking this deal.

Rakesh Makkar, the CEO-India of New York International Bank, was slated to move to New York and Kailash was keen to get that job. It meant a lot to him. Kailash had only a few years left before retirement. It was NYB's policy that anyone retiring as a Country Head would be entitled to retirement benefits that essentially took care of him for the rest of his life. The gross gain for Kailash would be much more than the half-a-million dollars that he would pay Naresh. And, in any case, this payout would not happen from his personal funds. If he did become the CEO, this amount would be paid by NYB. He would approve some marketing bills for Naresh's team over the next few months.

'Will you get Sundeep into your current role then?' Naresh was now cutting a deal.

'Ram, you know that I have just got back Swami from the US as the Head of Distribution. Both of them had joined the organisation together and are from similar backgrounds. This would not be fair to Swami. He cannot report to Sundeep.'

'Kailash, the call is yours. I know I can swing it for you. Half-a-million dollars and Sundeep in your role, and the job is yours. Think of yourself, Kailash. Why do you have to let this opportunity go because of that dog Swami.' Kailash wanted the job very badly and couldn't refuse. Naresh hated Swami and it was apparent. He wanted someone above Swami to manage him. Sundeep was the guy he wanted.

'I will call you tomorrow morning,' said Naresh before disconnecting the phone.

Naresh looked at his watch. It was 12.45 a.m. It would be early afternoon in New York. He dialled a number.

'Joseph Fernandes,' said the voice at the other end.

'Hi Joseph.'

'Hey Naresh. How are you?'

'*Yaar, ek baat bata*, are you guys moving Rakesh Makkar to New York?'

'Yes, the management felt that given the focus on the BRIC nations, he can be of significant value in driving our strategy in the emerging economies. But the move is not closed yet. We are meeting today to discuss the options. Rakesh has been spoken to and he is keen to move. But, this is classified info. How did you get to know?' Joseph was curious.

'Who are the candidates you are looking at for Rakesh Makkar's replacement?' He ignored the bit on this being classified information. He knew Joseph too well to let that impact his manipulations.

'Chetan Bindra and Suneel Dutt are the candidates. But they don't seem keen to go back to India for family reasons. We might just have to hold back Rakesh's move because we are not able to get the right guy to replace him.'

'Are you nuts, fatso?' Naresh went a long way with Joseph and hence could speak to him in this manner. '*Bagal mein bacha, gali mein dhindoora.*' Naresh was telling him that with the kid right there beside him, he doesn't need to go looking all over.

Joseph was silent. He didn't understand what Naresh was trying to tell him.

'You have the best guy in Kailash Advani and you are looking all over the place for a replacement.' Naresh spent the next ten minutes canvassing for Kailash, and by the time he hung up, he knew the deal was as good as closed. It now hinged on Joseph's ability to convince the management committee.

The next morning, when Kailash got up, his entire body was stiff from lack of sleep. In fact, he had tossed and turned so much in bed that his wife had to go to the other bedroom to catch some sleep.

He picked up the phone lying by his bedside and dialled Naresh's number. He tried calling Naresh. His phone was not reachable. He called Naresh's residence. His wife picked up the phone and told him that Naresh had gone out for a game of golf. Mobile phones were not allowed on the golf course. There was no way he could have got in touch with him. He left a message for Naresh and hung up.

49

Kailash was the first person to reach office the next day. It was 8.15 a.m. when his car entered New York International Bank's India HQ.

He was about to enter the lift when his phone rang. One look at the screen told him that it was not Naresh. The screen read *Private Number*. It meant that the call was from an international number. He let the lift pass and stepped aside on the corridor to take the call.

'Hi, is it Kailash Advani?' a heavily accented voice came on.

'Yes.'

'Calling from New York. Mr Bridge would like to speak to you. Should I connect you.' Tedd Bridge was the CEO of NYB globally.

'Sure. Sure.' Instinctively his hand went up to set his hair, when he realised that Tedd Bridge would not be able to see him. He cleared his throat instead.

Kailash could feel his heart pounding. He sat down on the sofa in the lobby. His legs were weak and could give way anytime. Anybody with a weak heart would have had a cardiac arrest.

'Good morning, Kailash.' Tedd Bridge's voice reverberated on the line. It was late at night in New York, but Bridge was still in office.

'Kailash, this is Tedd Bridge from New York. Hope I didn't disturb you too early in the morning.'

'No, Mr Bridge, it's an honour to receive a call from you. Wondering what I have done to deserve this call.'

'Hey Kailash. You haven't lost your touch, old man. Not changed one bit.'

Kailash had worked with Tedd Bridge when he was in New York. Being a career NYB guy, the seniors in the US knew him well.

'Kailash, a huge career opportunity has come up and hence we have decided to move Rakesh Makkar to New York.' Kailash had his heart in his hand.

'That's great for Rakesh, Mr Bridge. I am sure Rakesh will be thrilled and feel extremely challenged. What role will he be moving into?'

'Kailash, he will be moving into a strategic role. He will be driving our global strategy for emerging markets.'

'That's fabulous. He will stay engaged with India.'

'Yes, that's correct. I have just got out of a meeting with the leading team that looks after the emerging markets. Joseph Fernandes strongly felt that if Rakesh Makkar moves, you should get the top job in India. The committee discussed a few other candidates and eventually agreed with his recommendation. I just wanted to check with you if you have any reservations or concerns before I formally congratulate you on your appointment as the new CEO of NYB in India. This would, of course, be subject to regulatory approvals in India. Wanted your go ahead before we release this story to the press.'

Kailash was silent. Tedd Bridge's call had knocked the wind out of his lungs. He clutched the phone tightly lest he dropped it and the phone got disconnected.

'The press conference is in another fifteen minutes. You will have to make up your mind and call me back in the next ten minutes,' said Bridge, implying that he was disconnecting the call.

'Mr Bridge,' Kailash said hurriedly, 'It will be a matter of great pride and honour for me to lead the India team.' Kailash knew that anything could go wrong in ten minutes, if he didn't accept the offer then and there.

'That will be great, Kailash. We will make the official announcement soon. Please be discreet about it till it is formally announced. I have got to go now. Congratulations and best of luck.'

'Thank...' The line went dead even before Kailash could complete his line.

He went up the lift to his office. No one was around. He turned the key and opened the door to his room. What he saw surprised him. A smile came onto his lips. He was about to become a big man.

There was a large basket of flowers in his room. He couldn't figure out who had left it there. Who could it be? Maybe the security guys would know.

He was dialling the security extension when there was a knock at the door.

'Come in,' he thundered. He had the right to be loud, now that he was the CEO.

In walked a person who he had not expected in his wildest dreams to be there. In walked a beaming Ram Naresh.

'Kailash, I wanted to be the first one to congratulate the new CEO of India,' Naresh said and extended his hand in congratulation.

Naresh had taken the first flight out of Calcutta to be in time to congratulate Kailash. Joseph had called him a couple of hours after his call, to tell him that he had personally spoken to nearly everyone in the committee and they had all agreed to let Kailash become the CEO.

Kailash hugged Naresh and thanked him.

Naresh had swung one more deal. Now the CEO of NYB was in his pocket.

Naresh settled down on the sofa in Kailash's room and said, 'CEO *saab*, hope you remember our deal.'

'You will get your half-a-million dollars, my friend.'

'Half-a-million dollars, and Sundeep back in India as Head of Retail Banking,' said Naresh, reminding him about the second part of the deal.

'Of course. How can I forget that?'

That afternoon, a message from Tedd Bridge was sent to all employees of New York International Bank

Dear New York International Bankers,

It gives me great pleasure to make this announcement today. India is a strategic market for the group and we all recognise that in the coming years, India will be one of the largest markets for the banking industry in the world. We have had a fair bit of success in this market, especially over the last few years, wherein under the able leadership of Rakesh Makkar, we have emerged as the largest foreign bank in the country.

Rakesh Makkar has lead the country admirably in the last three years, wherein revenue has more than doubled and profits have trebled to $106 Mn. However, as all good things must come to an end, it is time for Rakesh to move on. I am glad to announce that Rakesh will move to New York Global Headquarters as Senior Vice President and Head-Strategy, Emerging Markets. His role will encompass both retail and corporate banks' expansion plans.

Taking over from Rakesh will be another star, who is a career New York International Banker, Kailash Advani. Kailash has demonstrated excellent leadership and vision in all the roles that he has held across India and abroad over the last twenty-four years with the bank. Kailash will take over from Rakesh w.e.f. close of business hours today. Please join me in wishing both Kailash and Rakesh the best in their new roles. We will be announcing Kailash's replacement shortly.

Regards,
Tedd Bridge

50

Naresh called Sundeep in London that evening. Sundeep was preparing to leave for work. Sundeep confirmed that Kailash had indeed called him to check if he would be keen to move to India as Head of Retail Bank. Sundeep was obviously expecting this call and readily agreed. Kailash hung up with a commitment to announce Sundeep's appointment soon. Sundeep had tried to call Naresh, but couldn't get through since Naresh was on a flight back from Mumbai to Calcutta.

'Naresh, I have been very curious to ask you something. I have been thinking about it for the last two days. How did you get to know about Rakesh Makkar's move before anyone got wind of it? And if you knew about it, why didn't you tell Kailash yourself, why did you ask me to tell him about it?'

'Sundeep, your work is done, my friend. Enjoy yourself. Leave all these things to me,' said Naresh and hung up, leaving Sundeep struggling to figure out whether he had used Naresh or gotten used by him. But, whatever be the case, it can't be denied he had gained from it. So, what the hell!

The moment Kalpana saw the mail, she called Swami. Swami hadn't seen it yet. He was too new in India for someone else to have called to tell him about it.

'Do you think they will give you Kailash's job?'

'Don't know, Kalpana. Ideally, they should. I am the senior most guy within the system. Unless they bring in someone from outside, I should get the job.' Swami seemed confident.

Both Kalpana and Swami had expected New York International Bank to back merit and be fair. But he had not bargained for an animal called Ram Naresh who decided careers in NYB for a price.

Swami called Kailash almost immediately.

'Congratulations Kailash. This is brilliant news,' said Swami.

'Thank you, Swami. A man is only as good as his team. I am reaping the benefits of all your efforts, which has made me look so good.' Kailash had to make the right noises.

'Kailash, have you decided on who is going to take over from you.'

'Not yet, Swami. We have been thinking of a few names.'

'Kailash, does my name figure in that list? If you recollect, I was part of the core team that started retail banking in India.' Swami was slightly embarrassed to push himself. He had never done that in the past.

'Swami, if you are lobbying for the job, I have taken note of that. But the decision has not been taken yet, and I will let you know once that's done.' Kailash was very curt. Swami was taken aback and could only mutter 'thank you' before disconnecting.

'Maybe I should not have called,' he thought to himself.

The same afternoon came a message from the outgoing CEO Rakesh Makkar to all employees of New York International Bank

Friends,

We have achieved a lot as a team over the last three years. I am proud to be part of this great and successful team. It is hence very difficult for me to leave it and move on. Change is inevitable, and the only thing about this change that makes me feel good is that I am leaving all of you in safe hands.

Kailash Advani is a great leader, a people's man. He has a history of building great teams and successful organisations in all parts of the bank that he has worked in. I wish him all the success in his new role and hope all of you will give him complete support and commitment just as you have done to me.

With Kailash's move, there will be some changes in the retail organisation. Replacing Kailash will be our very own Sundeep Srivastava, the current Head of NRI Business. Sundeep, who is currently based in London, will be relocating to India by the end of this month. Till that time Kailash will be directly running the retail business.

Pranoy Lal, currently managing the NRI business in South East Asia, will move to London to take over the NRI business from Sundeep Srivastava.

Rajendran, Head of Credit, Swaminathan, Head of Distribution, Pranoy Lal, and Amit Suri, Head of Cards, will report to Sundeep in his new role.

I would like to welcome Sundeep back to India and wish him all the best as he takes charge of his new role.

Regards,
Rakesh Makkar

Swami was shocked when he saw the message. He thought he deserved the role more than Sundeep. He had no ill feelings for Sundeep, was rather happy for him. That was Swami. He would never think ill for anyone. He just had no clue why Kailash did this to him. He decided to bide his time. He had wanted this move back to India. The organisation helped him when it mattered the most. He had to demonstrate his commitment towards the organisation and so he decided not to take up this issue with Kailash. Such was Swami. He opened his laptop and typed a message.

Sundeep,

Just saw this message from Rakesh. Congratulations. It's a great move and we wish you all the best in your new assignment. We look forward to welcoming you, Natasha, and the kids back to India.

Regards,
Swami and Kalpana

51

That evening, when Akshay and Anindyo Roy went out for a drink, their gossip was dominated by Kailash, Swami, and Sundeep.

'Amazing luck that guy has.' Bhalla was referring to Sundeep.

'Yeah. But his coming back will be good for us.'

Bhalla nodded. 'Life was a bit boring with Swami around.' It was a different issue that Swami had hardly been around long enough. Swami bashing and idolising Sundeep was the flavour of the discussion.

'I was talking to Sundeep when he was here in India a few days back and he told me, with Swami coming in, the bank will now move in slow motion,' said Anindyo and both of them burst out laughing.

Two things would have been very clear to anyone hearing the discussion. One, Swami lacked acceptance in the team despite his very good intent and great intellect. And, two, Sundeep had still not forgotten or forgiven Swami for his successes over him, including the biggest one—marrying Kalpana, and had been badmouthing him at every forum.

With Sundeep coming back, Swami would have to battle his own team to work with them. It was not going to be an easy time for him and he had no inkling of what was in store for him.

52
New York

'Sundeep, you have a meeting in fifteen minutes with Tedd and Michelle,' said Louisa, walking into Sundeep's room.

Sundeep looked at her blankly. 'What's the time, Louisa?'

'Just about three-thirty. Michelle just called me to remind you about the meeting. She said that the meeting would be in the board room at three-forty-five.'

'The moment of truth has arrived,' Sundeep thought. There was little he could do. He was responsible for things reaching this state.

'Can we postpone it, Louisa? Can you check with Michelle if she can give me some more time? I am not in a proper frame of mind to meet Tedd Bridge.'

'Sure, Sundeep,' said Louisa and disappeared for about a minute.

Returning, she said, 'Sundeep, the latest they can wait is six this evening. Apparently Tedd is travelling from tomorrow for the next one week and wants to settle this issue before he goes out. Should I confirm for six?' asked Louisa and walked out as Sundeep nodded.

He had got an extension of a couple of hours. For whatever they were worth!

53

Sundeep came back to India in August 2002. For him, it was a return to home territory, the fulfillment of a dream, a victory of sorts. He had come back as the head of the business that he and Swami had started along with Aditya. That Swami was going to work for him was the icing on the cake.

A huge reception awaited him as he walked out of the Delhi airport. Akshay, Anindyo, their key team members, and Ram Naresh were at the airport to receive Sundeep and Natasha. As they stepped out of the airport, a band started playing victory beats. A red carpet led them to a waiting car. Naresh had hired a Merc to receive him. Akshay took over the luggage trolley and pushed it all the way to the car. Those guys were willing to do just about anything to get his attention. It was a reception that would befit a head of state. Sundeep was floored. His chest puffed up a few inches. He liked these things, though Natasha was a bit embarrassed. She took the kids and went directly to the hotel. On the way she saw a large hoarding on the roadside, *New York International Bank welcomes Sundeep Srivastava back to India*. Somehow she didn't get a good feeling.

Sundeep's parents in Delhi were very happy that they were now back in India. They could now spend more time with their grandchildren. After a few days in Delhi, Sundeep and Natasha left for Mumbai.

The first thing Natasha did on landing in Mumbai was to call Kalpana. The two hadn't met for over four years. They had remained in touch, though, despite the strong undercurrents between Sundeep and Swami. They promised to meet that evening and hung up.

Sundeep walked into the plush office in Bandra Kurla Complex. New York International Bank had inaugurated this new office only a month back. As he walked into his large four hundred square feet cabin on the third floor, a sense of déjà vu set in. He felt like he had again walked into Aditya's room the way he had done many years ago. But now it was he, Sundeep, who was the Country Head of a large retail business. He had arrived in life.

Natasha spent the first few days in Mumbai house hunting. After her stint in London, Natasha was very particular about the type of house they would be staying in. She saw over a hundred apartments before she settled on one. Sundeep had his hands full on taking over charge of the Indian retail business from Kailash. On top of that, both Sundeep and Natasha had to attend a killing number of felicitations and welcome parties. The special one, of course, was a party hosted by Aditya. Apart from Sundeep and Natasha, the only other invitees were Swami and Kalpana.

'Sundeep, you now have a job that I held several years ago. It's a big job now. The lives of a number of individuals depend on you. You have to make sure that you do everything honestly, keeping the interests of your people and your customers in mind,' Aditya had said as they left.

'Aditya, everything has changed in the last ten years. I am sure I will be able to do a better job than you did,' said Sundeep, much to Aditya's surprise. Natasha was not amused, but she had learnt to deal with the egocentricities of a successful husband.

Sundeep indeed was a business-focused leader. He was a taskmaster, and a tough one at that. He reached out to the frontline sales directly and he dispassionately drove all businesses to ramp up the numbers. He travelled like crazy. He oozed infectious levels of energy. He would be on the road half the month. After a full day's work, he would set out at 1.00 a.m. to personally inspect all the ATMs of NYB. His approach would keep all his teams constantly on their toes. Productivity increase was only a matter of time.

He was also a lot more visible to the frontline staff as compared to say Kailash. He would review business performance directly with the business managers like Akshay, Vivek and Anindyo. Swami started getting marginalised, but didn't complain.

Sundeep wanted success at any cost. The mantra in New York International Bank became sell, sell and sell more... the customer be damned. Sundeep instructed all his sales managers to send him SMSs on his mobile phone every night, giving him details of daily sales versus targets. Anyone not meeting targeted numbers would get humped by Sundeep.

All this put tremendous pressure and stress on the frontline sales teams. Sundeep didn't imagine that he could be wrong. This was a costly mistake. The sales teams now wanted to do their numbers at any cost. It became acceptable to make wrong commitments to the customer as long as you closed a sale. The evening SMS was sacrosanct. You couldn't miss your target. Deals had to be done, by hook or by crook. Swami was totally against such an approach. But he was no match for Sundeep's aggression.

While Sundeep pushed people a lot, he would also celebrate success in a big way. The parties and celebrations that were in vogue when Suneel Dutt was around made a reappearance. But now, Naresh would organise the parties. And he made his secretaries an essential ingredient of the fun on offer. Sundeep's parties would start at 11.00 p.m. and go on throughout the night. He would be the last to leave the party in the wee hours of the morning.

In one such party Sundeep met Nitin. He was not aware then that this meeting would one day change his life.

54

The Chennai branch of New York International Bank had broken all records in personal loan sales in January 2003. Sundeep had gone down to Chennai to celebrate this success of Team Chennai. All the employees of Chennai along with the spouses of key employees were invited. The venue for the party was *The Club*, a happening joint on the outskirts of the city.

It was about 11.45 p.m. when Sundeep walked in. The party was just about coming alive. Sundeep was extremely tired. He had come after visiting all the ATMs of the bank in the city and had driven over 150 kilometres that day. His body was not willing, but he had pushed himself to attend this party since his presence would have motivated the entire team.

At quarter past midnight, in walked Nitin, the Chennai City Head for Personal Loans. Vivek Jalan, the personal loan head of NYB in India, introduced Nitin to Sundeep as the star of the personal loans team and the driving force behind Chennai achieving the desired numbers. Sundeep, the motivator that he was, showered praise on Nitin, who was quite flattered.

'Thank you, Sundeep.'

A young girl, who was standing quietly behind Nitin, listening to his conversation with Sundeep, came up and stood beside him.

'Oh, I am so sorry,' Nitin apologised for having forgotten something important. 'Sundeep, please meet my wife Karuna.'

She was ravishing. Gorgeous! Sundeep couldn't take his eyes off her. He continued to stare at her with his mouth open, as if in a trance. When it started becoming too obvious, Vivek nudged him knowing that Sundeep didn't realise that he was being noticed.

She was a pretty young thing, about twenty-five years of age and had got married to Nitin about six months ago. Karuna worked in the Branch Banking side of NYB.

'Hi Karuna. I must say you have a wonderful guy for a husband. He will go places. I am sure.'

'Thank you, sir. It's very kind of you.'

Vivek pulled Sundeep towards the bar to get a drink. On the way, he asked him, 'What are you up to, Sundeep?'

'*Kya cheez hai yaaaaar!*' Sundeep was clearly turned on by her.

'I don't find her too good looking,' Vivek contested, 'She is an eight on ten.'

'Vivek, I can read women better than you. I can tell from her looks, she will fuck well. She will be a ten on ten in bed. Wanna bet?' said Sundeep as they reached the bar.

'Every woman looks good at a particular age and she is at that age, Sundeep.'

Even while they were standing at the bar, Sundeep was constantly looking at her from the corner of his eyes. And even Karuna didn't miss this. Sundeep found her looking at him every time he glanced at her. She even managed to smile back at him a couple of times.

Sundeep called Nitin to the bar and said, 'Nitin, you have done us proud. You have done something that no one could have done. Beating Standard Chartered Bank in the Chennai market is something we had till now considered impossible. You need to do a bottoms up for this.' And he gave him a large glass of whisky and asked him to drink it on the rocks in one gulp. Nitin was too thrilled to refuse and did as he was asked.

Sundeep's trick was working. Now he called the entire Chennai sales team and asked them to do another round of bottoms up and, of course, Nitin was a part of the second round too.

In the next thirty minutes, Nitin had gulped down three bottoms up of whisky, two of vodka, and one beer. That he could stand straight despite that was the ninth wonder of the modern world. That he couldn't talk straight after three minutes was the wonder of mixing drinks.

By the end of the evening, Nitin was dead drunk. Karuna was worried about how she would cart Nitin home. That's when Sundeep offered to drop them home, an offer Karuna didn't refuse. Sundeep asked Vivek to go back to the hotel and wait for him.

Sundeep's cab zipped through the empty streets of Chennai at 3.00 a.m., with a drunk Nitin, who had completely passed out, belted up in the front seat. Sundeep and Karuna were in the back seat. Karuna looked stunning. Her t-shirt, wet with her sweat, clung to her breasts. He was reminded of her dancing to the wild beats earlier in the night. Every part of her body had been shaking invitingly.

She had even asked Sundeep for a dance, and when they had danced, they had set the floor on fire. Sundeep had held her tightly and close to him. So close that she had felt the movement in his crotch. She had come close to him and repeatedly rubbed against his erect manhood. Whether it was an intentional tease or a harmless dance, he couldn't tell. The sweat had made her shirt cling to her body and he could make out her contours in detail. She had a wonderful figure, a toned body. A sculpture guys would kill for.

'Have you ever learnt dancing? You dance very well.' Sundeep was trying to build a conversation with her. 'Not exactly. I am just a casual dancer. It's just that the number of parties one attends these days makes one a good dancer. You too are amazing on the floor.' Sundeep was thrilled by the compliment.

They reached Nitin and Karuna's house in ten minutes. 'Why don't you come up for a coffee,' Karuna offered and Sundeep was not a fool to refuse.

They both carried Nitin to their third floor apartment and tucked him into his bed. Karuna held Sundeep's hand and thanked him profusely. They sat down on the sofa in the living room and started talking. Karuna went to the kitchen and switched on the coffee machine. Then she excused herself, telling Sundeep that she would be back after a change of clothes as she was feeling very sweaty and sticky in her party wear.

She went into the bedroom and closed the door. Sundeep was very disappointed that the door was shut. Once inside, Karuna opened the bathroom door to go in to quickly wash her face. The suction on account of the bathroom door being opened slightly pulled in the main bedroom door. It opened slightly giving Sundeep a fair view of the bedroom. What Sundeep saw left him dumbstruck. Karuna walked out of the bathroom after a wash, with just a towel wrapped around her. The water dripping from the hair on her bare shoulder made her look divine. She had a fabulous body. Her assets were even better than what they seemed to Sundeep. Sundeep slowly walked up to the door. He didn't make any noise, but stood still at the door, watching her as she dropped the towel to pick up her clothes from the bed. Suddenly his mobile rang. Vivek was trying to reach him.

Karuna heard the ring. It was closer than she thought it to be. She looked up and was shocked to see Sundeep at the door, staring at her naked body. She screamed. 'Get away from here,' she screamed again. Sundeep quickly went back and sat down on the sofa. The bedroom door banged shut.

He sat there for a minute, then quietly got up and came out of the apartment and made his way back to the cab. 'Taj Connemara,' he told the cab driver and quietly came back to the hotel.

When Karuna saw that there was no one in the living room, she heaved a sigh of relief. She went to the kitchen, switched off the coffee machine and went to bed. She kept tossing in bed, feeling violated by Sundeep. However she decided not to tell Nitin, in the interest of his career.

55

It was three months since Sundeep had moved in. Sundeep was systematically going about creating his own empire. His equation with Swami was just about at the razor's edge. If it had not deteriorated, it was because of Swami's sanity and balance and definitely not Sundeep's.

That was the time when banks in India started selling insurance products. Banks were required by law to tie up with only one insurance agency. They were forbidden from entering into multiple tie-ups. NYB had tied up with KAIC.

The relationship manager from KAIC Insurance Company handling the New York International Bank relationship was a lady named Sharada Rajan. Sharada was a very efficient young woman who had risen to success in a short period of time. Firstly, she was one of the few experienced personnel in the insurance industry, and, secondly, she knew how to use her charms to get her work done. She got along gloriously with Sundeep Srivastava. Had to, since she was a good-looking woman and high on intellect too.

When New York International Bank started selling insurance policies to its customers, in no time the bank emerged as the single largest contributor to the insurance premium collected by KAIC.

Of all the bank assurance partners of KAIC, only NYB was meeting its insurance sales numbers. Nobody else was even close to getting there. Sharada was not happy. If she had to meet her annual targets, Sundeep had to do something special. He was her only hope.

She kept pushing Sundeep to help sell more insurance. Sundeep didn't know what to do. He was running out of ideas. He pushed all his channels, launched contests and incentives, looked the other way when insurance was wrongly sold. In short, did whatever he could. But the market had hit a plateau. The incentive that Sharada had offered him was also something special.

Sharada had promised him a 'full service' date, after they reach number one position in the banking industry. 'Sundeep, the day you become number one in the industry, I'll be all yours. Just you and me will go on a date to Switzerland. It will be no business and all pleasure,' she had teasingly said, running her fingertips over Sundeep's trousers. When it came to women, Sundeep just couldn't control himself.

Then he had his first run-in with Swami.

56

Amit Suri, the cards head, had gone on leave and Swami was temporarily in charge of credit cards as well. Sundeep pushed Akshay Bhalla to bundle insurance with home loans. He did the same with Vivek for personal loans. Both of them agreed and cross-selling of insurance was launched.

But that was not enough. NYB was one of the largest banks in terms of credit cards in circulation. It had over one-and-a-half million cards in circulation in 2004. When Sundeep didn't get enough joy bundling insurance with home loans and personal loans, he came up with an idea: why not sell insurance to cards customers! On the face of it, this was a normal idea that could be executed very easily.

However, there was one difference. Till date all cross-sell programmes to credit cards customers, or, for that matter, any cross-selling programme, would require the customer to come back and ask for the product being sold. Any normal offer going to a customer through a direct mail campaign would detail the features on offer and give a call-in number or mail-in address for the customer to order the product or service. The response percentage in such cases was around four to five percent. But this percentage of the cards base was not going to get Sundeep anywhere.

In the steering committee meeting held to discuss the cross-selling of insurance products to credit cards customers, Sundeep's devious mind came up with a different idea. Sharada had been thrilled when Sundeep had mentioned this to her.

Sundeep recommended that instead of asking for positive confirmation from customers, why not ask for a negative confirmation. He implied that the best way to do the deal was to send out a mailer to all customers that New York International Bank was offering a KAIC insurance to all cardholders and that the premium amount would automatically be debited from their credit cards. Customers were to be given an option of calling back and confirming only if they didn't want insurance. In case customers do not confirm back, they would start getting charged for insurance premium, month on month.

Sundeep was counting on the fact that many customers do not read mailers and many of them would not make the effort of picking up the phone and calling NYB. In case they did, he would happily reverse the premium charged and claim a refund from KAIC. He was counting on the inertia of people to make this programme a success.

Swami was taken aback when Sundeep recommended this. 'Sundeep, this is not right. We will be hauled over coal for doing something like this. Customers will lose faith in us.'

'But we are on the right side of the law, Swami,' argued Sundeep.

'But, only in the letter of it. I do not think this is in the right spirit,' Swami insisted.

'Swami, look at the revenues we will be earning. 1.5 million customers, at one hundred rupees per month, works out to forty million dollars a year in premium collections. Even if we get twenty percent of that from the insurance company, we will make a clean profit of eight million dollars. We have no other way of beating Citibank and coming on top. We cannot go wrong on this.' Sharada would have loved this argument.

'Sundeep, we do not need to beat Citibank in this fashion. And, surely, to beat us, they wouldn't do anything like what you are proposing. We might even get into trouble with the regulators and the consumer forums. Needless to say, our name will be hauled over coal.'

Vivek Jalan and Mohit Bakshi agreed with Swami. But Sundeep bulldozed them into accepting his stance. Swami was not convinced. He refused to toe this line, stating that this was morally incorrect.

Finally, after a heated debate, Sundeep said, 'Swami, I appreciate your views, but I am going ahead and doing this. You may choose to either be a party to this or stay out of it.'

'I will not be a party to this,' retorted an angry Swami and stomped out of the room. He couldn't believe that this was the same Sundeep with whom he had set up the retail business over a decade ago.

Once he got back to his desk, he shot off a mail to Kailash about this deal and his staying out of it. But he got an *Out of Office* response from Kailash's mailbox. Kailash was away on vacation and wouldn't be back for another two weeks. Sundeep was in charge. Despite wanting to do something, he couldn't.

Sundeep looked at Bakshi and asked him to move fast on the insurance cross-sell programme. Within the next two weeks the mailer was out. This was the first negative confirmation cross-sell of its kind in India. New York International Bank sold a million insurance policies to its cardholders, half of who didn't even know that they were paying for an insurance premium.

Sundeep had pulled off the biggest rip-off in the history of Indian credit cards. One million insurance policies sold with a monthly premium collection of close to three million dollars was not small game.

It was not long before the press and consumer activists got wind of it. New York International Bank's press office was flooded with complaints and calls seeking details of this scheme.

'NYB fleeces millions of unsuspecting Indians,' soon screamed the headlines in the *Times of India*. 'The great credit card rip off'; 'Insure against insurance frauds: Banks on the prowl'; 'Mis-selling, the NYB way'—nearly every newspaper published ugly articles about New York International Bank.

Sundeep was not flustered. He knew that all of this would die down. When Kailash called him about this, Sundeep requested him to give him a week. Kailash was worried that if the international media got to know about this, NYB would be screwed. It might even cost him his job. The only saving grace for him was that this entire programme was commissioned and executed when he was on leave.

Sundeep had already got his press machinery into an overdrive. The media relations wing of NYB called up all newspapers, magazines and tabloids, and threatened withdrawal of advertising support if they wrote anything derogatory. This worked on the smaller media and TV channels.

The larger ones took it upon themselves to wage a crusade against the tyranny of the MNC banks. They kept writing about New York International Bank for four-five days and then lost steam. It was no longer front-page news. The entire episode fizzled out. New York International Bank earned over five million dollars in the bargain.

This episode took place in the month of November. In India, NYB was well behind the targeted revenues for the year. So, the five million dollars they made in the entire bargain, despite the debatable means employed, didn't create any internal stir. On the contrary, Sundeep became a hero. 'Everyone told me not to do it, particularly you Swami. Despite that I went ahead and did the insurance deal. Now look. The bank has earned over five million dollars. You must take risks in business,' Sundeep thundered in one of his many speeches. He started touting the scheme as an innovation. This irritated Swami no end, but the nice Swami never responded to such provocations.

Sharada, true to her word, went on a 'full service' date with Sundeep. But, instead of Switzerland, they decided to make do with Sharada's posh home in Pali Hill, Bandra. Sundeep got his pound of flesh, literally, for his indiscretion.

57

Swami's open dissent on the insurance sales issue had majorly pissed off Sundeep. He was quite furious. But this issue was so sensitive that he didn't want to be seen taking a tough stance on Swami. He decided to wait for the right opportunity to get even.

A golden opportunity came his way.

The BPO wave was sweeping India. A number of companies from the west started outsourcing their back office processing jobs to India. Call centres across the world were relocating to India. India offered a splendid opportunity to cut costs. It also had a large population of English-speaking people, and so finding skilled people to do these jobs was not difficult.

NYB also wanted to shift some processes to India from across the globe. They decided to scout around and acquire a BPO in India. They would rather outsource to a company managed by themselves rather than to a third party.

Within ninety days a target BPO was identified and acquired. BOCA was a small BPO based in Delhi. Post acquisition by NYB, the responsibility for running it and getting cost efficiencies out of it was thrust on the retail side of NYB. Sundeep was asked to take it under his fold. Grudgingly, he accepted this. He viewed it as a pain rather than a challenge.

All the employees of BOCA were absorbed by the NYB group. Within two weeks of the BOCA acquisition, its leadership team was asked to make a presentation to Sundeep on the opportunities that existed in the BPO space, and how a bank like NYB could leverage on this acquisition.

Sundeep was not interested in the proceedings right from the beginning. The presentation took him through some slides on the evolution of the BPO industry in India and the nuances of operating a BPO.

Sundeep was thinking about the cards business. He was concerned that the new cards acquisition growth had not taken place in line with his expectations. His mind meandered to the insurance cross-sell tiff with Swami. All this while, some idiot was presenting on the BPO activities. Sundeep had not registered a thing. He was getting restless and upset on recalling his discussion with Swami.

And then, slowly but surely he broke into a devilish smile. He had found reason to be interested in the BPO business. For the next three hours he grilled the entire BOCA team on anything and everything about the business. When he got out of the BOCA presentation, he was convinced that this was a fuck all business.

BOCA requires someone from NYB to control it and run it, he thought as he was entering his office. He thought for some time and decided to send out an organisational announcement. Normally he would have called his secretary to dictate the message to her, but this was special. He had to do it himself.

After typing the message he thought for a second. Was he doing the right thing? Should he not first speak to the people who the message would impact? 'Fuck it,' he said to himself and pressed the send button on the screen.

Swami was in Chennai when this message reached the management committee of New York International Bank. The news spread like wildfire.

Swami was in a meeting with DBS developers, who were the leading developers in Chennai. His phone was on silent mode. It was a long meeting and lasted for over ninety minutes. They were discussing some complex financial deal. After the meeting when Swami came out and looked at the phone, he had twelve missed calls from Kalpana. He panicked. He immediately called her back. 'Swami, where are you? I have been trying to reach you for the last one hour.'

'What happened, Kalpana?'

'Haven't you checked your mail?'

'No.'

'Swami, there is a mail from Sundeep in your mailbox. See it and call me back. Right now.' There was panic in her voice, which told Swami that all was not well.

The moment Swami reached his office, he connected his laptop and opened his mailbox. There were forty-two unread messages. Most of them were normal mails. Or so it seemed till he reached the third last mail.

This was a mail from Sundeep on the acquisition of BOCA.

Friends,

As all of you are aware, we have today completed the acquisition of BOCA, which is a company into business process outsourcing in the banking and financial services industry. BOCA is a small company started eighteen months ago and has managed to get three key processes outsourced to it from New York International Bank in USA. We have completed this acquisition in line with our backward integration objectives.

This acquisition means a lot for the India business of New York International Bank. We will, over a period of time, transition most of our operations to this new company. BOCA will give us synergies in terms of cost efficiencies and technology. This company holds the key to our growth plans as we embark on a journey to become the largest financial services organisation in India.

Keeping in line with the criticality of this acquisition, we have made some key changes to the management structure in India.

Swaminathan, the current Head–Distribution, will move on as Managing Director of BOCA. He will be responsible for managing the integration of this business with our organisation. His vast experience will be completely stretched to ensure that we are able to manage this acquisition and derive the best value for our shareholders. His move will be with immediate effect. Akshay Bhalla, Vivek and Anindyo Roy will now report directly to me till such time that we announce a replacement for Swaminathan.

Please join me in wishing Swaminathan the best of luck in his new role.

Regards,
Sundeep

Swami couldn't believe it. He called Kalpana. 'What the hell is going on?' He sounded frustrated. He had been tolerating all the crap that Sundeep was throwing at him, but now it was getting too messy.

'Why don't you call Sundeep and ask him why he did this?' suggested Kalpana.

'No, I can't call him. It is very clear that he has done this intentionally. The least he could have done was call me before he sent out this mail. I don't think he can explain this, even if I call him.' The disappointment was pretty much evident in his voice. 'Anyway, I'll be back tonight. I'll talk to you then,' he said before disconnecting the call.

58

Swami was very disturbed. He couldn't fathom why things were going wrong for him ever since his return from America. The role which Sundeep had decided to move him to would befit someone five years his junior. He decided to make a call.

'Aditya,' said the voice at the other end.

'Hello Aditya, Swami here.'

'Hey man. How are you?'

'Not too good, Aditya.'

'I heard about the acquisition of BOCA and your move.'

'What do you think of it, Aditya? Why is Sundeep doing this to me? I haven't done anything to harm him.'

'Swami, let's meet up the day you return. We need to chat. Please do not do anything stupid before you speak to me,' Aditya knew Swami very well and was scared that he might quit in a huff.

'I'll be back tonight, Aditya,' said Swami.

'Then let's meet for breakfast at Taj Lands End tomorrow morning. Do not bring Kalpana with you.'

'Okay.'

He went to the airport and took a flight to Mumbai. He went home straight, as he did not want to meet or speak to anyone from the bank.

After his conversation with Swami, Aditya thought for a moment and then called another number.

'Aditya! What a pleasure!' It was Sundeep.

'Of course, Sundeep. How have you been?'

'I am doing great, Aditya. You seem to have vanished in thin air.'

'Just got a bit busy with my new venture. I called regarding something specific, Sundeep. Can we talk now or should we talk later?'

'Aditya, I'll drop everything I am doing to listen to what you have to say.'

'It's about BOCA, Sundeep.'

'What about it?'

'Sundeep, are you doing the right thing by moving Swami to the new company. I just heard about it.'

'Did Swami squeal to you, Aditya? Why can't he pick up the phone and speak to me, if he has a problem?' The irritation in his tone was very evident.

'No, I just heard about the mail you have sent out. My network is still active within your bank, Sundeep,' Aditya lied.

'Why would you think I am doing anything but the right thing?' Sundeep was not happy with the discussion.

'Aren't you being strangely vindictive with Swami? You are moving him to a role which even his juniors will not be willing to take,' Aditya asked him point blank, and Sundeep didn't like it one bit.

'Aditya, must I remind you that you are no longer with the bank?' Sundeep forgot for a moment that it was Aditya who made him what he was today. 'Concerning yourself with issues which are purely internal to the bank and hoping to be heard is very ambitious of you. Is there anything else you called me for? Else I need to go. I have people waiting for me.' Sundeep was really upset that Aditya had raised this with him.

Aditya was taken aback. He was deeply hurt and insulted and didn't know what to say. He decided to end this conversation and meet Swami the next day.

59

'Arre Hero.' Vivek turned when he heard someone calling him like this from behind. It was Sundeep. 'How is the month going?' Sundeep knew that it was a bad month for personal loans. Despite that he asked Vivek in full earshot of everyone. The intent clearly was to embarrass him. For him, Vivek was Swami's man. He was quite antagonistic towards him. Vivek knew that and tried his best to be professional in his approach, but he too was reaching his wit's end.

'Can be better, Sundeep. We have eight days to go for the month to end. Hopefully, we will achieve the desired numbers,' he said.

'Did your Mumbai guys screw up again?' asked Sundeep, raising his voice so that everyone around could hear him. He knew that Mumbai had not delivered on their numbers in the previous month.

'They are struggling a bit, Sundeep. But we have done some changes and they will soon come up the curve,' argued Vivek.

'Rubbish. *Yeh sab bakwas hai.* Let's do a complete review of the Mumbai business. I want to meet your entire Mumbai sales team,' said Sundeep, 'I am free in the second half today. Please fix up a review meeting with them.'

'Sundeep, they won't be able to come at such a short notice.'

'They better come if they want to keep their jobs. Six p.m. sharp, in my room.' Sundeep walked away without waiting for Vivek's response.

Vivek along with his Mumbai sales team met Sundeep in his large room at six in the evening. Sundeep made them wait for over an hour before granting them an audience.

The Mumbai personal loans business for New York International Bank was going through some pressure. Mumbai was a tough market to begin with. It was also home to a few of the largest banks in India, and the competition was intense. It was difficult for any new business to do well in Mumbai, and the personal loans business was no exception.

The head of the Mumbai sales team was a guy called Jinesh Shah. He had worry writ all over his forehead as he entered Sundeep's room. His team members were in no better state. Vivek was also finding it difficult to wipe the wrinkles off his face. Sundeep was not known to be considerate and understanding.

The meeting was a tough one for Vivek's team. From the word go, Sundeep was ballistic. It was difficult for him to accept that Mumbai personal loans was not doing well, and the fact that Vivek was Swami's man complicated matters.

Vivek tried defending his team. 'Don't get into this pissing match with me,' Sundeep had thundered, shutting off Vivek for the rest of the evening. 'Why am I taking all this shit? Why don't I just quit and go?' The thought of quitting crossed Vivek's mind at one point during the meeting.

When the meeting showed no signs of ending at 9.30 p.m., Sundeep's secretary walked into the room. 'Sundeep, do you want anything else? I am leaving.'

'Just hold on. I will be with you in a minute,' said Sundeep, turning back his attention onto the Mumbai sales team. 'I am just stepping out for the next five minutes as I have some work with Reena. When I come back, I want commitments from each of you on what we can do in the next two months. Else none of you needs to come back to work tomorrow.' He left the room in a huff, leaving the sales team shattered. That was the way he was. However, in this case it was different. It had more to do with Swami than Vivek. Sundeep was becoming meaner by the day. Success had gone to his head.

As Sundeep stepped out, the entire sales team started whining. 'Don't worry, I am here,' said Vivek, but nobody believed him. Jinesh Shah was close to tears. Sundeep had torn his reputation and self-confidence to shreds. The fact was that he had slogged his butt out for the bank and here he was, standing and listening to all the crap from Sundeep.

Sundeep had gone out of his cabin to speak to Reena regarding his tickets to Delhi the next day. Most of the office was empty. People had left as it was well past nine. Only the personal loans team was staying back.

'That's a nice bag. Louis Vuitton? Original, or from a Bangkok street?' A nice sweet voice filled the background. He looked up. When he couldn't see anyone, he walked around the partition to the other side of the hall, from where the voice had emanated.

'Of course, original. It's a genuine Louis Vuitton. Hubby got it from London.' Yes, he knew this voice. It was Sneha. He knew it because he heard it almost everyday. The girl sat opposite his office. But this was not the voice he was looking for. Who was the other woman with Sneha? He could now see two shadows and hear a few giggles.

When he went completely round the partition, he was thrilled.

'Hi Karuna. What are you doing here? What brings you to Mumbai?' He was reminded of the Chennai episode, in which he nearly, well nearly got into bed with her.

The Chennai incident flashed through her mind and she was embarrassed. She didn't know whether Sundeep was standing at her door intentionally or if he had wandered there unknowingly.

'Hello S... Sir,' she stammered. 'I am here on a training.'

'That's great. What training is this?'

'It's the Fundamentals of Banking Compliance programme. I am here for a week. Today was the first day.'

'Oh, that's great. Where are you guys put up?'

'Sundeep, my mom stays here in Worli. I will be going there for the night.'

'Karuna, if you are around for some more time, see me before you go.' Sundeep's scheming mind had already gone to work.

'Sure, sir.'

Sundeep went back to join the personal loans team back in his room.

'Vivek.' He called out as he entered the room. 'I have a idea. Can I ask the others to step out of the room while we talk?' Everyone walked out, wondering what was on Sundeep's mind. Jinesh Shah was particularly worried. He knew that Sundeep didn't like him. He had taken on Ram Naresh when he was in Calcutta as a sales manager, by refusing to sign some frivolous bills of his. Naresh had taken it upon himself to screw his career. As far as the bills were concerned, Naresh got Kailash to sign them off for him.

But Jinesh had stuck on. He was still an Assistant Vice President, whereas almost all his batch mates had moved on to become Vice Presidents, despite him clearly being the best in his batch.

'Why can't we move out Jinesh and bring in Nitin from Chennai?' Sundeep dropped a bombshell. He saw this as an opportunity not to get Nitin to Mumbai, but an opportunity to move Karuna within striking distance.

'That will not be fair to Jinesh, Sundeep.'

'But Jinesh hasn't delivered. He has failed to grow in a growing market.'

'And we don't even know if Nitin would be willing to move to Mumbai. His wife too works. That will bring in additional complexity. And Jinesh is genuinely a good guy.' Vivek made a passionate plea.

'Look Vivek. Don't get emotional about people. Listen to me and get Nitin here. His wife works for us only. If we do not have any opening for her, I will make her my chief of staff. She can work in my office as my executive assistant.'

Now Vivek understood Sundeep's game. Sundeep was playing this entire game to get not Nitin but his wife Karuna to Mumbai. 'What a son of a bitch!' thought Vivek.

'And you don't worry about Jinesh. If he is so good, I have a role in mind for him. Government of India has given foreign banks an option of bringing in a capital of one hundred million dollars and set up a private bank subsidiary in India which will be at par with the local private banks. Let Jinesh do the project paper for this subsidiarisation project. If he does this well, I will make him in-charge of the roll out. As a start-up, I want to set up seventy-five branches in rural India. Let's see how good he is.'

Vivek knew the moment he said this that it was a made up project and was not going to take off.

'And I will talk to Nitin. You don't mention it to him.'

The discussion between the two of them lasted a few more minutes during which Sundeep checked Nitin's career record, his experience and level in the organisation hierarchy.

As Vivek left, he saw Karuna walking towards Sundeep's room, and he knew his inference was right. 'I wish my wife was also beautiful, I would have been the CEO,' he said to himself in jest and walked away.

60

'Hey sweetheart. You look stunning.' Sundeep was drooling as soon as Karuna entered his room. She was a indeed a bomb. She had an awesome figure and her clothes accentuated her contours. She looked gorgeous and stunning in an orange chiffon saree. 'Gravity defying sarees,' Sundeep thought. 'How do people manage to hold these five metres of cloth five inches below their navel,' he wondered.

'I am going to town for dinner. Do you want me to drop you?' asked Sundeep. His apartment was in Bandra, which was three miles from work. Peddar road was over ten miles in a different direction. The drive was his opportunity to have her all for himself.

By the time they went down the elevator, the car was in the driveway. A spanking new Mercedes E class sedan. Ashish Baruah was standing in the driveway along with a couple of others waiting for their cars when Sundeep and Karuna passed him.

Sundeep asked his driver to get off, gave him a hundred-bucks note, and asked him to find his way back home all by himself. He got into the driver's seat and Karuna into the seat beside it. This was the first time she had got into a Mercedes, and she was awestruck. One day I will also have such a car, she thought to herself.

'Today is Christmas. Santa Claus has just paid a visit to Sundeep's house.' Ashish Baruah looked at the guy standing next to him and grinned. Such was Sundeep's reputation. No one doubted his banking intellect, but it was this side of him that made people wonder how he got this far.

In the car, Sundeep looked at Karuna with lust in his eyes. She was too taken in by his stature and the car to really think about anything else.

'I am sorry about that night. I was just coming in to tell you that I was getting late and had to leave. The door was open and before I could turn back, you screamed. It was unintentional and I'm really sorry for the confusion.' Sundeep apologised for the Chennai incident.

'You are embarrassing me, sir. I should have ensured that the door was shut. As far as I am concerned it is a closed chapter.'

'Thanks for being so understanding,' said Sundeep as he lightly pressed her hand with his for a moment, before moving it back to the steering of his car.

'How do you like Chennai?' Sundeep asked her.

'It's a nice city, but not too good from a career perspective,' said Karuna. 'If you have to make a career in the banking industry, one has to be in Mumbai. This is where all the action is,' she said.

In one stroke she had made Sundeep's job easier. 'Is that why Nitin is still a manager and has not become an AVP?' he asked.

'The titles depend entirely on people like you, Sundeep.' Karuna was falling in his trap. And like a lion waiting in ambush for the poor deer, Sundeep was waiting.

'Oh, come on, Karuna. Nobody can hold back titles from deserving guys. Nitin is such a great guy. Why doesn't he move to Mumbai? I will give him his title. He can run my personal loans for Mumbai. What do you say?' His hand brushed against her thighs as he changed gears. Thank god! Automatic transmission cars were not popular in India.

'I will ask him. But if he does move, Sundeep, I will also have to look for a change.'

'You can be in my central team,' he said instantaneously, and almost immediately felt that he should not be moving so fast.

Karuna looked at him and smiled.

'What are you doing for dinner tonight?'

'You had a dinner to attend, Sundeep.' Karuna was wondering what made this man change his mind.

'I will cancel it, if a beautiful lady like you gives me company.' Karuna blushed at this compliment. Sundeep was waiting for her response. She picked up her phone and dialled a number. 'Ma, I will not be coming home for dinner. Don't wait for me,' she said and kept the phone down. 'So where do we go?'

Sundeep took her to Indigo, a happening pub in South Mumbai. They freaked out on the floor. Sundeep was an amazing dancer and so was she. Both of them danced till the wee hours of the morning. Sundeep's hands were all over her, feeling her up in the name of dancing. Once when he tried to kiss her, she stopped him. She thought he was drunk. But Sundeep was not. He had not had a single glass of alcohol. He was drinking apple juice and passing it off as whisky. He did not want to get drunk that night. Karuna didn't want to offend him. Someone had spoken to her about Nitin's promotion for the first time.

He didn't push his luck. He dropped her home at half past three in the morning.

61

While Sundeep was dancing the night away with Karuna, it was a restless time for Swami and Kalpana. Neither could get a wink of sleep. Both of them were worried at the turn of events. This was not what they came back to India for.

Kailash was in London when Swami called him at 4.00 a.m. It was late night in London. Kailash heard out Swami.

'Swami, I understand what you are saying. Please understand, we need someone operationally strong like you to manage the integration of BOCA with our organisation. You are the best person in the entire bank for this job.'

All his reasoning fell on deaf years. Rather than listen to Swami's concern, Kailash was trying to convince him that this was indeed the best deal for him. Soon he realised that Sundeep had completely taped up Kailash and he was not going to get any help from him.

When he met with Aditya for breakfast, he had almost made up his mind on quitting the bank that very afternoon. Aditya too was visibly peeved with Sundeep. He told Swami about their conversation.

'Aditya, I will get to office and submit my resignation. I cannot take this humiliation any more. I would rather come and work with you.'

'Grow up, Swami. Don't be stupid. You are behaving like a sulking kid. Such decisions are not made emotionally.' He pulled out a paper napkin from a stand kept on the table and gave it to Swami. He also gave him his Mont Blanc.

'Now write,' he said. Swami was confused.

'Write down the number of your stock options that will mature in the next two years.'

Swami did some calculations and wrote down a figure.

'How many more years do you have to serve the bank to start getting pension for life?'

'Pension at NYB starts post fifteen years of work experience. I complete fifteen years of service next year. To answer your question, I have one year to go,' said Swami.

'Assuming you live till seventy, write down the approx value of pension you will get from now till you are seventy.'

He looked at Aditya, then took some time to do the maths, and eventually wrote down a number.

'Great. That was quick. You are four months away from getting your bonus for the year. Write down the bonus you expect to be paid this year.'

Swami wrote it down. He was now smiling. Aditya had his own way of making him understand.

'How much do all these add up to?'

'Over two million dollars.' Swami's face lit up.

'If you want to give up two million dollars because of some son of a bitch, please go ahead and do so. Come tomorrow morning and collect your appointment letter. And now Mr Swaminathan, I am getting late and hence I must leave.'

Swami got up too. He had got the message. He was going to have some fun.

Kalpana was leaving when he bumped into her in the lift of their apartment. 'All well?' she asked him and was surprised to see him smile. 'Call me when you get to office,' she screamed as the lift started moving.

It was 9.45 a.m. when Swami walked into office. He went straight to Sundeep's room. Sundeep was on the phone, talking to Natasha who had left with the kids on an early morning flight to Delhi. Sundeep had not got up by then. And they had left without saying bye to him. Sundeep was glad that Swami walked in. He could use that as an excuse to cut the phone call short.

'So Swami, how do you feel about your new assignment,' fingered Sundeep, expecting Swami to plead with him to revoke the announcement.

'Wonderful, Sundeep. It's a god sent opportunity. No doubt, a challenging assignment. Fair bit of learning for me. I have tremendous faith in your leadership and am confident that you will support me completely in making this venture a success.'

Stumped, Sundeep's could only say, 'Yes, of course, Swami. You are the best man for this job.'

Pleasantries over. They decided that Swami would move over to the new assignment from the first day of the next month. Since Sundeep was a very hands-on boss, Swami didn't need to give him an extensive handover.

And so Swami moved to his new role as MD of BOCA.

62

Karuna moved to Mumbai into Sundeep's team. Nitin was not that fortunate. The Regional Head for North India quit around the same time that Nitin was supposed to move to Mumbai. Sundeep was quick to seize this opportunity. He moved him to Delhi, the Assistant Vice President title thrown in as a carrot. Karuna in Mumbai and Nitin in Delhi... Mission accomplished for Sundeep.

This move upset Karuna a bit, but she couldn't complain. Sundeep had promised to move Nitin to Mumbai at the first available opportunity. Karuna bought that. Hadn't Sundeep kept his promise of giving him the AVP title?

She became a core member of Sundeep's coterie. Sundeep involved her in every decision, every meeting. She started enjoying the power and adulation that came with being in Sundeep's team. This was almost becoming an addiction. Working with Sundeep meant regular parties and frequent night-outs with Sundeep. She was having a ball and Sundeep had his arm-candy to tout all over the town.

'I am going to Chennai for a branch banking offsite tomorrow. Do you want to come with me?' Sundeep asked her and she said yes. In Chennai, their work got over by 6.00 p.m and they hit the bar at seven. They were drinking till about nine when they realised they had a dinner to attend. The dinner was being hosted for the participants of the offsite. Sundeep and Karuna went in late and were partly sloshed by the time they reached. The music was heavy. They started drinking again. Sundeep and Karuna were the first ones to hit the dance floor. He held her by her arm and she was willingly sticking to him. He didn't leave her for a moment. Even when he was not dancing, he didn't let go of her hand. Karuna was enjoying it too.

The bhangra beats brought out a different animal in Sundeep. Then the music changed to a slow number, and Sundeep turned to Karuna, one arm on her waist and the other on her shoulder, and began a languorous dance. Karuna also had one arm on his waist and the other on his shoulder. Sundeep's arm moved from her waist to her back and pulled her closer to him. She could feel the bulge in his pants. A month had passed since Nitin moved to Delhi. She hadn't had a guy for thirty days and was partly drunk too. The wind was chilly. Sundeep could see that she was getting turned on. Not one to ever miss an opportunity, he suggested a walk on the beach.

They quietly disappeared from the crowd. While they were walking on the sand, Sundeep pulled her towards him and kissed her. She didn't react. Sundeep held her face in his hands and kissed her once more on her lips even as his hands wandered from her face to her back and then down the elastic band of her skirt.

'This is not right. I am married.' She desperately tried to free herself, even though a part of her wanted to be held. She was terribly confused, scared of turning down her CEO and, at the same time, afraid of violating her own sense of morals.

Sundeep was a smart cookie. He didn't want to force himself on her completely. He wanted her to yearn for him. 'Sex is fun if the other partner wants you. Else you can always buy it.' That was his philosophy.

She finally managed to set herself free and started walking away from him towards the hotel room. Sundeep followed her. 'Karuna, I could feel it. I know that you want me, desire me. I could sense it when we were dancing. I could see it in your eyes.'

She didn't turn back.

'Come back, Karuna! I will not say a word about it to anyone. I want you.'

Still no response.

'I promise you, if you do what I say, I will move Nitin back to Mumbai within the next one week.'

Now she slowed down. Why not? The Head of Retail was pleading with her. She can now call the shots. She can extract whatever she wanted from him. Now was the time.

'I will do whatever you want me to, Karuna. You know I can work wonders for your career. I will also move you to an AVP position.'

Now Karuna stopped. Her back was towards Sundeep. The deal now looked good.

Sundeep quietly moved from behind and hugged her from the back. His hands caressed the bare neck and came to rest on her breasts. She could feel his dick growing against her ass. She closed her eyes in pleasure. She didn't want to miss this opportunity and neither did Sundeep.

She woke up the next day in Sundeep's room. 'You were wonderful last night,' said Sundeep as he made her a cup of coffee. She looked at him and smiled. The smile told Sundeep that he was wonderful too.

Her mobile phone was on the table. It showed three missed calls. All of them from Nitin. She looked at her watch. It was six in the morning. She wanted to get out of Sundeep's room before the others got up. She got dressed and was about to leave the room when Sundeep held her hand and pulled her back. She kissed him on his lips.

'You were wonderful. I will see you tonight. I have got to go before the others see us.' She tiptoed out of the room.

Though it was only six in the morning, there were a few branch managers, the early risers, who were out for a jog. They saw her coming out of Sundeep's room and it didn't take them much to put one and one together, given Sundeep's reputation. The news spread like wildfire. But it didn't matter, because no one told Nitin.

True to his word, Sundeep moved Nitin back to Mumbai as Mumbai Sales Head for Personal Loans within the next one week. He had, however, tasted the forbidden fruit, and now he wanted it more. Karuna was anyway in his team and would stay in his vicinity, day in and day out. She would be in his room almost all the while. He would take her with him on all his branch visits.

On days she was not chatting with him in person, she would be chatting with him on SMS.

All the employees of NYB started treating Karuna with respect. A respect derived out of fear, on account of her closeness with Sundeep. The addiction was getting into her head. She was hooked on the attention she was getting from everyone else in the bank.

Karuna was also beginning to get emotionally involved with Sundeep now. Sex with a powerful guy was a huge turn on. Making love in weird places, by taking risks and hoodwinking people, became a favourite pastime for both of them. They even made love in Sundeep's office at 12.45 a.m., after covering the security camera with Karuna's jeans.

Nitin noticed his wife's rising influence, but was blinded by his love for her. He thought that his wife was capable and hence was rising up the system.

For Sundeep, this was nothing but pure, unalloyed pleasure. He was in it solely for the kick of it. The fun of feeling big and powerful. He felt no emotional connect with Karuna, just the massive ego kick of bedding a lovely, married woman. Making love to her made him feel like God—the God of Banking.

63

The first few days that Swami spent at BOCA were uneventful. He was trying to learn the tricks of the trade. He had never worked in a BPO earlier.

The environment at BOCA was a lot different from the bank. The average employee age here was less than twenty-five years, while at NYB it was closer to thirty-five. The way the employees were treated and their aspirations were totally different. Swami had to struggle hard in order to associate himself with the employees of BOCA.

The business model of BOCA was completely different from the way businesses at NYB were run. Despite being a financial wizard, Swami couldn't figure out the ways and means of making a significant profit at BOCA, large enough to justify his posting there.

'An MNC manager is only as good as the money he makes,' Aditya had once told him. He had also said, 'if ever you get stuck in a business that does not make large profits, either change your job or work hard at making money in the same business. More often than not, the latter is the easier option.'

Swami was getting stuck in the BPO. He somehow pulled through the first three months, trying to understand operations, financials and process flows, but soon started getting frustrated.

God came to his rescue. In the form of Aditya.

After quitting the bank, Aditya himself had started a BPO. His experience came in handy.

'Don't just depend on Sundeep for your business. Make it an independent profit centre,' Aditya advised Swami.

Swami sat down with all the business managers in the bank and individually worked out all the processes that could be migrated to BOCA. He also went and spoke to such outfits of competing banks. He went and personally visited the Citibank Operations and Processing Enterprise in Chennai to figure out how they managed their processes and made money. He made every effort to understand the financial dynamics. He finally realised that he will not make enough money by migrating bank processes alone. The core intention of banks in migrating these processes was saving of cost and they would never pay him enough to make a decent profit. If he had to make money, he had to bring in business from overseas and transition processes to BOCA from various other countries where New York International Bank operated.

For that he needed resources. He needed people who would go and sell the outsourcing concept to various other countries. He needed a guy who would be 'his guy.' Someone he could trust. He went back to Sundeep and asked him to move Vivek to BOCA. Sundeep was only too happy to oblige and so was Vivek.

Vivek became Swami's hit man for selling the India BPO proposition to other New York International Bank countries. Vivek and Swami went together to make presentations to the CEOs of various countries. They put their heart and soul into it. They would travel for over twenty days a month. Kalpana lost track of Swami and which part of the world he was in.

In the next three months they were able to convince people from across the globe to transition to India two back office operations and one outbound calling activity from UK, four processes from the US and three more from Argentina. They were in business. They delivered these transitions within ninety days of getting the orders. Revenues started flowing in.

In no time the gross monthly revenues of the BPO started crossing ten million dollars. The business was operating at a margin of thirty percent. BOCA became a star, the biggest and the best performing business for New York International Bank in India. Swami was again a hero.

The phenomenal run of BOCA left Sundeep wondering what went wrong in his assessment. He had sent Swami there to make life miserable for him, but Swami had actually turned it into a golden opportunity.

When he saw BOCA taking centre stage in the India business, he wanted his share of the pie. He started interfering in the day to day running of BOCA. Swami was not one to get into a direct conflict and tolerated this interference for some time, till he received this e-mail from Sundeep's secretary.

Swami,

Sundeep has scheduled a full review of BOCA, this Saturday from 9.00 a.m. to 4.30 p.m. He has asked me to request you to be present with the BOCA management team at the conference room #2 on the third floor of NYB HQ.

Regards,
Reena

Two things about this mail pissed off Swami. First, it came from Sundeep's secretary. If Sundeep felt that it was important, he should have called himself. Secondly, the least Sundeep could have done was to check with him if he was free on that day for a review. He decided to take Sundeep head on. He decided to send this e-mail to Sundeep.

Sundeep,

The senior management team of BOCA would be glad to discuss their progress and success with you on Saturday. Any inputs for running this business or improving its current traction will be really appreciated. However, I would like to make one thing amply clear: BOCA is an independent business and, in this company, I am the boss. The final word rests with me. If you keep that in mind when you meet my team, that will help.
Look forward to seeing you on Saturday.

Regards,
Swami

64

BOCA became one of the largest BPOs in the country and Swami one of the most sought after individuals in this space. His turnaround experience was worth its weight in gold. Swami was inundated with offers from other BPOs, and at times he contemplated starting his own, but he was wedded to the bank. He would not and could not leave it under any circumstance, irrespective of whether it was Suneel Dutt or Sundeep who tried to push him out.

Sundeep didn't like it one bit. But he was the one who had moved Swami to BOCA. And Swami had made a mockery of him. The business grew to such an extent that the NYB board under Kailash Advani decided to divorce it from Sundeep and spun it off into an independent business unit. Swami now reported directly to Kailash. Sundeep went crying to Naresh, but in this case even Naresh couldn't do a thing.

Aditya watched the game from the sidelines. It was he who had taught Swami the tricks of the trade and had worked closely with him. He was the prime driver in Swami's getting all the overseas contracts that had come BOCA's way. He had leveraged his contacts with seniors in NYB to get those deals for Swami. He had worked behind the scenes for Swami's success. He was spurred on by Sundeep's nasty conversation with him, when he had called him about Swami's move. Sundeep might just have lost a friend for life.

65

The sleaze fest between Sundeep and Karuna showed no signs of abating. Whenever Sundeep was travelling and Karuna was not with him, he would send her an SMS from the airport. Once he was off on a two-day trip to Delhi. He was at the airport, waiting to board the flight.

Beep. Beep. Karuna's phone woke her up. She reached out for it. 'Miss U honey.' This was the SMS Sundeep had sent her from the airport. She quietly deleted the message, worried that Nitin might see it.

Beep. Beep. It was Sundeep again. Another SMS: 'I am HOT and waiting.'

Karuna replied: 'Go jerk off.'

They would exchange twenty or more such messages, almost on a daily basis.

Karuna had finished her work at office by lunchtime and was feeling very bored. She dialled Sundeep's number. 'Hey sweetheart, missing me?'

'Was feeling bored! Have nothing to do. Should I come over? I'll do some shopping in Delhi and wait for you at the hotel.'

'No, honey. I have a dinner with the branch managers and Anindyo Roy at the hotel tonight. I will be very late. I'll try and come back early tomorrow. Send Nitin off on some training and we will have some fun.' He spoke to her for a while and disconnected.

At about seven in the evening, she got a call. It was from Anindyo Roy.

'Hi Anindyo. How are you?'

'Karuna, couldn't get through to Reena and so I'm calling you. Any idea where Sundeep would be? He is not reachable and we do not know where he is?'

'Wasn't he supposed to have dinner with you and the branch managers tonight?' Karuna asked.

'No, he sent me an SMS this morning from Mumbai airport asking me to cancel it.'

'No, Anindyo. I have no clue where he is. Sorry. If you do get through to him, please ask him to give me a call. I have also been trying to get in touch with him.'

She was quite surprised. 'Where is he? Why did he lie to me?' thought Karuna as she took the taxi back home.

A couple of days later, an SMS was waiting for Karuna when she woke up in the morning. It was from Sundeep. She had come back early the previous night as she had a terrible headache. There was no incentive for her to stay back in office as Sundeep was travelling. She had gone off to sleep and had put her phone on silent. Nitin had come back home late and had found her asleep. He didn't bother to wake her up.

The message read: 'Let's meet at ten. I haven't had you in a while. Am desperately waiting.' She saw the message and smiled. It was actually over a week since she had made out with Sundeep. Despite the headache, she got dressed and went to office. She reached office at nine sharp, hoping to see Sundeep there. But there was no sign of him.

At ten, she tried calling him on his mobile. His phone was off. She was a bit worried. Sundeep had sent a message asking her to meet him at ten. He hadn't come in yet. This had never happened in the past. In the past, whenever he was running late, he had called. Why not today? Finally she went to Reena.

'Reena, where is Sundeep?'

'He is in Delhi. Will be back only tomorrow,' she said and added sarcastically, 'Why? He didn't tell you?'

Karuna was a bit taken aback. She was confused. If Sundeep was in Delhi, why would he ask her to meet him at ten? She opened the message and read it again. Yes. She had read it correctly. Why did Sundeep do this?

As she read the last portion of the message where the sent details normally appear, realisation dawned on her. The message was not for her. She read the message once more.

'Let's meet at ten. I haven't had you in a while. Am desperately waiting... Sent 6.30 p.m. Sundeep had sent it to someone in Delhi last evening at half past six and by mistake the message got sent to her. She had wrongly assumed that it was sent in the morning. The world collapsed around her. Sundeep was two-timing her. Whether it was two-timing or more, she couldn't say.

She couldn't even go and confront him on this. After all, he was the boss. That she had no *locus standi* was something she never thought about. Sundeep was probably doing to her what she was doing to Nitin.

66

NYB was a business leader in almost all the business segments it operated in. Sundeep drove his people to perform consistently at high levels. It's branch banking business was the best in India. The customer service at NYB was legendary. It was also the most preferred bank for people to work in. The intellect quotient in the bank was enormous. NYB was a place where people could make a career for themselves. They were the only organisation in India with a large bench strength. If one person went out to a larger job overseas, five guys would put up their hands to take that job, and each one would be equally competent. Such was the environment in which NYB operated.

Around the same time Citibank started revamping its retail business and started investing in India. The global brand came in with an aggression rarely seen since the days when Sundeep and Swami had launched NYB's retail business in India. They started eating into NYB's market share rapidly and, in less than a year's time, they overtook NYB in all aspects of the business. This was bad news for Sundeep.

The worst hit was the branch banking and wealth management business. Citibank had deep pockets and was definitely a better brand. They started hiring the best people from NYB. Anindyo had no clue as to what was going wrong.

Sundeep would go on the rampage in the branch banking meetings. '*Kuch bhi karo. Citibank ko khatam karo.* We will have to beat them at any cost.' He became ruthless with the people in charge of the businesses. Despite the fact that Anindyo and Sundeep were good friends, and despite the fact that they would sleep with the same relationship manager at night, Anindyo started feeling the heat.

Good-looking women dominated the Relationship Management team in NYB. Sundeep's policy was to hire pretty girls, with plunging necklines, who would smile at the customer and make him swoon and sign up for investing through NYB. This policy paid rich dividends for some time, but when Citibank came up with better products and services, NYB did not know what hit them. The pretty girls were no match for the qualified and trained financial advisors at Citibank. The pressure soon started telling on NYB's RMs. The good ones quit and joined other banks. The ones left behind were the average ones. In their quest for success, they started resorting to unethical means to get in investments and sell insurance. The number of dissatisfied and disgruntled customers started growing by the day.

Anindyo Roy tried his best to control the team, but it was too large a team. The attitudes he and Sundeep had imbibed in them were difficult to change in a hurry.

Malintent combined with a rampaging bull stock market was a deadly combination. There were some quick bucks to be made. The wealth managers in NYB started forging customers' signatures and transferring funds from their savings accounts to various mutual funds. It was just a matter of time before the bubble burst.

67

NYB had three categories of customers—Value Plus customers, Super Value customers, and Club Class customers. Customers were graded as per their relationship value with NYB. Customers with relationship value of over one million dollars brought up the Club Class. They were the most pampered customers.

Legend had it that NYB once hired a helicopter to ferry a Club Class customer from Mumbai to Pune, when a landslide had blocked the highway.

Arun Jain was a Club Class customer of the Nehru Place branch. He had a relationship value in excess of two million dollars. He had a set pattern as far as his banking habits were concerned. He would go to the bank every Monday morning to check the status of his deposits. He hadn't missed his weekly visit even once in the last two years.

He would leave home at 9.25 a.m., reach the bank ten minutes later, have a cup of coffee with the branch manager, and then leave with his statement of accounts. His relationship manager was a cute little girl, Nidhi Agarwal. She was one of the top performing relationship managers with NYB and was also one of Anindyo Roy's favourites.

Arun Jain had been banking with NYB for over a decade. Today he swore by the bank. All the new foreign banks in India had been chasing him for his money, but he never moved his money from NYB. He was a seventy-year-old guy and all his children—two sons and one daughter—were in USA. The last time he visited them was four years ago.

When his daughter was expecting her first child, Arun Jain and his wife decided to pay them a visit and help them out. They packed their bags and left for the US. They planned to be there for six months.

Before he left, Arun met the branch manager and Nidhi Agarwal together. 'I know my money is safe with you guys. Please take care of it.'

He handed them a small piece of paper. 'This is my e-mail ID and my daughter's phone number. Please get in touch in case you need anything from me. I will come back and see you.'

'Not to worry, Mr Jain. We will take care of your money as if it's our own. Do let us know the progress of your daughter's delivery. Give her our best wishes,' Nidhi told him as she shook his hand outside the main door of the bank.

The equity markets in India were going through a bull phase. Investment products and insurance sales were the mantras and every bank was selling them as if they were going out of fashion. Customers were being convinced to move money from fixed deposits to mutual funds. This was not without reason. The mutual fund companies paid the banks a commission for every rupee of mutual funds sold. The money that the banks made on mutual fund sales was more lucrative than holding them as deposits.

Of course, there were a few banks that would look at the risk appetite of customers before recommending them a mix of deposits, debt funds, and equity mutual funds. These banks would endlessly research the markets and advise customers appropriately, even if it meant throwing away a chance to make a few dollars. NYB was definitely not one of them.

Sundeep was different. For him the result was more important than the means. He pushed his people to sell as much of these products as they could. To energise the sales fraternity, he launched a sales contest titled, '*Hawa se Hawaii*.' The objective of this contest was to motivate employees to become heroes from zeroes. It was a three-month contest with a trip to Hawaii as the bumper award for the winner. '*Hawa se Hawaii*' was an instant hit. Sales of investments and insurance products skyrocketed.

For the next two months, NYB was the largest distributor of mutual funds across India. Sundeep and Anindyo kept the interest in the contest alive, by publishing weekly results, announcing spot incentives, holding impromptu get-togethers, and more.

As the contest entered the last week, there were two contestants in the race, Nidhi Agarwal from the Nehru Place branch and Pooja Deshmukh from the Bandra branch in Mumbai. Pooja was leading by 2.2 crores in mutual funds. This being the last week of the contest, daily results were being posted on the NYB intranet. By the penultimate day, Pooja had sold 1.3 crores worth of mutual funds more than Nidhi. Nidhi had managed to pull back but she had not done enough.

On the last day Nidhi needed to sell Rs 1.3 crore more of mutual funds as compared to Pooja to win the contest. No one gave her a chance. But she had an ace up her sleeve. One of her biggest customers, a factory owner in Gurgaon, was supposed to give her a cheque of Rs 5.1 crores for investment in Franklin Blue chip fund. He had committed to those funds on the last day of the contest.

She landed at his house in Sector V of Gurgaon at a quarter to ten in the morning. Mutual funds normally accept investments till three in the afternoon. She had given herself enough time to collect the cheque and bank it with the fund house.

As she turned right from NH 8 and entered the approach road, she saw more activity than usual. She crossed two vans that looked like mobile TV crews. 'Looks like this guy has closed another deal today,' she said to herself, looking at the huge contingent of media vans outside his house.

When she reached his house, she was surprised to find it surrounded not only by TV cameras and a horde of curious onlookers but also police jeeps. She didn't know what was going on. She pushed her way through and reached the main gate of the bungalow, only to be told by the security guard that income tax personnel had raided her customer late last night and that he had gone underground.

Her head started spinning. She was banking on this guy for a large sum and if she didn't manage a replacement deal, she would lose the contest. She couldn't let it go after coming so close. She had been the Number One Relationship Manager all her life.

Driving back in her red Hyundai Accent, she was wondering what to do. She stopped for a fuel refill. While she was flipping through the pages of her diary for last-minute referrals on investment deals, a piece of paper slipped out. She picked it up from the car floor and looked at it. The piece of paper was saying something to her. As she looked at the paper, a low whistle came out of her mouth. She put her Accent into top gear and soon hit the highway headed towards Delhi. Once she reached the branch, she signed a few papers and gave them to the branch service guys, and then went back home smiling. The markets had jumped another 120 points on that day.

The next afternoon, the results of 'Hawa se Hawaii' contest were announced. And the winner was Nidhi Agarwal. She was thrilled. Her phone was constantly ringing that day. She got over a hundred congratulatory messages. Not only were her colleagues at NYB congratulating her, but people from the mutual fund fraternity were also calling to congratulate her. She had sold twenty-seven crores of mutual funds in the last thirty days, of which five-odd crores came in on the last day, and that was a record for any individual.

The stock market gave her a twenty-one-gun salute and surged even further.

She was basking in this newfound glory, when she got a call from Anindyo Roy's office. It was his secretary Melanie.

'Nidhi, Anindyo wanted to meet you today. He was wondering if you could see him in the next fifteen minutes. Why don't you run up to his office.'

'Five minutes,' and off she went dashing towards the main door.

Anindyo's office was on the fifth floor of the same building. In the next five minutes, she was standing outside Anindyo's office.

When Anindyo saw her waiting, he got up from his chair and hugged her. 'Well done, Nidhi. I am proud of you.' The hug lingered for longer than normal.

'Thank you, sir. It wouldn't have been possible without your encouragement.' Anindyo didn't release her from the hug, neither did she try and move away.

'So when are you planning your trip to Hawaii?'

'Sir, I plan to leave next month. I need a favour from you.'

'Can I refuse you?'

'After my trip to Hawaii, I was planning to take two weeks off and do a trip to Rio. No point going that far and not go to Rio.'

'I too have always wanted to go to Rio, but never got a chance,' said Anindyo.

'Sir, why don't you come now? It's off season and we will get good deals,' said Nidhi.

'How can I join you? You might be going with your family,' said Anindyo coyly.

'Sir, *aap ishara to karo, sab ko chod ke aa jayenge.*' Nidhi was teasing Anindyo.

'*Toh theek hai*, I will confirm to you by tomorrow. Only you and me. Is that a deal?'

'Copy that.' Nidhi gave him a thumbs up and the discussion ended there.

Anindyo called up Sundeep the moment Nidhi left his room. '*Yaar, Nidhi apne saath Rio bula rahi hai.* She said she will ditch her family if I go with her to Rio.'

'Then what are you waiting for? She is a hot babe, Mr Roy,' said Sundeep.

'Why don't you get KAIC to sponsor my trip?'

'No problem, Anindyo. I will tell Sharada. She will organise it. What all you guys get me to do to motivate you!'

After exactly a month, Nidhi was off to Hawaii, and three days later, on a Sunday, Anindyo was off to Rio to join Nidhi.

68

The day after Anindyo left for Rio, North Korea tested a nuclear bomb. This was entirely unanticipated and took the world by surprise. America made noises about launching a military attack on North Korea.

The impact of this was felt on the stock markets. The entire Asian markets tumbled and India was no exception. The sensex fell by over four hundred points on a single day.

That same morning the finance ministry had decided to withdraw tax concessions given to the foreign institutional investors who had routed their investments through offshore companies registered in Mauritius. These FIIs were the ones driving the market into a bullish phase. Once the concessions were removed, they started dumping stocks and exiting their positions. The next two days were disastrous for the markets. The stock market fell by thirty percent in just over seven trading sessions. There was mayhem on dalal street.

While all this was happening, Arun Jain walked into the Nehru Place branch of NYB. Since Nidhi was away, he went and met Mr Shankar Mittal, the branch manager.

'Mr Jain, what a surprise! How come you are back early?'

'My daughter had a miscarriage, Shankar. She was miserable and didn't feel like living in the same house. We brought her back for a change.'

'I am so sorry, Mr Jain. May god give her the strength to come out of this unscathed.'

'Thanks, Shankar. I am in a bit of a hurry. Can I get my regular statement, please?' Jain was in no mood for pleasantries.

Shankar consoled him and pulled out his deposit status. He put it in a cover and handed it over to him.

'There you go, Mr Jain.'

Jain casually removed it from the envelope and opened it. He turned the paper around to see if there was any print on the back of the paper. It was blank.

'There seems to be a mistake, Shankar. This is not complete.'

'I am so sorry, Mr Jain. Let me check and get back to you in a minute.' Shankar went to the customer service representative and came back in three minutes.

'Mr Jain, this indeed is the correct status.'

On the deposit status sheet, Mr Arun Jain's deposit showed Rs 4.2 crores whereas when he had left for America he had Rs 9.6 crores in his account. He was shocked and speechless. He picked up a glass of water and gulped it down.

He opened his briefcase and pulled out an old statement that had been given to him before he left for America. He passed it on to Shankar. That showed Rs 9.6 crores.

Shankar went back again and this time he had another sheet of paper with him.

'Got it, sir. The balance 5.4 crores are invested in mutual funds through us.'

Jain gave Shankar a blank look.

'2.4 crores in HDFC top 200 and the balance in Franklin Index-linked funds.'

'Are you kidding? What is wrong with you, Shankar?' Arun Jain was screaming at the top of his voice. The banking hall suddenly fell silent.

'In my entire life, I have not touched any shares or share-related instrument, and you are telling me that I have invested over five crores in mutual funds. Are you out of your fucking mind?'

'Mr Jain, I am sure there is some confusion on this one. We do not invest any of our customer's money into mutual funds without their mandate. I am sure we will have an instruction letter for this investment. Let me try and pull that out for you.'

Mr Jain was already shivering with rage. He paced up and down Shankar's room, waiting for the so-called document to arrive.

'Old man is out of his mind. Pull out the letter he gave us,' Shankar muttered to the customer service officer responsible for filing all such documents. 'Thank god, he is Club Class.' Normally, NYB would have sent the customer instruction letter to their centralised operations unit in Chennai, from which retrieval would have taken at least a week. For the Club Class customers, NYB had the practice of retaining a copy of the customer instruction at the branch for six months. Hence it was not too difficult to retrieve a copy of the same.

When Shankar produced the same to Mr Jain, the later was left speechless. He didn't know what hit him. Right in front of him was a paper which had his signature, but one he had never signed.

He looked at Shankar and, his voice belying the storm within, said, 'Shankar, I haven't signed this. On the day this transaction was effected, I was in America. I have never invested in any mutual funds ever.'

'Mr Jain, did you ever call and give instructions to anyone in this branch, Nidhi maybe?'

'Son, I may be seventy years old, but my memory is still going strong. I haven't asked for this transfer. Now will you figure this out for me or should I call Mr Sundeep Srivastava?'

Shankar was a worried man. How could something like this happen? 'Sir, we can withdraw the amount and credit your account back immediately. I will sort this out.'

'You better do that young man, else I will have to do whatever I can to get my money back, and that may not be something you will like.'

Shankar returned in a few minutes. The look on his face told Jain that all was not well.

'Now what?'

'Mr Jain, the 5.4 crores that was invested in your name is now worth only 3.9 crores. The stock market has fallen by over thirty percent since we invested. This has impacted the Net Asset Value of the mutual funds as well.'

'Thank you.' Jain got up from his seat. 'My lawyers will now talk to you. I will make you guys pay every pie of it.' And he stomped out of Shankar's room.

The moment he left his room, Shankar picked up his phone and dialled Anindyo. He couldn't get through to him as he was in Rio. The next call was to Sundeep.

Sundeep initially didn't believe what he heard. He thought that the customer was trying to create a scene since he had lost a lot of money in mutual funds. When Shankar explained to him, he was concerned. He was too smart not to have understood what would have happened.

They tried calling the hotel in Hawaii where Nidhi was staying. She had just stepped out to the beach. They left a message for her. In an hour she called back.

'Sundeep, were you trying to reach me?'

'Yes, Nidhi. What's the story on Arun Jain?'

'What about him, Sundeep?'

'He claims that he never gave instructions to transfer money to mutual funds from his deposit account.'

'Oh that. Sundeep, this is the same guy I spoke to you about, on the last day of the contest. You had asked me to go ahead. Don't worry, Sundeep. I will come and manage it.'

'Bitch, you stay in Hawaii and do not come back, because if I see you, I will slaughter you,' said Sundeep. He was furious. He knew that she had forged the signatures of Arun Jain and transferred his money to mutual funds. He knew that the moment Shankar told him that the amount was transferred on the last day of the '*Hawa se Hawaii*' contest and that the RM was Nidhi. She had taken his approval on this, but he didn't realise that this would blow in his face.

She had bet on a booming stock market, but the market let her down. He decided to terminate her. He had no option. If he didn't, it would come back to hurt him. It was sad because she was a great fuck.

A termination letter was faxed to Hawaii, where Nidhi found it on her table when she returned from a swim. She knew it had to happen. Irrespective of that, she decided to go ahead with her trip to Rio. Any bank would give her a job on her return. Anindyo was a big guy. It was more important to keep him happy. And, who knows, maybe one day Sundeep would come back to her too.

The bank decided to pay back Arun Jain and take a hit of over two crores. Shankar communicated the same to him. It had taken the bank two days to make up their mind, and Arun Jain had already complained to the police. He had pressed forgery and cheating charges against the bank. The media too had caught on.

The morning newspapers the next day carried banner headlines, 'NYB wealth managers caught in a major fraud: Rampant forgery of customer's signatures.' Trouble was brewing for NYB. Once this headline hit the newspapers, a number of customers came back to the bank to check on their deposits and found that their funds also had been invested and lost in mutual funds. A problem that began with Arun Jain was snowballing into a major controversy. In a matter of three days, the bank had logged in 359 cases of forged signatures—all from wealthy customers. It was becoming a big credibility issue for the bank.

What had gone wrong? The wealth managers had bet on a bullish stock market and assumed that they would be able to make their customers happy by transferring some money from their accounts to mutual funds. The customer's wealth would go up and they would make significant incentives in the bargain. Typically a bank is paid two percent of the amount invested through them in equity mutual funds, and often upto twenty percent of that amount makes its way back to the wealth managers as incentives.

In the case of Nidhi, the Rs 5.4 crores that she had clandestinely moved to mutual funds gave NYB Rs 10.8 lakhs in revenue. The incentive Nidhi made on this would have been Rs 2.2 lakhs—not a small sum of money by any standard, certainly not for a Wealth Manager. People were bound to fall prey to temptations of that order. But, in the case of NYB, it was not the lure of money alone that was responsible for this. The pressure, which Sundeep put on the system, was enormous. It was assumed that only the results mattered, not the manner in which they were achieved. This was partly responsible for the systemic collapse.

The bank was expected to build in processes to ensure compliance and put controls in place. Sundeep pushed all his people for numbers, but didn't put in adequate controls.

Sundeep moved fast, and created a task force and a core team to deal with this debacle. But this one refused to die down. They tried to hush it up the same way they had killed the insurance cross-sell issue, but were unsuccessful. When Global HQ got to know of this, they were very embarrassed. They wanted to know who was the person responsible for this entire episode. With 359 reported cases across the country, the only person they could point a finger at was Sundeep. He had fostered a culture built on low morals and low integrity, and now it had come back to hurt him.

The media glare brought with it a host of new problems for Sundeep. The whole issue blew up into an ideological debate on national television. It snowballed into a discussion on whether the controls in the financial system were adequate to ensure that the people's trust was in safe hands. Talk show after talk show debated for days on whether the banks were a safe place to invest any longer. NYB was being compared to the plunderers from the West who had looted India in the past. A number of caricatures of Sundeep and Kailash with moneybags and the NYB logo in the background dominated the print media.

The media seemed to suggest that the banking regulators had no means of protecting the consumer's interest in such cases. They also raised fingers at the regulators for letting the foreign banks off the hook so easily. The banking regulators were obviously peeved.

They came sniffing with a vengeance, right to the doorsteps of NYB. They went on record stating that they will not allow NYB or any other bank found guilty of any malpractices to open new branches and ATMs. They had to be seen to be taking action against the guilty. NYB at that time had licenses to open four new branches. All of them were withdrawn without an explanation.

A team of Reserve Bank of India (RBI) auditors landed at NYB for a surprise audit. During the audit, a number of other issues cropped up. NYB was found to be flouting the *Know Your Customer* norms, which had been mandated by RBI. The inspection found a number of loopholes in the way NYB was being run. They were extremely unhappy and said so in no uncertain terms.

If NYB didn't face a run on the bank, it was only because of its reputation as one of the largest and best banks in the world. But Sundeep was in trouble.

All this happened in a matter of one week.

69

The situation was becoming too hot to handle. Kailash was under tremendous pressure to act. He called Sundeep into his room. Kailash had hired Sundeep into this role and so he wanted to protect him.

'Where the fuck is that bitch Nidhi?' Kailash was furious. Sundeep was not listening. He was looking at the crystal vase in the corner of the room. Natasha had bought it when she was the secretary to Aditya Rao.

'Sundeep, where the fuck is Nidhi?'

'Kailash, you are aware that we sacked her four days ago. We haven't heard from her yet, but the hotel has confirmed that they have handed over the fax of the termination letter to her.'

'The matter has reached such a state that now we have to demonstrate to the media that we have taken some action. If we don't, then we will be taken to the cleaners. It will be disastrous for our franchise. It will be in your best interest if we quickly find something for you to move out to.'

Sundeep didn't like this. Kailash was politely asking him to fuck off from there. But he had anticipated this. He was a smart guy. 'Kailash, Martin Sanders is looking for a Head of Retail Bank for UK. I heard that last night. I was myself going to talk to you. Do you think you can get me that job?' It was actually Naresh who had told him about that opening in the UK. Thanks to Naresh, Sundeep was trying to turn adversity into opportunity.

'I don't promise, but I will try. You must be prepared to move at a short notice, Sundeep.'

'Maybe we should not have come back to India,' Natasha blurted out at the dinner table. Their kids had just settled down in Mumbai and their school.

'It was a bad idea, I agree,' said Sundeep. 'What have I not done for this organisation? I gave it my best, I pushed everyone and got revenues doubled in eighteen months, but at the first sign of a problem, they drop me like a hot potato.' Sundeep was not too happy with the way Kailash had spoken to him that morning. But he had only himself to blame. He was the one who drove people madly and looked the other side when they made mistakes. He realised that he was lucky to have survived this.

He washed his hands and walked into his study. His cell phone was blinking. He had put it on silent mode. He picked it up. Karuna was trying to reach him. He disconnected the phone. He was in a very foul mood. He did not want to speak to anyone. The phone blinked again. He looked at it and again disconnected Karuna's call. He switched off his phone and threw it on the table. He had some important work to do.

He picked up the cordless and called Naresh. He was the one who could do something for him.

70

After Sundeep had left the room, Kailash called his secretary, 'Aparna, can you get me Chetan urgently.' The phone in his room beeped. 'Kailash, Chetan Bindra's secretary on the line.'

'Good morning, Margaret from Chetan Bindra's office,' came an anglicised Indian voice from the other end of the line.

'Margaret, can I speak to Chetan Bindra?' Chetan was the current Head of Retail Bank for NYB for the international markets—that is, all countries except the US.

'Hey Kailash. How are you, old man?' It was Chetan Bindra, in his usual high-energy tone. Chetan had joined the group twelve years ago as the marketing head for India, and now he was the king of retail bank across the globe for NYB. His rise had been spectacular.

'Good evening... I'm sorry, good morning Chetan,' said a nervous Kailash, mixing up the time zones.

'I just had a word with Sundeep and have told him that he must bail out and take the first job we are able to get him overseas. This will divert a fair bit of attention from the core issue.'

'I feel sorry for him. He is a bit like me in his approach. I see myself in Sundeep. I like him,' said Chetan, 'It's a bit unfortunate that he got caught in this controversy.'

'He is a great talent and a good leader, but he lacks controls, Chetan. I have counselled him on a number of occasions to be careful and discreet.'

'Good.'

'Chetan, the purpose of my call was to discuss about who we should bring to replace Sundeep.'

'What's the doubt? You clearly need to bring in a mature guy like Swami.'

'But Chetan, he is not a great leader. He doesn't know how to keep his people happy. He cannot run at the same pace.'

'Kailash, you have seen the problems you have to deal with if you run with a guy like Sundeep. I would rather take a balanced approach rather than a cowboy approach. This time we were fortunate to have escaped. Our stock price didn't get impacted. But we might not be so lucky next time around. Our stocks will take a pounding and the loss in market capitalisation will be far more than the miniscule gains we will make in India. Not worth the risk, my friend. Get Swami. He has run operations in the BPO. Is process oriented. Has migrated process from overseas to the BPO. Knows how we as a bank operate in other countries and is very high on integrity. And most importantly, he was the one who launched retail bank in India.'

'OK Chetan. I will communicate accordingly. But what about Sundeep. Where will he go? He was telling me about a position in UK with Martin Sanders, as Head of Retail for UK.'

'Oh, of course. How could I miss it? I am okay giving that role to Sundeep. It is a big role. The business in UK has stagnated for the last three years. Sundeep will be able to kick start it. That business has the potential to become one of our largest businesses. I will speak to Martin. You go ahead and commit the role to Sundeep.'

'Thanks, Chetan.'

'Aparna,' screamed Kailash. She came in running. 'Can you get me Swami?'

'Sure, Kailash.'

'No. Don't connect him to me. Ask him to see me tomorrow morning at nine. I want to meet him in person.'

71

Between that night and the next morning, two big deals were closed. Sundeep was to move to UK as Head of Retail Banking and Swaminathan was to become the next Head of Retail Bank for India.

Despite the screw up, Sundeep was saved the ignominy of an ouster from the bank.

When Swami came out of Kailash's room, he called his mother. 'Amma, I have made your dream come true. I have today become the Head of Retail Bank for one of the biggest banks in the world.' His mother was in tears. She decided to go to the temple of the family deity and do an *Abhishekam*, a traditional bath given to the lord by the devotees.

When Kalpana heard about this, she didn't know how to react. She knew how bad Swami had felt when he had to report to Sundeep. She also knew how Swami had felt like quitting when he was shunted out to BOCA. She had been his source of support and motivation. She just hugged him and wept. She was very happy for him. Life had come a full circle for him.

Sundeep had to move to UK in a few days' time and so he could not give a complete handover to Swami. He was under such a pressure to move quickly that his team could not even give him a farewell.

The first thing Swami did on taking over was to make sure that the business numbers didn't go down. Recovering from a downward slide was more difficult than recovering from a growth trajectory.

He hit the road and went to every branch and reassured every employee that all was well. He reiterated the importance of training, compliance, and doing business the right way. There was a stretch when he visited eleven cities in six days and held town-halls in every one of them. All employees of the bank attended these town-halls. The passion with which he delivered the speeches in these town-halls was very unlike Swami.

He took a very smart step. He roped in Aditya as a consultant for the bank. Aditya too was glad to be of help. He wanted to set everything right in a business they had started from the scratch.

Swami realised that Sundeep was only a people's guy. He had not gone into the nitty-gritty of the entire business. He now started asking tough questions from his team. Every cost was questioned. Non-compliance became a bad word. People were running scared of doing anything unethical. Swami would hound them.

The rampant frauds in Ram Naresh's unit were dealt with very strongly. With one crack of the whip. Swami made Akshay Bhalla fire a team of over 125 people from Naresh's team, as they were suspected of rigging personal loan files to make them fit for approval.

Naresh called Kailash to crib about Swami, but Kailash couldn't do anything about it. He tried talking to Swami, but Swami was like a man possessed. Kailash decided to lay off. On matters of integrity it was always safe to side with the person who has an honest reputation.

Time flew. People forgot about the whole mutual fund debacle. Swami became a hero once again. He had two successes in a row—the BOCA turnaround, followed by the retail bank success. He had shown that to be a leader you don't have to be flamboyant or sexy. You have to honestly apply your mind.

72

One thing happened before Sundeep left for his new assignment. Something that Sundeep hadn't imagined would happen.

That night when Sundeep, after his morning discussion with Kailash, had refused to take Karuna's call repeatedly, Karuna had something very important to tell him.

She would have called him at least twenty-five times. His phone was switched off. 'Who is he sleeping with now?' she had thought in desperation. She called the landline at home and Sundeep had picked up. She was a bit relieved that he was not sleeping around with anyone in Mumbai.

The previous day when Sundeep was in office, Karuna had walked into his cabin. Sundeep was looking very irritated and had walked off with Anindyo for lunch. They had stepped out to the Café Coffee Day outlet, just opposite their large HQ for a sandwich. He had forgotten his mobile behind.

The moment Sundeep stepped into the lift, his mobile started ringing. Karuna heard it ring and picked up the phone. She looked at the screen and saw the number flashing. She did not know whose number it was. She let it ring for a while. She was not sure whether to pick it up or not. Finally she decided to pick it up. The moment she picked it up, she heard a woman's seductive voice, 'Hi honey, I am back in Delhi. *Kab aa rahe ho?*' Karuna hung up. The phone rang again. It was from the same number. She put the phone on silent. Reena was typing something for Sundeep's visa in her cubicle outside Sundeep's room. Karuna quietly pocketed the phone and walked out.

She had to go to some place where no one would see her. The rest room! Yes, the toilet was the best bet. She walked straight to the toilet and locked herself in. Then she opened her purse and took out her own mobile. She retrieved the number of the last received call from the call log on Sundeep's phone. Then she keyed in the same number in her mobile phone and pressed the dial key.

Now, if the number you are dialling is already stored on your mobile, the person's name appears on the screen when you press dial. The screen on the mobile blinked and a name flashed on the screen. It was someone she knew. Her jaws dropped and eyes popped out. The name on the screen was 'Nidhi Agarwal - Delhi.' Now it became very clear to her. The person on the phone was Nidhi Agarwal! Sundeep had recently changed his phone and hence all the names were not keyed into his phone memory. That's why his phone didn't display Nidhi's name when she called. She went into Sundeep's messages and read all his sent messages. There were messages sent to Nidhi in Delhi, Priya from BOCA in Mumbai, someone called Kalpana, and, of course, to her.

Was this Kalpana Swami's wife? For a minute she thought anything was possible, but on closer examination she realised it was some other Kalpana.

All almost at the same time. At times even the same message had been sent to multiple people. She was almost about to break down when the main door of the bathroom opened and someone came in. She flushed and came out quickly. She had to keep the phone back before Sundeep returned from his lunch.

She quietly walked into Sundeep's room along with a few papers, kept the phone on his table, and walked out before Reena could realise what was going on.

That night she had rung him at home to confront him. But Sundeep had refused to pick up his phone and had disconnected. She was very upset, but had felt utterly helpless to do anything.

73

Chetan Bindra moved on to replace the Worldwide Head of Retail Bank. It was a very big move for him, reporting directly to Tedd Bridge, the CEO. He was very excited. The job he was currently doing came up for grabs. Chetan was clear. He wanted an Indian to do the job, probably a reflection of his nationalist sentiment. The good thing about NYB was that there were many Indians in senior positions, and they would help fellow Indians get larger roles, because they genuinely felt that Indians were better and intellectually brighter than most of the other people in the world. And, most importantly,

Indians were a loyal breed, who would slog their butts out if you did them a favour.

But there was no one across the globe who could fill in such a big role. He split up his job into two: Managing Director-Retail Banking (Emerging Markets) and Managing Director-Retail Banking (Rest of International). The former's brief was to cover the emerging economies like India, Brazil and China, and the latter's to manage all the developed economies except USA.

He decided to move Sundeep to New York and give him one of the roles. At that time Sundeep was based in London. He was also very impressed by Swami. The way Swami turned around the India retail bank business stood him in good stead. He settled on Swami for the second role. Kailash Advani was asked to sound out Swami about the role.

'I do not think I would be keen to move out of the country at this time,' Swami had responded. His mother was growing old. She refused to move out of the country, and, for Swami, moving back to New York would have meant moving away from her again. He did not want to do this to someone who had struggled all her life to make him successful. He let the opportunity pass.

For Sundeep, this was a big break. He had expected the India incident to wreck his career, but it seemed to have worked well for him. He jumped at the opportunity and grabbed it with both hands.

Sundeep moved to New York as Managing Director of Retail (Emerging Markets). His family relocated to America almost at the same time.

74
New York

From the corner of his eyes, Sundeep looked at the trophies that adorned his cabinet. Louisa walked in with a few e-mail print outs and left them on the table.

Swami's and Sundeep's careers had been neck to neck till this very moment. 'Had Swami accepted Chetan Bindra's offer, he would have been sitting in the cabin next door,' thought Sundeep. When he looked back at it, Sundeep felt that he had more regrets about his career as compared to Swami, who seemed to be more at peace with himself.

If God gave him a chance to be a banker again, he would prefer to live Swami's life rather than his own. Swami also had Kalpana, whom Sundeep so desperately wanted. He would have then had a friend like Aditya, who stood with Swami through the thick and thin and helped him sail through bad times.

He was sitting on his table, head between his hands, staring at the carpet below. He did not know what to do.

75

The year 2005 was a great year in the history of NYB in India. NYB reclaimed its position as the leading foreign bank in India, a position it had lost in the aftermath of the mutual fund debacle. Swami was on cloud nine. The entire success was being credited to him. He was now hailed as a visionary, a balanced business builder, an honest professional with great values. He was seen as a role model for the burgeoning middle class. Stories of how Swami, a regular middle class guy from Chennai, went on to head the retail business of the largest foreign bank in India made folk lore. He would be invited to all the financial services awards ceremonies. Customers who had left NYB in the wake of the mutual funds scam, returned to the bank. Assets grew, deposits grew, and so did profits.

Swami became very people oriented. He started getting involved in everything that concerned his people. He worked with his team on resolving issues, encouraged collaboration among his team members, frowned at distracting organisational politics, and rewarded hard work and effort, even if they did not bring in the desired results.

In all this, Kalpana was a major source of support for him. In her role as an HR compliance officer, she helped Swami put together the compliance hotline service for all staff. Swami used it to cleanse his system. A compliance hotline was nothing but a toll-free telephone line with a recorder at the other end. The number of this telephone was widely publicised among the employee community. Anyone who found anything fishy taking place in the system could call on this line and complain. A process was put in place so that all these queries would be looked at and addressed at a senior level.

Swami never killed the messenger. He never went looking for good news. His philosophy was that good news travels to you, even if you do not ask around. It is the bad news that one has to hunt for, as it hides below files and paper. Swami diligently went about finding the bad news and fixing things.

Once NYB employees started trusting the system, they began to come out in the open. Swami had tremendous faith in this system and ownership of the process at the top helped. He would seriously monitor each and every complaint that came in.

Aditya was Swami's aide. Swami would bounce all his ideas off Aditya before he implemented them.

A key focus area for Swami was cost control. His past experience also helped him here. He started doing away with the business intermediaries. He had spent enough time in BOCA to know that scale in outsourcing always helps. He set up his own telecalling team in BOCA rather than rely on what was left of Naresh's call centre. He also set up an in-house sales channel which was more productive and hence cost effective as compared to a DSA outfit.

He dramatically cut down the payments made to the Nareshs of the world. When they came complaining, he categorically told them that the bank could not afford anything more than what was being offered and that it was up to them to either take it or leave it. Naresh was very upset. He complained to Kailash. But even Kailash, who was now close to retirement, told him there was little he could do to help him. This was the first time in over a decade that even Naresh was helpless.

NYB had a very efficient system of global audit. This audit would grade countries by effectiveness of control, adherence to policy, and efficiency of operation. Basing on the above three gradings, countries would be classified into low, medium and high risk categories. The global audit team would audit the high-risk countries once a year, and the medium risk countries would be subject to audit once in two years.

After the mutual fund fraud, the rating of the India business was changed to high risk and towards the later half of 2005, the global audit team decided to visit India.

Global audit was a very serious exercise, which was at times career threatening. There had been instances in the past in which a poor global audit had led to shutting down of businesses or sent high-flying careers tumbling down. Everyone, including Swami, was paranoid about the consequences of a poor global audit.

Around the same time Mona Albance, a member of the Global HR team, was expected to visit India for a week. She was in charge of diversity and work environment.

76

Ekta was one of the senior most female employees of NYB and was the Head of Training for India. As Swami would be tied up with preparations for the global audit, he requested her to manage Mona's visit.

Preparations for the audit had begun in earnest, over a month before the team actually landed. Though Kailash was not too concerned about NYB clearing the audit, Swami was not taking any chances, the perfectionist that he was. Although the preparedness, the controls, and the basic banking discipline had improved since Swami took over the reigns, there was always work to be done till the last day.

All critical areas were checked, documents revisited, key files eyeballed again, and any shortfalls taken care of. All processes were critically re-examined for compliance with regulatory requirements. Nearly half the bank was working on getting in shape for the audit. 'You can always make up for lost business, but can never make up for a screwed up audit,' Swami had once said.

Ekta had handled many visitors from the group, but she was a bit foxed on how to handle Mona. Mona hadn't given her a brief on what she wanted to achieve in those five days. How long can you spend on diversity related issues? At most you could give her a diversity-related presentation for a few hours and sit through a couple of meetings. But, five full days on diversity-related issues was a bit too much. Ekta had no clue. She did, however, line up a five-day agenda for her and sent it to Swami. Swami sent it to Mona without giving it a second glance. He was too preoccupied with audit-related issues.

The agenda read as follows:

Day 1 Monday
9.00 a.m. Pick up from the hotel by Ekta and drive to NYB HO
10.00 to 1.30 Meeting with Swami and introduction to the senior management team
12.00 to 1.00 Meeting with HR Head (Abhinav Mookherjee)
1.00 to 2.30 Lunch with Ekta and the training team
2.30 to 3.30 Free time to catch up on e-mails
3.30 to 5.30 Talent management update

Day 2 Tuesday
9.30 to 12.30 Meeting with HR Managers of other financial institutions, followed by lunch
3.00 to 5.00 Review of recruitment policy, equal opportunity employer
5.00 to 6.00 Discussion with Swami

Day 3 Wednesday
Day visit to Agra, see Taj Mahal

Day 4 Thursday
9.00 a.m. Drive to South Mumbai branch, interact with the branch team

12.45 p.m. Lunch with South Mumbai branch team
2.30 Drive back to the HO with Manager-Women's Accounts
3.30 to 5.00 Meeting with Vivek J and Akshay Bhalla to understand their business needs
7.30 Dinner with key women executives of the bank

Day 5 Friday
Morning-Meeting with three women executives of the bank
Lunch with Swami at Taj Lands End
Wrap up and free time
7.30 p.m. Drive to the airport with Ekta

Mona Albance landed in India three days before the audit was supposed to begin. As her flight taxied into Terminal A of the international airport, she took a deep sigh. She had come here on a mission. No one in the India team was aware of her mission. Actually, not many people anywhere knew anything about it. This was her first visit to India, and not many from the India management team had ever met her. The impending audit had ensured that her visit kept a low profile. She reached the hotel well past midnight. The jetlag didn't let her sleep.

Monday morning, when Ekta went to pick her up from the hotel, she was surprised. She was expecting a fifty-year-old woman. On the contrary, she found Mona to be a young and attractive woman in her mid-thirties.

As they drove in Ekta's Merc to the head office of the bank in Bandra Kurla Complex, Mona was a little taken aback by the obvious poverty on street display. The south Mumbai hotel where Mona was staying seemed to be an upmarket location lined with high-rises, sprinkled with buildings with a colonial architecture. On her way to the hotel last night, she had seen a number of slum dwellers sleeping on the pavement.

'How come there is so much disparity in the lifestyles of people?' she asked.

The Indian corporates are always ready for these usual questions from visiting foreign dignitaries. Ekta gave her a prepared speech on population growth, lack of infrastructure, India's GDP, its purchasing power parity and so on. Mona wasn't satisfied, but she didn't want to embarrass Ekta and kept quiet.

They reached the HO fifteen minutes late. Swami was waiting for her in his room.

'Welcome Ms Albance, it's a pleasure to have you with us.'

'Pleasure is mine, Swami.'

'Hope you had a comfortable flight to Mumbai. Was it on time?'

'Oh yeah. BA is normally on time.'

'And the hotel? Hope your room is comfortable too.'

'Thanks for asking, Swami. Yes, it was very comfortable.'

The pleasantries went on for a few more minutes, after which Swami's management committee also joined in.

Mona seemed quite happy to meet Swami and his team. 'Is this the team which worked with Sundeep too?' she asked.

'Part of this team also worked with Sundeep,' said Swami.

Mona did notice the squirming at the mention of Sundeep's name. Was 'Sundeep' a dirty word? She didn't know.

After a round of basic introductions, Swami gave her a small docket.

'Mona, this is the itinerary that Ekta has drawn up for you. We had e-mailed it to you earlier. We have covered all that we thought would be relevant to you and where we would need your support. It will also help you spend your time here effectively. Do let us know in case you want to cover anything more and we will be happy to provide you with all the inputs that you may need.'

She opened the docket and quickly glanced through the agenda.

'Thanks Swami. This looks fairly extensive. I just have one comment. I pretty much know what I need to do in these five days. I do not want anyone to baby sit me or manage me. I will pretty much manage on my own. I might need some support in these five days. It would be nice if you could assign someone to work with me while I am here.'

'We have assigned Ekta to take care of all your needs. She will be with you for the next five days.'

'Swami, I drove in with Ekta this morning. She is a wonderful woman. I need someone junior, someone who can take calls, call in people, draw up notes, etc. I don't think it is right nor is it possible for Ekta to do all this. I need someone junior.'

'Sure. If you could share the agenda with us, we will be able to streamline things.'

'I will let you know as we go along. It will help if we identify some support staff quickly.'

Swami looked at Ekta. 'Karuna? Do you think she would be able to work with Mona.'

'Not a bad idea. Let me check if she is around.'

Once Ekta came back with Karuna, Swami stepped in. 'Ekta, why don't you take Mona to meet Abhinav, by which time I will brief Karuna. You guys are already ten minutes behind schedule.'

'Thanks, that will not be required, Swami. I will brief Karuna myself,' Mona interjected. She didn't want to give anyone any time to react or over-manage issues when she was there.

Swami was a little hurt, more by the manner in which she spoke rather than what she said. He didn't like the arrogance in her tone. 'Fine,' he said, shrugging his shoulders. 'American!' he thought as she left his room.

Mona walked down the corridor to Ekta's cabin. Coffee was served on the table.

'Mona, I do not know why you reacted the way you did, but Swami is not the kind who will mislead you on anything. He is the most upright banker I have ever seen. I have no clue what was going through your mind, but your manner of speaking was very insulting, specially to someone who was looking forward to your visit. And, more importantly, it's inappropriate to talk like that to a country Retail Business Head.' Ekta's pride was also hurt a bit when she heard that conversation.

'I am sorry, Ekta. I will also apologise to Swami if you feel that it has not gone down well. My intent was to drive home a no-nonsense message to his direct reports. From the looks of it, I have managed to do so.'

'You seem to have come with an agenda. What is it?' Ekta was getting more and more curious by the minute. This was not the way normal overseas visitors would behave.

'I have five days to go, Ekta, and you want to know everything on the first day itself?' And both of them laughed.

'We are getting late for the meeting with Abhinav Mookherjee. Let's go.'

'Sure.'

On the way Mona gave instructions to Ekta for the remaining days of the visit. 'Please cancel all internal meetings. I will let you know who all I want to meet. I will keep all external appointments already fixed. It will be an embarrassment for the bank if we cancel them.'

Ekta nodded.

The meeting with Abhinav Mookherjee was a very pleasant one, but lasted only fifteen minutes. Abhinav had prepared a stand-up presentation for her. She politely thanked him and requested for a print-out of that. She said she would go through the print-out and get back to him in case she had any questions.

On the way out, she looked at Abhinav and said, 'Mr Mookherjee, I will be needing lots of information. I will give the list to Ekta. It would be nice if you could get someone to generate all the data and give me the information within twelve hours.

'Sure Mona,' said Abhinav. The moment she left his room, he dialled Swami.

'Give her anything she wants,' said Swami, 'and make sure that you give it to her on time. She is here only for five days. I don't want her to go back with a feeling that we have denied her anything she wanted.' Swami had nothing to hide.

Mona opened her briefcase and took out a sheet of paper for Ekta. The paper listed out everything that she wanted. Ekta was wondering what Mona was up to. She didn't know and Mona was not telling.

Ekta gave Mona's list to Karuna.

'Karuna, will you please speak to Abhinav and get this data organised quickly.'

Karuna glanced at the list:

1. List of all women employees in the organisation with name, date of birth, date of joining, background, designation and salary;

2. List of all women employees who have been promoted in the last three years;
3. List of salary hikes given to women employees in the last three years;
4. Names of women employees who have resigned in the last three years;
5. Performance appraisal reports of all women employees for the last three years;
6. List of women who have moved into Head Office in the last three years;
7. Gender mix, unit wise, in the last three years;
8. Compliance hotline complaints for the last three years;
9. List of all bank employed drivers (both on rolls and contractual) for senior management along with their phone numbers...

Besides the above, there were seven other heads under which Mona wanted information. The gossip was that she was a member of the Tedd Bridge coterie, and so no one screwed around with her. She always got what she wanted.

'Why last three years?' Karuna wondered. 'Maybe the last audit happened three years ago,' she told herself as she walked into Abhinav's room.

Ten minutes later she was back in Ekta's room. She looked at Mona and said, 'Abhinav said that he would be able to give you all the required information by this evening, except for the performance appraisal reports. That he would be able to get only by tomorrow night. They are stored at an offsite location and it will take some time to get them photocopied and brought here. Will that be fine?'

'Where is the storage for the bank?'

'In Thane. It is about an hour's drive from where we are.'

'Then tell him not to worry about photocopying them. I will go to the storage tomorrow evening and see the reports there. I don't need to see all of them. I might actually end up seeing only a few of them. Just get me the individual performance ratings by tonight.'

'I think that should be doable,' said Ekta.

'The first lot of data should be in by the time you head back after your lunch with Ekta,' Karuna told Mona.

'Ekta, are you fine if I also invite a couple of guys from Swami's team for lunch? I would like to spend some time with them too.'

Lunch was at the Grand Hyatt hotel, which was just two blocks away. Reena had reserved a poolside table for them. It was a quarter to one and the restaurant had just started filling in. In fact, they were the first ones to walk in for lunch.

'So Akshay, I am told that the mortgage business in India is booming.'

'Yes Mona, the housing industry boom in India is just about taking off. There is expected to be an unfulfilled demand for housing to the extent of twenty million units by 2010. Prices are expected to go up and so will the demand. This will translate to increase in credit. Mortgage is expected to drive the growth of retail credit in India.'

'That's great. India is an exciting market. I am glad I got an opportunity to come to India. Have you all ever been to the States?'

'What does she think? We all are suckers, who have been cocooned in our own country? Bloody descendants of Christopher Columbus who set out in boats fitted with ancient fishing nets, to fish and eat when food runs out? Got marooned in America, when they set out to find India!' thought Akshay, but he didn't say that. 'Of course. We have had the privilege of visiting the US a few times. It's indeed a wonderful country.' Now he was truly behaving like a sucker.

This discussion lasted for over an hour. Then Mona asked Ekta, 'How do you feel working with these guys? I mean do you ever feel threatened, intimidated by these guys.'

'No. Not at all. Akshay's a sweetheart and Vivek is a gem,' said Ekta. 'But why do you ask?'

'You have been very quiet throughout this lunch. That got me wondering.' Mona grinned.

Ekta knew that she was lying. There was something she was up to and she was not telling. She knew that her question was a loaded one. There was something more to it than general curiosity. What did the next five days have in store for all of them?

As committed, the data was waiting when they returned from lunch.

The gender mix in the Indian operations of New York International Bank was very good. About thirty-two percent of its employees across all businesses were women. That compared very well with New York International Bank's global average of 24.6 percent. This ratio dropped dramatically at senior levels where only eight percent of the India leadership team and their direct reports were women. A large population of women worked in BOCA and in the Branches. Indian women seemed to love the service sector.

'Do women normally prefer softer jobs in India?' She looked at Karuna.

'Pardon me.' Karuna didn't understand the question.

'I do not see too many women working in cards sales, asset sales, front line jobs, leadership positions, etc. Is it a cultural issue in India or does it reflect on the approach that we as a bank have?'

'I guess it's more cultural. Women in India normally prefer desk jobs. They at times lack the opportunity and the drive to go ahead in their careers. Family pressures, an archaic male dominated society lead to a number of women giving up their careers for the sake of their families. But all that is changing now. We have role models in people like Naina Lal Kidwai.'

'Yes, I have heard about her.'

'She is the CEO of HSBC in India and is also on the global board of Nestle. One of the fifty most powerful women in the corporate world globally. Wish she was working with us and not with competition. You have a number of women rising to the forefront. They have learnt to manage the travails of a corporate life along with their families. They still have to face a lot of challenges at the workplace, but things are improving,' Karuna continued.

'What kind of challenges?' Mona was enjoying this discussion. This was the kind of discussion that would normally lead to exposures.

'India is an evolving society. It is a culture where brazen adaptation of the Wild West is looked down upon. Women are still expected to get married early and raise a family. Men and women are not equal. Why outside, within our organisation, do we treat men and women as equals? We don't.'

'But we intend to,' said Mona.

'So many times women lose out on senior positions because someone senior says, "Forget it, she is married and she will not be able to give it her best." Or "She will not be able to travel to the extent we want her to and so she will not be able to deliver." We have created a glass ceiling that is very difficult for any woman to break out of. How many women are there in our own management committee? Have we checked how much time it takes for a male to get there and how much time it takes for a woman with equal capability to get there? Women normally compromise and keep quiet, because if they make a noise, it may adversely impact them.'

'You seem to feel very, very strongly about it. Have you been wronged ever in this organisation personally?'

'No. No... Not at all,' she said, trying not to look at Mona.

Mona didn't push it. She didn't want to make it uncomfortable for Karuna. But Mona could guess something was wrong.

She went back to her data to begin her analysis.

'Karuna,' she called out after some time. 'What are you doing tonight? Free for dinner?'

'I have a nine-month-old baby. Don't have help at home. Don't think I will be able to come.'

'Not a problem, Karuna.'

'Hold on, I have a solution. The hotel where you are staying is very close to my house. Why don't you come home for dinner? I will ask Nitin to pick you up.'

'Nitin?'

'Oh. Forgot to tell you. Nitin is my husband. He also works for this bank. He heads personal loans for western India. Just got moved up recently.'

'That's great. I'll see you tonight then. I normally hit the bed early. Hence a dinner at seven-thirty or thereabouts would be great.'

'Sure, Mona. I will check with Nitin if he's free to pick you up. Else I'll give directions to your driver and he will bring you there.'

'See you at seven-thirty.'

The rest of the day was uneventful. Mona spent most of her time closeted in her room, analysing the data that had been provided to her. The India management had been quite cooperative and had given her whatever she had wanted.

Towards the end of the day she walked into Swami's office. 'Swami, I am sorry about this morning. I was probably a bit curt and rude. I shouldn't have been. Actually most of the work I do is so negative that a bit of it rubs off on my normal behaviour as well. One starts suspecting each and every individual. I am really sorry.'

'You are embarrassing me, Ms Albance.' Swami was indeed embarrassed.

'I have heard so much about you from Chetan Bindra. I was actually looking forward to meeting you, Swami.'

At that precise moment, Kalpana walked in.

'Come Kalpana, let me introduce you to Mona.'

'Of course, I know Mona. We have met when I was working for the New York HR compliance team. You ran the company that carried out various employee vigilance activities for us.'

'Oh my god, yes. How nice to see you again!'

'I knew someone was coming to India from the New York team, but I didn't know it was you.' Swami and Kalpana rarely discussed work at home and hence Kalpana didn't really know who was coming.

'And what on earth made you to shift from New York to Mumbai?'

'Well, this gentleman in front of you. He moved to India and I had to shift with him... given that I am married to him.' Kalpana's radiant smile flashed on her face.

'How nice! I didn't know of this connection. How does it feel to be husband and wife working in the same organisation?'

'Not great. But with him around as Head of Retail Bank, no one else will hire me. I have seen Swami running around in circles, trying his best to accommodate an extremely good and efficient person whose spouse left us to join at a senior position in ABN AMRO. Not everyone will be so accommodative. You know, Mona, I quit the bank over ten years ago when we got married, because I didn't want the two of us to work in the same organisation. But now, I have joined back. Thank god, we have a rule which states that related people can't report to each other. Otherwise, imagine, he would be my boss in office too,' joked Kalpana. All three had a hearty laugh at this. Mona now felt a lot more comfortable with both Swami and Kalpana.

'Kalpana, why don't you join me for dinner tonight? Karuna has called me for dinner. You also join me. I am told the place is close to the hotel where I stay. If it is convenient to you, that is,' she said looking at Kalpana. 'But, Swami, you stay out of this.'

Kalpana looked at Swami first, then at Mona, and nodded her head.

'Great, then we will leave from here at around half past six,' said Mona as she walked out of the room.

'Sweet girl,' said Kalpana looking at Swami.

'I am a bit worried. Just be careful about what you tell her,' said Swami.

77

The doorbell at Karuna's house rang at 7.30 p.m. Mona walked in with a nice little bouquet of flowers. Karuna was surprised to see Kalpana with her. Ekta was already there waiting for them in the living room.

Karuna had invited people from various units of the bank. There were a few people each from the branch banking side, the assets side and the customer service side, and some from BOCA as well. There were about twenty people in her small, warm, tastefully-done house.

The living room was a wee bit tiny for so many people. Mona didn't mind it though. The powerful AC in the corner of the room made it less stuffy.

Mona met Nitin, who seemed to be a nice young lad. He seemed energetic and capable. 'Nice couple,' she thought when she saw Nitin and Karuna together.

The food was good. It was a mix of continental and Indian fare. Ekta had told Karuna to get the best food and not to worry about the expenses as the bank would pick up the tab.

Mona also noticed that Kalpana was very gentle and nice with everyone. She mixed around well without really throwing her weight around. She had no airs about being the wife of the Head of Retail Banking. People were not running away from her. In all, a balanced personality.

When they were all sitting around after dinner Mona suddenly announced: 'We will now play a quick game.' The room went quiet.

'I will give you two minutes before we start. Go get your next round of refills, bio breaks, anything you want, before we begin. The game goes as follows. Starting with Nitin, I will ask everyone one question. The question may or may not be different from what I have asked anyone earlier. You will in one word, I repeat, in one word, give me an answer. If you use more than one word, you will be out of the game. If you do not answer in five seconds, you will be disqualified. Do not bluff, because I reserve the right to ask you to elaborate why you chose the word that you uttered. So two minutes from now we start this game.'

No one moved.

'Okay, here we go. Nitin, what's the best thing you like about your wife?'

'Eyes.'

'Ooooohh...' A moan went round the room and Karuna blushed.

'Kalpana. Your question. What do you find in Swami that you don't find in men around?'

'Honesty.'

A round of applause, and Kalpana felt proud that she was married to such a man. She coyly smiled when she remembered how she had proposed to him on the beach and how clumsily he had behaved.

'Ekta, your question now. What do you hate in your husband?'

'Pony-tail,' and everyone burst out laughing.

'Priya, your turn. One word which would describe how the bank has changed in the past two years.'

'Safer.'

There was silence. For a moment even Mona was quiet. She didn't know how to react.

'Arvind, you are next. Why did you join NYB?'

'Money.'

'Romil, what will make you leave your wife?'

'You.'

'Ooooooooh...' The room went in raptures again. Romil was the head of collections for NYB. Collecting from delinquent customers makes you a tough guy. This hint of romanticism was something one would never have expected from Romil.

'Well said.' Mona was also beginning to enjoy this visit.

This went on for another twenty minutes before she decided to call it quits. It was already approaching ten, well past her bedtime. It was a fifteen-minute drive through the streets of Mumbai before she could get into bed.

She had enjoyed the evening thoroughly, but one thing was bothering her. Normally in other countries wherever she had used this Quick Answer Game, or QAG as it was called, she had got very innovative answers. For 'what has changed in the bank in the last two years,' she would get words like aggressive, hunger, drive, motivation, empathy, perception, pay, etc. Never had she got 'SAFER' as an answer.

QAG normally reflected the mindset of the individual. Given that people did not have time to react, the answers were normally top of mind, and hence most people would subconsciously answer what they felt most strongly about. Five seconds was not time enough for people to cook up their response, and so, unless they were masters at the art of deception, people would not lie.

Priya must have meant that the bank had become a safer workplace in the last two years. Did it mean that two years back the bank was an unsafe place? Mona didn't know. She was too tired by the time she reached the hotel. She went off to sleep the moment she hit the bed.

78

The next day Mona was supposed to meet the HR representatives of other banks. The meeting was to extend till lunch. Karuna had picked up Mona from the hotel to take her to the meeting. As Ekta was travelling, it was just the two of them.

'Karuna, who was that girl Priya I met yesterday at your place?'

'Oh, Priya. She is a good friend of mine. She is a part of BOCA, the BPO that we acquired. Her story is a bit tragic.'

'Why, what happened? She seemed to be a sweet girl.'

'She got married only two years ago and is now divorced. Her husband works in the bank. In branch banking. He is a cluster manager. Manages three branches in Mumbai. They made a nice pair. Even their careers were going great guns, and then suddenly one day she comes and drops this bombshell. Don't know what went wrong with them,' said Karuna.

They reached the hotel, where the HR heads of all the foreign banks and a few BPOs were waiting for them. Ekta had lined up this meeting for Mona, for her to get a perspective of women working in banks and BPOs, and the challenges they face. They moved to the conference room, which had been blocked for this meeting. The discussion centred on how to make banks a better place for women to work in. How to provide them with essential services so that they don't feel the stress? What do women look for at their workplace?

It was a good discussion and by the end of it, Mona had accumulated enough knowledge about the Indian work environment from the point of view of women. She could now write a book on it.

On the way back, she again tried asking Karuna about Priya. But Karuna couldn't say much. That afternoon Mona sat down with the list of women who had been promoted in the last two years. She went through it name by name. Her eyebrows, which were fairly static all along, went up as she read one name there: Priya Mehra. Priya had been promoted twice in the last two years. Something which was not too common in NYB. She decided to meet Priya separately.

She went through the balance list and came across seven names whose cases she wanted to investigate further. She handed the list to Karuna.

'Can you ask Abhinav to get the appraisal documents for these seven employees to be faxed to our office here? I will not be heading to the storage this evening.'

'Sure.'

'And also ask Priya to meet me at two this afternoon.'

'What should I tell her if she asks me why?'

'Never mind that. I will tell her. You just ask her to come and see me.'

Priya was slightly nervous when Karuna told her about Mona wanting to meet her, but she didn't have much of a choice.

That afternoon, Priya knocked very nervously on the glass door of the room that Mona was using. Mona looked up from her laptop, smiled, and got up from her chair.

'Come in, Priya. It's excellent to see you again.'

'Oh, thank you, maam.'

'Mona. Call me Mona. And by the way, you were looking gorgeous yesterday,' she said, trying to put Priya at ease.

'Is there a coffee shop close by, Priya? I am missing my daily dose of Starbucks caffeine.'

'Yes, Mona. There is one outlet of Café Coffee Day, the Indian Starbucks, just a five-minute walk away.'

'Why don't we go there and chat? That is, if you are fine with it.'

'Perfectly fine, maam,' said Priya.

'Give me five minutes. I just need to send this mail in a hurry. We can leave immediately after.'

In five minutes both of them were walking briskly towards the nearest outlet of Café Coffee Day, unwary of the summer heat. 'Mona is quite a sport,' thought Priya.

At the coffee shop, Mona ordered a Cappuccino and Priya asked for a cold coffee. They settled down at a table in the corner. The coffee shop was not too crowded as it was lunchtime and not many Indians like to have coffee at that hour. There weren't many people who could overhear their conversation.

It took them over an hour and a half and a few glares from the coffee shop executives, before they decided it was time to leave. They walked back to their office.

'It was a long discussion. What did she want to know about?' Karuna asked her when Priya was out of hearing distance of Mona.

'Well, nothing much. She wanted to know what should the organisation do to make this place more attractive for women to work here. She was enquiring about what other organisations in India do in this regard.'

That evening Karuna offered to drive back Mona to her hotel. On the way Mona asked her about her relationship with Nitin. She was testing the Indian family fabric. From the discussion, Mona could make out that Karuna was extremely fond of Nitin and her kid. They were her family and she had no qualms about throwing away her budding career for the cause of her family. Hats off to Indian women, she thought as she entered her room and switched on the lights.

The next day at work was a little different. When Karuna came in, Mona asked her for a telephone with an interstate dialling service.

'Karuna, you be at ease. I will call you in case I need anything. I guess, I will be able to manage pretty much on my own today.'

She called up a few people from the list of those who had quit NYB and moved on, a list that HR had provided. She focused on those who had got a promotion and then quickly moved.

She called seventeen people. All through this, she kept taking serious notes in her diary. By the time she was through with her calls, it was three in the afternoon. She had an evening dinner which Swami and Kalpana had planned for her at their residence. She had lots to finish before that. She thought about it and immediately left for the Bandra branch. She had an appointment with the cluster manager.

Everyone in NYB was wondering what she was up to.

Swami hadn't called many people for dinner. It was only Swami, Kalpana, Aditya and Mona. The latter two hit it off very well.

Swami was a man of simple tastes. His house was done tastefully, and not extravagantly. No expensive furniture for him. Everything was purely functional.

Aditya knew a number of people who worked with Mona, and that was a good starting point. Mona took pains to explain how she was in love with India and that it is a great country with great people.

'She must be giving this speech in every country she goes to,' thought Aditya.

After a long time, Mona had attended a party at a residence of someone senior in the bank, where no liquor was served. Swami never felt the need to indulge himself or others to move ahead. He had stuck to his principles and this was something that even Mona had come to appreciate over the past few days. She had started admiring Swami and Kalpana.

'Swami, I am cutting short my visit by one day.' She took Swami by surprise. 'I will be leaving tomorrow night.'

'Why is that? Are my people not taking good care of you?'

'No Swami, that's not the reason,' said Mona, 'the work that I came here for is more or less done. I just need to go back and complete what I had set out to achieve.'

'And what is that?' It was Aditya this time.

'You will get to know soon,' she said and smiled.

After dinner, Kalpana brought out a nice piece of Bidri work which she had bought that morning for Mona. Mona was moved by the love and affection showered on her. Swami and Kalpana were an awesome couple.

Kalpana also gave her another packet. 'Can I take the liberty of requesting you to hand this over to Natasha, Sundeep's wife, once you get back.'

'Oh sure.'

'If you get a bit tight on your luggage, please don't hesitate to leave it behind.'

Mona nodded.

When Aditya offered to drop her back, she didn't refuse.

On the way to the hotel Mona asked Aditya, 'Are Sundeep and Swami great pals?'

'Well, they are adversaries. Sundeep is forever competing with Swami. But Swami looks at him as a friend. More importantly, Kalpana and Natasha are great friends. They are bosom buddies.

One good thing which I would hand out to Sundeep is that he did not to interfere in his wife's relationship with Kalpana.'

'Aditya, you have worked with two of the brightest guys we have, Swami and Sundeep. Do you see any difference between them?'

'Oh tons. The key is short-cuts. Swami will never take a short-cut. Sundeep will always find reason and method to beat the system. Swami is a horse for the long race.'

'Who will you back, if you had a choice.'

'Undoubtedly Swami, because he has virtues of CHILD.'

'Child,' queried Mona.

'Yes, because of his Commitment, Honesty, Integrity, Leadership and Dedication. I would rate him higher than Sundeep on most of these,' elaborated Aditya as the car drove into the lobby of the hotel.

'Thanks Aditya. I will speak to you later. I might need some stuff from you. I'll call you. Good night.' She walked into the hotel as Aditya drove off.

79

The next morning, the Group Audit team walked in. This fifteen-member team was led by an Indian, Ravi Subramanian. Ravi had worked in India before moving out about eight years back. His path had often crossed Swami's. And their interactions had not always been cordial.

Ravi and Swami often had very acrimonious discussions, mainly on audit findings. Ravi was a very tough-nosed auditor, clerical at times, and Swami would normally take him head on, and, as you would expect, Swami would win those arguments. But the best thing about this relationship was that they would go back home together to the warm idlis and sambar that Kalpana would make for them.

'Swami! Wonderful to see you again.' Ravi grinned as he walked into Swami's room. They hugged each other. 'How are you Ravi?' Swami asked fondly. Despite the various professional disconnects, they liked each other. The entire audit team waited in the auditors' conference room as Ravi and Swami caught up with each other and their coffee.

Just as they were to step out to meet the rest of the audit team, Mona walked in.

'Hello Ravi.'

'Hey, Mona darling. How are you? What are you doing in India?'

'Ravi, I knew you were coming in today. I came in early so that I could get out by the time you get in.'

'Are you here for long?'

'Got in last Sunday, am leaving tonight. I need to have a word with you. Need some time and it is urgent.'

'Swami?' Ravi looked at Swami, wondering what schedule Swami had planned for him. Swami shrugged his shoulders and said, 'Ravi, you have been through many of my audit opening speeches, and they are all the same. I can handle it without you. Why don't you go ahead and finish it with Mona. You can join us after lunch.'

Ravi went with Mona to her room.

'Yes Mona, how can I help you?'

'Ravi, Global HR knew that India is going to be hit by an audit from today. That's the reason why I was sent four days before you arrived. I was asked to prepare some groundwork for you. To give you some specific areas that we would want audit to focus on.' She started narrating all that she did in the last four days. Ravi had a shocked look on his face. He didn't utter a word.

Mona kept on talking and Ravi was listening. When Swami came back from his introductory session with the audit team, and tried walking into the room, he was asked to stay out. 'What the hell is going on? Why doesn't someone tell me anything in my own company,' thought Swami as he walked back into the corridor.

Finally when they came out of the room, it was well past lunch hour.

'Is there a problem?' asked Swami when he saw them. Ravi didn't say a thing.

Mona looked at both of them. 'No Swami, I just wanted him to cover something from an HR perspective in his audit.' Swami could make out that she was lying. If that was the case, she wouldn't have asked for fifteen minutes with Ravi and taken over four hours.

Swami didn't press the issue, but there was something at the back of his mind. There was something that these guys were hiding from him. He was hoping that Ravi would tell him about it once Mona was gone.

80

Mona was back at the NYB Global HQ in New York the next day. She was to meet Tedd Bridge and Michelle in two days. She was both excited and worried about the findings from India.

She spent the next two days documenting all her findings and preparing an interim report. The final report would not be out till the audit team came back with their findings, and that would not happen before at least three weeks from now.

However, the interim report was to be presented to the management ASAP.

On the morning of 6 October 2005, Mona's heart was pounding as she walked into the boardroom. She was going to make a presentation to Tedd Bridge for the first time, and he was known to be a very sharp guy. He could rip apart any hypothesis to shreds within minutes. She was prepared.

Michelle called on Mona's mobile at around 8.00 a.m.

'Should I get Tedd in?'

'I am ready, Michelle,' said Mona even as her knees became jelly. She wanted to leave everything and run. 'God, am I nervous?' she wondered.

By the time Michelle and Tedd Bridge walked in at quarter past eight, she had regained her composure. For the next forty-five minutes Mona spoke to them on her findings and what she thought had happened in India. Her findings were inconclusive to the extent that she wanted the Group Audit findings also to come in before making any serious inferences.

'I will need three weeks before submitting my final report. Group Audit report will come in by then.'

'I will be off on my annual vacation from the first of November. I need to close these outstanding issues before I leave. Please ask the audit team to prioritise these and send in all the information that you need by then.' Tedd gave her a fortnight to put together her final report. If Tedd Bridge said fifteen days, it had to be fifteen days.

81
New York

It was ten minutes to six. Sundeep got up and walked into the rest room. He had a meeting with Tedd Bridge at six. He washed his face. Work had taken a backseat. No e-mails, no conference calls, nothing.

He had just revisited the story of his life.

He was about to set out on the long walk to Tedd Bridge's room, when the phone in his room rang. Louisa was not around, and so he picked up the call himself.

'NYB. Good evening. Sundeep here, how may I help you?'

'Hello.'

'Natasha, where are you?'

'Sundeep, when are you planning to leave? We are in the neighbourhood. Two blocks away. If you are planning to leave soon, we will come over to your office.'

'Natasha, I will be delayed. I am just stepping into a meeting with Tedd Bridge.'

'Okay. We will find our way back. Call me if you will have some dinner at home. I will make something,' said Natasha and hung up.

Sundeep dragged himself out of his room and walked towards Tedd's.

'Go on in. They are waiting for you,' said Tedd's secretary, as soon as she saw Sundeep.

Sundeep knocked on the door and entered the room. There were four people in the room. Tedd Bridge, Chetan Bindra, Michelle, and, in the corner sat Aditya Rao. Sundeep was quite stunned to see Aditya. What was he doing there?

All of them were seated in the lounge sofa that was on the right side of Tedd's room. Sundeep had harnessed a dream of one day occupying this corner office. He was wondering what would happen to it now. But Aditya's presence was adding to the suspense. Why was he here?

'Hi Sundeep.' Michelle was the first one to speak. 'Please make yourself comfortable.'

'Thank you.' Sundeep sat down on a single sofa on the left to everyone else.

'Coffee?' It was Michelle again. Tedd hadn't spoken yet.

'No thanks. I am fine,' said Sundeep, a meek copy of his usually arrogant self.

'Sundeep, you might be wondering why Aditya is here?' Tedd spoke for the first time.

'He is the one who hired you in the bank and he is the one who knows you and your family better than anyone of us. That's why I requested him to join us today,' Chetan Bindra clarified.

'Hi Aditya. Good to see you after a long time.' Sundeep was being polite. Aditya nodded.

'Shall we start?' said Michelle seeing that the pleasantries were over. Tedd nodded. He was quite cold towards Sundeep today. Normally he was a very friendly sort of person. But today was different for everyone.

'Sundeep,' began Chetan, 'today is the culmination of a process that began over six months ago. After you moved into New York, one day there was a phone call which came into the Global Compliance Hotline. We had received many similar calls on the compliance hotline against you, but we had, after initial investigations, ignored them. We couldn't establish the validity of what was being said in those calls. We thought some professional rivalry was instigating these calls. Complaining on the compliance hotline against successful individuals is a very common occurrence these days. Hence, while we act instantaneously on the calls on the hotline, we also discount them if they are found to be false.

'In all we have received eighteen complaints on the hotline, all levelling various charges against you. The one which came in six months back on the eighteenth of June was one that was very unclear, and so we decided to ignore it. We thought that it was a disgruntled employee speaking and we couldn't do anything about it. Here is the transcript of the call.'

Sundeep extended his arm and received the copy of the transcript:

I am calling from India. My life has been screwed by the irrational and rash behaviour of a senior member of NYB in India. When this person was in India, he pressurised me into having a relationship with him. Now because of him, my marriage is on the rocks and I am close to a divorce. He has screwed many lives in India. He is corrupt to the core. I have heard that he is hand-in-glove with some vendors and has made millions in the bargain. Such people are not worthy of holding high offices in the group. They have messed up lives and they will mess up the bank.

Sundeep read through the entire transcript with a blank face. He didn't know who the person was and why it was being shown to him.

'The same person called back on twelfth of July and left another complaint in an extremely agitated tone. We suspected it was the same person and confirmed it by running a voice analyser test on the two messages. They were indeed from the same person. Here's that transcript.' Chetan handed over the second page to him.

I had called earlier as well. My life is ruined thanks to this gentleman who works in New York. He is a maniac.

Has no respect for women. He has screwed my life. My husband today has filed for divorce, because he got to know of my relationship with him. This person threatened to ruin my career if I didn't oblige. He forced me to sleep with him. He chased me even when I told him that I was not interested and now I have nowhere to go. If you do not take any action against Sundeep, I will be forced to take it up with the legal authorities in India. It is not fair that I get screwed and he has all the fun in life. The organisation owes it not only to me but to other women in the organisation as well.

'Chetan, Tedd, Michelle, Aditya! Is this the basis for all the conversations that we are having today. Pardon me for saying this, but here is a girl who is not happy with her family life and has convinced herself that I am responsible for her screwed up life, and all of you happily believe her.' Sundeep said in a tone stinking of ridicule, and looked straight out of the window.

Tedd was a bit peeved at this attitude. 'Sundeep, I do not particularly appreciate your attitude. Respect the collective intelligence of four people in this room. This is not it. There's more to it. Do you want to take it one at a time, or do you want to see it all at once. The choice is yours.'

Sundeep realised that Tedd was not impressed by his belligerence and decided to apologise and keep quiet.

Aditya was silently watching all this from his sofa by the window.

'Can we proceed?' Chetan looked at Sundeep and then at Tedd. Both nodded.

The door opened and Tedd's secretary walked in. 'Mona Albance is here.'

'Send her in,' said Tedd.

'I am terribly sorry. I was stuck in a traffic jam two blocks from here. Have I held all of you up?'

'No Mona. Join us.' Tedd moved and made some space for Mona to sit down.

Chetan introduced her. 'Sundeep, meet Mona Albance, our Manager, Diversity Initiatives. She works with Michelle.' She was the key player in the drama that was unfolding.

'Go on.' Tedd was getting impatient.

'Mona Albance was in Mumbai for a week. She met a lot of people there and investigated this whole issue threadbare. We will be showing you the findings shortly.' Chetan wanted to make it known that it was only after lots of deliberations that they had come up with the findings.

'Sundeep, what do you know about Priya Mehra?'

'Priya Mehra...' Sundeep pretended to be thinking. 'I can't seem to remember,' he finally said.

'Priya was a Manager in BOCA, the BPO that was bought in India when you were working there.'

'Oh yes. Now I remember. Didn't her husband also work in the bank?' asked Sundeep.

'Of course, he did, Sundeep. You gave him a job. When he was out of a job and looking for one. And you extracted your pound of flesh from Priya, didn't you?' Mona Albance started off. She was too emotional about the entire sequence of events.

'No. That's rubbish.'

'Are you sure, Sundeep?' Mona taunted him.

'Yes.'

'Well, then what is this?' She handed him a few sheets of paper.

It was the extract of Sundeep's mobile bills when he was in Mumbai. Sundeep couldn't believe his eyes when he saw it.

Along with the bills was a separate summary sheet, which had been made in-house. It had a table:

	Total SMSs sent	Sent to Priya
Nov 2003	680	426
Dec 2003	793	562
Jan 2004	624	412
Feb 2004	694	430
Mar 2004	745	545

'Between November 2003 and March 2004 you have sent Priya over 2300 SMSs. If you call that normal, then my name is Mother Teresa. That's not normal. If I look at the calls you have made to her, the picture looks quite similar. You haven't got back so much of a response from her. She hasn't sent messages to you, hasn't called you so often. I have seen those messages, Mr Srivastava, and they are extremely vulgar. You have solicited her umpteen number of times. The messages were so explicit that I am a bit ashamed reproducing the same here. You not only hired Mehra but also hired him at a level he didn't deserve, all because you had your eyes on Priya. Do you want to know who gave me copies of these bills? Priya's husband. When he found out about you, he wanted an end to their relationship. You killed their family, Sundeep.'

Sundeep didn't answer. He was staring blankly at the ceiling.

'Do you need any more evidence, Mr Srivastava?'

No answer. 'Bitch,' thought Sundeep.

'Sundeep.' Tedd stepped in. Sundeep didn't answer.

'Let's go on.' This time it was Chetan.

'Sundeep, what's your relationship with Ram Naresh?' Mona asked him.

'He is a vendor of the bank, who was introduced to me by Suneel Dutt.'

'Is that all?'

'Yes. Along the way he became a personal friend, but that never interfered with our professional relationship.'

'Is it true that you paid him more than normal for buying out his call centre at a time when you need not have paid that? You paid him six million dollars at a time when his infrastructure was not worth more than two million dollars.'

'That's not true. The entire deal was evaluated and the laid out process was followed when we bought the call centre.'

'Maybe you would remember something more when you see this document.'

It was a print out of Naresh's bank account. Two entries were highlighted in the bank statement. One was the credit of six million dollars into Naresh's account and the other was a debit of two million dollars. The day Naresh was paid six million dollars to buy out his call centre, an amount of two million dollars was transferred to the credit of an account in the name of S Srivastava in New Jersey.

'I do not know. That's not me,' said Srivastava. No one believed him.

'Maybe you would like to let the group know why Ram Naresh was paid over three times the amount you would pay any other sales agent? This is obvious from the bills that Mr Naresh has raised on NYB while you were in office. The Group Audit which is currently on in India has validated this.'

For a similar volume of personal loans originated by Naresh's unit and other DSAs, Naresh has been paid five percent as professional fees, whereas the others have been paid less than two percent. This disparity had been raised many times by the internal audit team in their reports to you, but you chose to ignore the same.'

'The payout requests are normally put up by the respective sales managers to the Business Heads, who review it and recommend it to me. I often go by their recommendations.'

'No Sundeep, I have a copy of this mail from Vivek Jalan to you, in which he has asked you not to pay him so much money, and you have asked him to mind his own business, stating that you are routing some other payments through Mr Naresh.'

'I do not remember,' said Sundeep.

Mona promptly produced a copy of the e-mail. She had laid her hands on it when she was in India.

'Is it not true that Reena, your secretary, quit because she felt that you were making her raise bills and do things that contradicted her own sense of ethics? That's not it, she was also fed up with your making suggestive passes at her. Your financial impropriety and personal advances made her quit.'

'That's conjecture. She quit because of personal reasons,' said Sundeep.

'I have a statement from her. She quit without a job in hand, and that too at a time when she was going through personal stress in her family life. She desperately needed the job, but, despite that, she quit.'

She gave him a copy of his secretary's resignation letter. It had Sundeep's signature on it. 'Received Sd. Sundeep Srivastava.'

In that letter she had categorically stated the reason for her quitting to be a dangerous conflict with her ethics and values. She had clearly said in that letter that she was quitting because of Sundeep.

Mona's hand went into the folder. She rummaged through the pile of papers that she had and came up with another document. 'Now read this.'

Sundeep took the piece of paper from Mona. This was the resignation letter of Reena which was pulled out from HR records. Sundeep could make that out because it had HR notings on it. According to this letter, Reena was quitting due to personal reasons.

'The second one is the letter that HR gave me when I asked for it and the first was the one Reena gave me, when I met her. That was her copy of your acknowledgement. And Sundeep, the two letters are different. You switched the two letters, got Anindyo Roy to document her exit interview, without even doing one, and relieved her in a single day because she had pointed a finger at you. She knew something that could have landed either you or Ram Naresh in trouble.'

'Is this still conjecture, Sundeep?' asked Chetan.

Sundeep didn't respond.

'We haven't spoken to Mr Naresh because he was partnering you in your misdeeds.' Mona was in no mood to relent.

'Sundeep, we have no business to interfere in your personal life. It's your look out. But the moment it starts reflecting on your work, it moves out of the realms of privacy.'

'We decided to act only when it became too serious to ignore. You have been with the group for over a decade and have done very well professionally. We use you as an example when we go to Ivy League campuses for recruitment, as the guy who has made his career with NYB in a short time through dedication and hard work. And here we are. Sundeep, we did not expect this from you.'

'Do you want to say anything or should we proceed?' Tedd was getting impatient. Aditya hadn't spoken yet.

'That's not it,' continued Mona.

'When will this end?' thought Sundeep. He showed no emotions.

'Nidhi Agarwal,' said Mona.

'What about her? We sacked her for her involvement in the mutual fund scam,' Sundeep asked.

'She produced a mail in which you had asked her to go ahead and transfer funds from deposit to mutual funds without the customer's consent. She did what you told her to. When it became too hot to handle, you sacked her. But that was an act meant for public consumption. You gave her a raving recommendation and helped her get a job with ABN AMRO Bank.'

'Your indiscretion screwed up the bank's reputation in India and had it not been for Swami's efforts, we would have had to exit the Indian market. I am sure you remember what happened to Citigroup in Japan. The CEO of the group was called to testify in a case in Japan. All this because they were indulging in certain advisory services without having the license to do so. They had to shut shop in Japan because of that. We came very close to that in India. You instigated your team to sell 'at any cost' and they got you the results. But, at what cost?'

'Someone is framing me. Nidhi is disgruntled with me for having sacked her from NYB.'

'Here's the mail, Sundeep. It has been taken out from the company's server wherein we have a record of every e-mail in and out for the last eight years. And your mobile phone records show that you were in touch with Nidhi Agarwal even after she was sacked. You would not be on phone from 11.00 p.m. to 1.00 a.m. with an employee who you sacked a few days back. Not normal behaviour, I must say, Mr Srivastava.'

Sundeep retorted: 'Do not forget that I managed to deliver a 124-percent growth in one year when I was the Head of Retail Bank. I am sure that counts for something.'

'That's the reason why we are even sitting and talking to you.' Tedd was beginning to get irritated.

'We have evidence of many more acts of indiscretion. June 2004. Offsite at Goa. You got a stage artist to do a risqué private show for you. Anindyo Roy, Mohit Bakshi and you billed the bank forty thousand rupees for it. When your relationship manager managing the offsite raised a bill for that, it was turned down by the Financial Control unit. You got Anindyo Roy to raise it and signed it yourself. Ravi's audit detected this impropriety. The issue is not the amount, but the way the money was spent and the way it was billed to the bank. The bank is not here to satisfy your libido, Mr Srivastava. You pay for your personal quests.'

'And the worst is yet to come.'

Sundeep had almost slumped in his chair, overwhelmed by the multiple exposures. He had no choice but to resign himself to his fate.

'Karuna, the pretty girl you moved to Mumbai from Chennai. Do you remember her? You met her at a Chennai party and shifted her to Mumbai and her husband to Delhi so that you could have a free run?'

'Yes. But we moved her husband, I think his name was Nitin, to Delhi because the regional sales person in Delhi had resigned.'

'That's what everyone thinks. You got Vivek to terminate him so that you had an excuse to move him to Delhi.'

Sundeep was quiet now.

'Three days back Karuna tried to commit suicide. And before she attempted that, she sent me an e-mail. She had become a good friend when I visited India.'

Sundeep had his head in his hands now. Not knowing what to say or do.

'Do you want to know why she attempted suicide?'

Silence.

'Come on, read this.' She handed him an e-mail print out.

Sundeep knew what the mail would say, because she had called him earlier on the same day and he had ridiculed her.

Mona,

When you were here two weeks back, I was trying to tell you something. But I couldn't. I could sense that you wanted to ask me something, but you never asked till the last day. And when you asked me, I lied. I did not tell you anything. Maybe I should not have lied. But life doesn't give you a second chance.

If there is one person who has made my life miserable, it's Sundeep Srivastava, the current Retail Business Head of emerging markets. I was happy in Chennai, when he brought me to Mumbai and enticed me into a relationship with him. He sent my husband off to Delhi and took advantage of my being alone and him being a senior.

It didn't take Swaminathan more than a week to bring Nitin back to Mumbai and help me settle down in my life again.

Within a few weeks I realised I was pregnant. With Sundeep's child. When I spoke to him about it, he chided me saying how can one be so sure. Why will a girl lie on these things?

Now I am at a crossroad. My husband has stumbled on a few mails that I had written to Sundeep during my pregnancy, which, by the way, Sundeep never responded to. Nitin now knows that Ayush, my son, is not his child. He is extremely hurt and has stopped talking to me. I have been living like this for the last one week. This feeling of guilt has been killing me every single moment. I cannot continue to live like this and have decided to end my life. By the time you see this, I may not be alive. But please ensure that devils like Sundeep are eradicated from this system. I knew you came to India on a mission. Don't know whether you accomplished that. But please, please, help me achieve my mission. Ensure that Sundeep is punished.

Sd
Karuna.

'Sundeep, you nearly killed that sweetheart. How could you? You are nothing but an animal.' Tedd was extremely upset.

'You can do anything to be successful. I did not suspect anything when Ram Naresh kept calling me to recommend you, but now I know. You were paying Naresh a price for taking care of you, or, should I say, NYB was paying Naresh to be a spokesman for you. I am ashamed that you are a fellow Indian.' Chetan's voice thundered across the room.

Aditya had never seen Sundeep in such a position. Cornered from all sides. He was known to fight his way out of situations. Here, he was being clobbered and could not do anything whatsoever. The Sundeep he knew was a very confident mercenary. He was aggressive, pushy, and would have his way at any cost. But today he was a broken man. Sundeep was struggling to hold back the tears that were coming out of his eyes. His past was catching up with him, and there was no place to run and hide. There was no Ram Naresh to save him.

There was no Joseph Fernandes to push him up the corporate ladder.

He did not know what to do. He got up, excused himself, and went to the washroom. He locked himself in and wept. Wept like a child. If he had the option to relive his life, he would have lived it differently. He would have been loyal to Natasha and the kids. He would not have fallen a prey to Naresh's temptation. He would not have indulged in a reckless pursuit of success, fame, power and money.

When he was finally able to control himself, he went back to Tedd's room. No one had moved.

'Sundeep.' It was Tedd's turn to speak. 'Our initial thought was to terminate you and put this out in tomorrow morning's press briefing. But we were forced to hold back our decision.'

For the first time, Sundeep looked up. Was he going to keep his job? Were they not going to sack him after all?

'You need to thank this gentleman,' Tedd pointed to Aditya Rao. Aditya figured for the first time in the discussion.

'He flew in this morning with two pieces of paper. The first one is a request from Karuna, who is at Jaslok Hospital in Mumbai, asking for her mail not to be made public. And she has been nice enough not to press charges against you, Sundeep. And the second is from Swaminathan, who has sent in an e-mail, a copy of which Aditya carried with him. He says that you have been drawn into your deeds by uninhibited passion for growth and your interactions with a suspect set of people. He has also said that it was Suneel Dutt who led you on in your relationship with Naresh, without you really knowing what you were getting into, and that once you got stuck, there was no getting out. He has stressed, which we also agree with, that you have been a different person once you moved out of India.'

'Why did Swami do all this?' Sundeep couldn't help wonder.

'So Sundeep, based on Aditya's request and Swami's report, we have decided to give you the option of an honourable exit. You will put in your papers today, and you will cease to be an employee of this bank from close of working hours today. You will not work with any competing organisation in the financial services business in India or abroad for a period of eighteen months from today. You will give us a written statement that you are resigning of your own free will and you have no issues pending with NYB.'

Tedd paused. 'Is it acceptable, Sundeep?'

No answer.

Tedd waited for half a minute, letting it sink in. 'Sundeep, is this acceptable?'

No answer.

'If this is not acceptable to you, Sundeep, we will terminate you with immediate effect and, as per the terms of our contract with you, you will be paid a month's salary in lieu of the notice period.'

'Tedd where will I go at such a short notice. I have worked in this organisation all my life. I don't even know how other organisations look like. Everyone makes mistakes. Can't I be given an opportunity to correct what I have done? You yourself mentioned that I have changed in the last eighteen months. I deserve one last chance, Tedd. My family will be devastated.'

'Given the variety of issues that have cropped up, Sundeep, I would like to believe that giving you another chance would be very inappropriate. I do not think we would even like to discuss it.'

'Where will I go, Tedd? Who will give me a job at such a short notice?'

'I will.' It was not Tedd. Aditya had spoken for the first time. Sundeep looked at him in bewilderment. Had Aditya really spoken what he thought he heard?

'I have always admired your energy, passion and drive. I have always been amazed at your will to achieve things. Surely, I have not always subscribed to the means that you have used to get to those goals. Sundeep, I hired you. You and Swami will always remain my protégés. When Chetan and Mona called me about this three days back, I knew that something would go wrong. So I asked him if I could join in and I'm thankful to Tedd that he agreed. You will come back with me to India and help me build my company. I expect you to be honest to yourself and go back to your roots and your family. No one needs to know about what has transpired in this room today. It will be difficult for me, but I will ensure that you maintain your current standard of living. Your salary will adequately cover your expenses.'

Sundeep was left speechless. Aditya was the God who had come to fetch him out of the depths of ignominy that his career had plummeted to. And Sundeep had treated the same Aditya so arrogantly when he had called him about Swami's move to BOCA. The same Aditya had come all the way to battle for him. To help him find his footing in life, even at this juncture.

'What will I tell Natasha? She will never forgive me.' Sundeep seemed repentant.

'No one needs to know. Right, Tedd. Only the people in this room will know,' said Aditya.

'Aditya, Sundeep is a closed chapter for us. What he does outside the organisation is none of our concern, unless the bank's name gets dragged into it,' Tedd confirmed.

Sundeep got up and hugged Aditya. Tears flowed from his eyes. 'Thank you, Aditya. In my wildest dreams I would not have imagined that you would come to my rescue. I have never been a believer in God. Aditya, today I know, if God was a banker, he would look like you.'

'Sundeep, I think you should thank Swami for this. Swami was the one who flagged this off with me and his mail to Tedd about you was the key influence on Tedd's decision not to publicly condemn you.' Sundeep had learnt that he had committed a grave mistake in distancing himself from Swami.

'That's the end of the discussion, and, if you guys don't mind, I'm getting late for my supper,' Tedd said as he walked out of the room.

A second later he returned and looked at the group, 'Michelle, will you take this to a logical closure?' She nodded.

'Thanks,' said Tedd and disappeared for the day.

Aditya's phone beeped again. It had been beeping throughout the meeting, but he had not taken the call as Tedd was in the room. This time he picked it up. It was Swami. All the previous calls were from him too.

'Hi Aditya. How's it going? How is Sundeep?'

'What we expected has happened. Speak to him.'

'Hey Sundeep. How are you, my friend? Don't lose heart, Sundeep. Come back to India. Come on mate, we haven't spent an evening together in a long time. Natasha and Kalpana will also be happy to be together.'

Silence on Sundeep's end.

'Sundeep! Sundeep. Are you there?'

Sundeep couldn't hold back his tears. He couldn't utter a word. Tears were steadily streaming from his eyes. Aditya took the phone from him. 'Swami, I will call you later.'

The exit formalities were over in an hour. Aditya stayed with Sundeep throughout the process and also drove him home. Sundeep had to leave back his car as it belonged to NYB.

Aditya helped Sundeep regain his composure before he entered his house.

'Natasha, look who is here.' said Sundeep as soon as she opened the door. He was not at his best, but acting came naturally to Sundeep.

'Aditya, what are you doing here?' Natasha hugged him. She was thrilled to see him at her door. Any visitor from India was welcome, and if that visitor was Aditya, then it had to be special.

'He has come to take us back to India. I have decided to join Aditya's business. Are you with me in this decision, Natasha?'

Tears rolled down Natasha's eyes as her dream of returning to her homeland was about to come true. She knew the background to this all along, but didn't want to embarrass Sundeep. She was confident that, with Aditya around, they were all in safe hands now.

82
Epilogue

Sundeep now handles business development for Aditya's BPO in India. He travels all over the globe, but irrespective of where he is, he calls Natasha every night to say '*I Love You*' before he hits the bed.

Swaminathan is still the Country Head of Retail Banking for NYB in India. He is in line to become the CEO of NYB when Kailash retires. Kailash is expected to retire in another three months.

Swami and Sundeep today admire each other. Sundeep really looks up to Swami and holds him in high esteem. He is now genuinely trying to emulate Swami in his personal life as well.

Natasha and Kalpana are today the best of friends. Kalpana couldn't conceive in the normal process. Swami and Kalpana went to the UK to undergo an IVF and are now proud parents of twins—Akruti and Jagruti.

After Karuna attempted suicide, Nitin understood the true meaning of love. The very thought of losing her shook him up. Both of them have quit NYB and are now in Florida with their son Ayush. Nitin teaches at a university there while Karuna works in a local bank. They are very happy to be together.

Naresh was the worst hit. All the business that he was doing with NYB has been withdrawn and passed on to another vendor. Given his background, Swami made sure that he did not get any business from any other bank in the country. He is struggling to make ends meet now.

Aditya, the God for both Sundeep and Swami, leads a contented life. Both Sundeep and Swami are his closest confidants, despite the fact that Sundeep works with him. He is the affectionate grandpa to their kids. He makes sure that the five of them and the kids spend at least one weekend in a month together. What he doesn't tell anyone, because everyone knows it, is that his company, which recently got listed, has become one of the largest and most admired software services and back office processing companies in India.

Life goes on, but everyone has become smarter from the learnings at NYB.